U0074169

凱信企管

**用對的方法充實自己，
讓人生變得更美好！**

凱信企管

**用對的方法充實自己，
讓人生變得更美好！**

全方位英語大師

1200 詞素卡 × 多功能字卡

唯一一本雙卡牌單字書，
完整解構基礎單字，增強
記憶學習效果

單字

學習寶典

使用說明 User's Guide

1200 基礎單字為語料，融入語素、字源、構詞音韻及語意關聯等元素；
不僅是字彙學習的房角石，更是流暢閱讀的起手式

01 | 完整解構 1200 基礎單字，有效增強記憶效果

- 依據 1200 字表實詞的字源語意整理 40 主題，語意導向，情境呈現，
  增進記憶與運用效果。

- 記憶技巧涵蓋字源、詞素、構詞音韻等面向，破解詞素與單字語意
  關聯，多元解構單字，多層學習體驗，直擊形音義，記憶力度大。

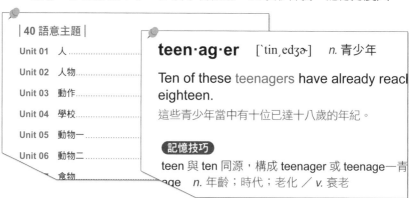

| 40 語意主題 |

teen·ag·er　[ˋtin͵edʒɚ]　*n.* 青少年

Ten of these teenagers have already reach
eighteen.

這些青少年當中有十位已達十八歲的年紀。

（記憶技巧）

teen 與 ten 同源，構成 teenager 或 teenage—青
ㄅge　*n.* 年齡；時代；老化 ／ *v.* 衰老

02 | 相關字彙羅列於例句中，拓展單字學習至閱讀層次

標題字及其同源字、下層字、反義
字等共同編寫例句，相關字彙高密
度羅列於題材多元、文筆流暢的例
句中，拓化單字至閱讀層次。

un·cle　[ˋʌŋkl̩]　*n.* 叔叔；伯父；

My uncle died young, and my aun
by herself in the past few years.

叔叔早逝，嬸嬸過去幾年來一直獨力撫養

反義字　**aunt**　*n.* 嬸嬸；姑姑；阿姨

相關字　**cousin**　*n.* 堂（表）兄弟；堂

03 完整鋪陳單字的元素圖譜，
呈現字彙學習的網絡圖騰

字彙為中心，增列衍生字、同反義字、聯想字等，學習面向更完整。

衍生字
增列該單字與 1200 字表所含字首或字尾詞綴，輕鬆擴增單字，培塑構詞概念。

同源字
列舉 1200 字表中的同源字，藉由「音相近、義相連」的同源關聯，達到新舊單字連動記憶。

聯想字
藉由語意層面的同義字、反義字、上下層字及類別語意字，拓化字彙學習面向，深化語言認知層次。

save [sev] *v.* 拯救；儲存；節省

A brave man saved the kid from （ was set down in a safe place.
一位勇敢的男子從危險中救了那名孩童，
的地方。

| 同源字 | safe *n.* 保險箱 ／ *adj.* 安全的
safe·ty *n.* 安全
| 反義字 | dan·ger *n.* 危險
dan·ger·ous *adj.* 危險的

04 40 組歷屆國中基測或會考題組＋
全新編寫近 300 題測驗試題

· 配合單元主題搭配一篇歷屆基測或會考題組，單字連結閱讀，情境強化字彙學習成效。

· 近 300 單字測驗試題：依據 108 課綱國中英語教科書逐冊編寫，切合測驗與評量精神，符合日常表達用法，鑑別度高。

小試身手 ★ 出自 93 年第二次基測

Kelly is a very special **student** i
American, and her mother is a Chin
was born in New York and finished
Then the family decided to move to Ta
father found a new job in Taipei. Kelly could
her parents did not send her to a **specia**

Test 1

____ 1. The _____ is an animal in A
horse.
(A) lion   (B) monkey   (C) zel

____ 2. A(n) _____ can grab leaves
long trunk.
(A) koala   (B) giraffe   (C) hi

前言 Preface

依據美國國家閱讀審議會（National Reading Panel）的報告，閱讀包括五基本要素：音素覺識（phonemic awareness）、聲韻分析（phonetic analysis）、閱讀流暢性（fluency）、字彙發展（vocabulary development）及理解（comprehension）；Mathes 與 Torgesen 也提到理解及成功運用拼音文字原則（alphabetic principle）是成功閱讀的重要因素之一；Moats（2004）提出閱讀教學策略應包括音韻覺識（phonological awareness）教學、重視字義、結構及字源的字彙教學等。

綜觀上述所言，閱讀導向的字彙學習應包含語素（morpheme）、字源、音韻覺識（phonological awareness）、聲韻分析（phonetic analysis）等核心知識，當然，這些**字彙內部的元素不僅是字彙的房角石，更是流暢閱讀的起手式。換言之，擴及這些面向才是完整的字彙教學或學習，進而達到閱讀流暢的目標。**

共同作者蘇秦老師於 2015 年與國立高雄師範大學英語系忻愛莉教授及高雄市立右昌國中英語科林健豐老師共同參與國立臺灣師範大學外語領域教學研究中心辦理的教學實驗研究案中，提出「全方位英語字彙教學：整合音韻覺識、結構分析、詞彙語意、閱讀流暢性之實驗教學」構想，並執行課堂教學，證實國中階段字彙教學若涵蓋上述語言要素，全方位協助學生字彙學習，學生的識字與閱讀表現則優於同儕。該實驗教學成果並以壁報發表方式參與 2019 年南臺灣教育學術研討會，希冀包含構詞、字源、音韻、語意等面向的「全方向」字彙教學理念與實踐能夠普及至更多的國中校園。（教學／研討相關證明文件、證書附件於後）

《全方位英語大師 1200 單字學習寶典》一書乃以 1200 基礎單字為語料，融入語素、字源、同源字、構詞音韻、語意關聯字等元素，由於卓越的教育信念、堅實明確的理論基礎、創新獨特的教學設計，本書將成為當代字彙教學的優良教本，值得廣大字彙學習與教學者參考研讀。

《全方位英語大師 1200 單字學習寶典》的特色：

一、以 1200 基礎單字為語料，將名詞、動詞、形容詞、副詞等實詞分成 40 語意主題，每一主題列 15 標題字，每一標題字增列其同源字、轉音關聯、同（反）義字、上（下）層字，解說字源構詞過程，甚至提及構詞音韻—詞素黏接時的音韻變化，猶如以字彙為中心，鋪陳其內部蘊含的元素圖譜，呈現字彙學習的網絡圖騰—這是字彙教材的圭臬，也是字彙學習的藍圖。

二、將標題字及其同源字、下層字、反義字等共同編寫例句，將相關字彙高密度羅列於題材多元、文筆流暢的例句中，藉由句子連結相關單字，達到深化單字學習並拓化單字至閱讀層次—這是字彙教法的創新，也是字彙學習的進化。

三、每一單元皆搭配一篇主題相關的歷屆國中基測或會考題組，適合 1200 單字階段讀者藉由主題情境延伸單字學習，對於國中同學，更是能夠增進學習動機，提升學習成效。另外，作者依據 108 課綱國中教科書編寫近 300 題單字測驗試題，題目設計符合課綱導向，有助於讀者精熟 1200 基礎單字與擴增字彙。

四、隨書提供詞素卡及多功能字卡的製作及桌遊活動建議，為學習者鋪設一條寓教於樂的學習林蔭大道，讓大家在愉悅的情意中內化字彙學理、在互動中激發學習動機，體驗「始於歡樂，終於智慧，達到熟習」的成功學習歷程。

五、本書附錄述及單字學習的核心知識，針對音節、詞素、同源字等提出簡要說明及明確的學習指引。誠如國內語言學專家湯廷池教授所言「一個人的『母語』，可以不必靠學習也會不知不覺地學會，而『外國語』則非靠有知有覺得學習不可。」舉凡音韻、構詞、句法，乃至溝通模式皆應理性探討方能理解，進而操練熟習而達到運用活用的語言學習目標。

時值本書付梓出版之際，由衷感謝讀者們對於吾等新近著作的支持指教及邀約演講的學校及團體的激勵。另外，共同作者蘇秦老師於國立高雄師範大學進修學院開設的「高效單字記憶與擴增特訓課程」以及配合勞動部勞動力發展署產業人力投資發展方案，提升勞工自主學習計畫而開設的英文單字教學訓練實務課程中，學員的回饋及互動著實深化基礎單字教學的思維、拓化教學作為的能量。

　　由於這些正向力量，成就了《全方位英語大師 1200 單字學習寶典》的單字教學理念與教材教法，臺灣這塊土地若能因本書而使英語字彙教學精進往前，則善莫大焉。

蕭泰　周儀弘

庚子　正月初一　曾文溪畔

※ 感謝您對本書的支持，現在只要掃一下 QR CODE，加入「全方位英語學習」粉絲專頁，即可獲得本書 40 主題的 quizlet 連結；更能隨時和我們一起分享切磋，輕鬆學習基礎單字。

★ 因各家手機系統不同，若無直接掃描，仍可以電腦連結搜尋 https://tinyurl.com/ubs5gtn。

附件（一）

國立臺灣師範大學

服務證明

感謝　蘇泰　老師在本校外語領域教學研究中心所辦理之教學實驗研究案，
提出「全方位英語字彙教學：整合音韻覺識、結構分析、詞彙語意、閱讀流
暢性之實驗教學」構想，並執行課堂教學 5 小時，對國內外語創新教學貢獻
良多，謹此證明。

校長　張國恩

中華民國 105 年 6 月 17 日

附件（二）

2019 年南臺灣教育學術研討會壁報發表

全方位英語字彙學習之實驗教學研究

國立高雄師範大學 忻愛莉、高雄市 蘇泰、高雄市右昌國中 林健豐

摘要

　　語言的切入點以聽與說是最自然的方式，本研究的實驗教學為字彙教學，以強調聽與說的教學方式來聯結英語單字中的形、音、義的
關係，以及單字如何由語素編碼解碼的關係，藉以建立學生學習英語單字的良好基礎。簡言之，本實驗教學整合了音素覺識、結構分析、
詞素語意和閱讀流暢性，目的在探討其對於學生英語字彙學習成效之影響。本研究以高雄市一所位於郊區的國民中學二個二年級的班級學
生作為研究對象，一班為實驗組(N=25)，另一班為對照組(N=27)。實驗教學實施約半年，由兩位臨床教師先示範此實驗教學之重點，完
畢後再由一位協同教師於日常課程執行每一部分之細節，並且經常為之，使為常態教學模式。本研究採用準實驗設計，檢驗學生在教學實
驗介入前後之變化與差異。本研究亦借助訪談學生及教師反省誌作為質性的資料。根據資料分析，本實驗研究發現此字彙教學，對於國中
二年級學生的字彙學習是有助益的。可幫助學生了解單字之構成；可幫助學生成功地唸出已學過之單字及文章；可提升學生唸讀未學過的
單字及文章的能力及信心。本研究亦發現學生及教師本身的態度也是成功學習的關鍵。教學者須注意學生上課的專注力及學生對任課教師
的信任度；教學者須擺脫傳統式的單字教學並有信心及能力。本實驗教學的研究結果可作為教育相關工作者日後實施英語字彙教學之參考。

關鍵字：字彙教學、音素覺識、結構分析、語素語意、閱讀流暢性。

附件（二）

壹、 研究動機和目的

一、 研究動機

語言的學習可經由多種方式，聽、說、讀、寫最好都能兼備，但在台灣因為英語是學校一門重要科目，考試亦多以紙筆方式，故造成英語教學較偏重讀、寫。其實語言的切入點以聽與說是最自然的方式，本實驗教學就是想以強調聽與說的教學方式來聯結英語單字中的形、音、義的關係，以及單字如何由語素編碼解碼的關係，帶領學生感受英語語素的語意以及拆解分合，藉以建立學生學習英語單字的良好基礎。

二、 研究目的與問題

（一）研究目的

本研究目的是探討藉由強調聽與說的字彙教學方式，

1. 學生是否能習慣英語聲音與字母的關聯，能經由英語發音大致正確地拼出單字(聽寫單字)；
2. 學生是否有信心唸讀不曾見過的單字(唸讀單字)；
3. 學生是否能體會英語單字裡常由許多語素組成，這些語素常可拆解，並跟其他語素合併，構成另一單字(字首字尾與語素語意)。
4. 學生是否有能力正確地、快速地閱讀文章(唸讀短文)。

（二）研究問題

本研究的四個研究問題如下：

1. 應用此教學實驗方法，學生的聽寫單字能力是否顯著進步？
2. 應用此教學實驗方法，學生的唸讀單字能力是否顯著進步？
3. 應用此教學實驗方法，學生的字首字尾與語素語意判斷能力是否顯著進步？
4. 應用此教學實驗方法，學生的唸讀短文能力是否顯著進步？

貳、 文獻探討

一、音素覺識

能察覺和辨識出單字中字母的發音，能釐清字音和字母間的關係。National Reading Panel (2000)回顧音素覺識相關文獻總結下列重點：(1)教學必須能教導學生音素覺識，有效察覺和辨識出字中字母的發音 (2)教導辨識音素-文字的發音，這技巧會持續地協助學生學會閱讀 (3)有效的教學重點在教導學生辨識字音，在課堂上可使用小組教學 (4)音素覺識是個入門方法而不是最終成果，學生持續運用音素技巧，將可轉換成經驗到閱讀和寫作上 (5)分割音素的訓練會對學生的閱讀成就產生正面的影響。

二、結構分析及語素語意

結構分析(structure analysis)是教學生使用字中較多的部分來進行解碼以學習生字，例如辨識字根(root words)、字首(prefixes)、字尾(suffixes)、複合字(compound words)、縮詞(contraction)和複數型(plurals)。結構分析字義部分，那就是語素(morpheme)。語素是一個字中所具有語意最小的單位。可單獨成立的字根為自由語素(free morphemes)，詞綴(affixes)與其中的字首和字尾被歸類為黏著語素(bound morphemes)。黏著語素一定要跟著自由語素才可成立。

三、閱讀流暢性

閱讀流暢性(fluency)的定義是「有能力正確地、快速地閱讀文章，並能表達出文意。」「正確性(accuracy)」「速度(speed)」和「表達能力(expression)」這三要素是閱讀中不可或缺的能力(Bursuck & Damer, 2007)。更具體地說，此三要素是識字量、速度和閱讀表達。

参、 研究設計與實施

一、 控制變數

1. 實驗組與對照組在同一學校，家長社經地位相似，班級為常態編班，兩班學生英文程度落差不大。
2. 實驗組與對照組的教學內容、教學進度、與教學時數相同。
3. 實驗組及對照組兩位教學者的性別、教學年資、學歷相同而且年齡相仿，可以降低不同教學者對實驗造成的干擾。

二、 研究方法

採用 t 檢定檢驗學生在教學實驗介入前後之變化與差異，瞭解學生的後測是否達到與前測有差異的顯著水準。本研究亦借由訪談學生及教師反省誌作為質性的資料。

三、 教學實驗策略及步驟

對照組的教學內容、教學進度、與教學時數和實驗組保持相同，只有教學方法不同，實驗組教師的字彙教學融入九項策略進行教學，對照組教師的字彙教學沒有融入實驗組的教學策略。

四、 研究角色及分工

教師	研究角色及分工
K	對照組教學者
L	實驗組主要教學者/協同教師/研究者
C&S	臨床教師(入實驗組示範教學第四次)/研究者 試題評分者(評分第一、二、三大題紙筆測驗)
Y&T	試題評分者(評分第四大題唸讀短文)

肆、研究結果與討論

一、 學生學習成效評估

1. 兩個班級在聽寫單字、字首字尾、唸讀單字、唸讀短文A與唸讀短文B後測總分皆高於前測總分，但皆未達顯著差異。
2. 在語素語意此一評量向度，兩個班級在後測總分得分皆高於前測總分得分，並且皆達顯著差異。表示學生對英語單字之構成有基礎的認識，其效果最為明顯的是語素及其語意。
3. 實驗組班級在聽寫單字、字首字尾、語素語意後測得分皆高於對照組班級，但皆未達顯著差異。原因可能是教學時間還不夠長和學生對作答的題型不熟悉。
4. 實驗組班級在唸讀單字、唸讀短文A、唸讀短文B之後測得分皆高於對照組班級，且皆達顯著差異。表示學生對已學之英語單字有良好的唸讀能力，學生對未學之英語單字亦有唸讀信心，並能展現八成正確的唸讀能力，受實驗之學生有比未受實驗之學生更好的英語單字彙及文章唸讀能力。

二、 教師反思和學生訪談

教師：提升學生音素覺識及落實閱讀流暢性教學，有助於提升學生識字能力。應用結構分析及語素語意的策略，能有效幫助學生學習字彙。**學生**：經過此字彙教學之後，學習上不同成就水準的學生都感覺到英文課變得比較有趣，也更有興趣學習英文，有些甚至覺得自己的英文能力進步了。

伍、結論與建議

本實驗教學之研究結果，已實際驗證整合音韻覺識、結構分析、詞彙語意、閱讀流暢性之教學策略有助於學生提升英語字彙學習成效，尤其是在幫助認識英文單字之構成及唸讀英語單字和文章部分。本研究依據研究結果再接續發展出輔助學生有效學習單字的三項學習資源：詞素卡、多功能字卡、Quizlet單字學習軟體。

目錄 Contents

附錄

★ 多功能字卡範例下載

★ 詞素卡下載／遊戲示範影片
　／ 1200 詞素卡語料說明

★ 同源字教學建議

（完整內容收錄在雲端）

★ 因各家手機系統不同，若無法直接
　掃QR code，仍可以電腦連結網址
　https://tinyurl.com/skutlrj 雲端下載

40 語意主題

1200 基礎單字為語料，將名詞、動詞、形容詞、副詞等實詞分成 40 語意主題，融入語素、字源、同源字、構詞音韻、語意關聯字等元素，乃字彙學習的進化，也是字彙學習的藍圖。

★ 因各家手機系統不同，若無法直接掃描，仍可以電腦連結 https://tinyurl.com/rtqc934 雲端下載

🎧 Track 001

peo·ple　[`pipḷ]　*n.* 人們；民族

Twenty people came to the celebrity's house-warming party last weekend. Several of them are important persons who came along with their personal assistants.

上週末有二十人來參加那位名人的喬遷派對。其中幾人是重要人士，他們的私人助理跟著一起來。

> 聯想字　per·son　*n.* 人
> per·son·al　*adj.* 個人的；私人的，al 是形容詞字尾

---

ba·by　[`bebɪ]　*n.* 嬰兒；幼小的動物

Newborn babies spend a lot of time sleeping in a crib.

剛出生的幼小動物花很多時間在巢穴裡睡覺。

> 衍生字　ba·by·sit　*v.* 暫時照顧孩子
> new·born　*adj.* 剛出生的，born 表示出生；天生的

▶ baby 是指剛出生的嬰兒，出生是 born。

---

child　[tʃaɪld]　*n.* 小孩；兒童　複數形：chil·dren

They have a child of 15, and he is still childlike, and even showing childish behavior sometimes.

他們有一個十五歲的孩子，還很天真，有時甚至會露出幼稚的舉動。

> 衍生字　child·like　*adj.* 天真的；孩子般
> child·ish　*adj.* 幼稚的
> 同義字　kid　*n.* 小孩，包括 boy 男孩、girl 女孩。

teen·ag·er [ˋtinˌedʒɚ]　*n.* 青少年

Ten of these teenagers have already reached the age of eighteen.

這些青少年當中有十位已達十八歲的年紀。

記憶技巧

teen 與 ten 同源，構成 teenager 或 teenage—青少年的。
age　*n.* 年齡；時代；老化 ／ *v.* 衰老

guy [gaɪ]　*n.* 人；傢伙

This morning, I saw a nice guy helping an old lady cross the street.

今天早上我看到有位善心人士協助一位老太太過馬路。

man [mæn]　*n.* 男人；人類　複數形：men

Sir, there are two men and three women waiting in your office.

先生，有二位男士和三位女士正在您的辦公室等待。

反義字 **wom·an**　*n.* 女人　複數形：wom·en
相關字 **sir**　*n.* 先生

記憶技巧

1. woman 原意是作為妻子 --wife 的人類 --man，wo 是 wife 的意思，而 man 是指人類。

2. woman 的重音節是封閉音節，母音是短母音 /ʊ/，因此音節劃分為 wom·an，複數形 women /ˋwɪmɪn/ 則劃分為 wom·en。

fam·i·ly [ˋfæməlɪ]　*n.* 家人；家庭

I missed my dear family very much when I was studying abroad.

我在國外唸書的時候非常想念我親愛的家人。

聯想字 **dear**　*n.* 親愛的人 ／ *adj.* 親愛的

par·ent [`pɛrənt] *n.* 父親；母親；總公司

My parents are both teachers. My father is teaching in a college, and my mother is teaching in a senior high school.

我父母都是老師，我父親在一所大學教書，我母親在一所高中教書。

相關字 **parenting** *n.* 養育子女

▶ parent 是指 father 或 mother，father 也稱為 dad 或 daddy，mother 也稱為 mom 或 mommy。

記憶技巧
parent = par + ent，par 是 give birth to-- 生產的意思，ent 表示人。

---

grand·par·ent [`grænd͵pɛrənt] *n.* （外）祖父；（外）祖母

My grandparents are both healthy. My grandfather is in his early seventies, and my grandmother in her late sixties.

我祖父母都很健康。我祖父七十出頭，我祖母則將近七十歲。

記憶技巧
grand 主要是形容詞，表示首要的、壯麗的，當作字首時，原意是「較……年長的一代的」，因此 grandparent 是指（外）祖父或（外）祖母，grandfather 是指（外）祖父，grandmother 是指（外）祖母；後來延伸為反義的「較……年幼的一代的」，因此 grandchild 是指孫子（女）或外孫（女），grandson 是指孫子或外孫，granddaughter 是指孫女或外孫女。

---

hus·band [`hʌzbənd] *n.* 丈夫

George and Mary are husband and wife. Mary has been a housewife since they got married.

George 和 Mary 是夫妻。自從他們結婚以來，Mary 一直是家庭主婦。

聯想字 **mar·ried** *adj.* 已婚的
反義字 **wife** *n.* 妻子，housewife 是指家庭主婦。

記憶技巧
husband 是一家之主，而家就是 house。

son [sʌn] *n.* 兒子

When their son was abroad on business, Mr. and Mrs. Lin took care of their grandson.

林姓夫婦的兒子到國外出差時，他們照顧他們的孫子。

---

daugh·ter [ˋdɔtɚ] *n.* 女兒

The president's daughter is the marketing manager of the company and her granddaughter is a trainee in the customer service department.

總裁的女兒是公司的行銷經理，孫女是客服部門的實習生。

---

broth·er [ˋbrʌðɚ] *n.* 兄；弟

My roommate has one brother and two sisters.

我的室友有一位哥哥及二位妹妹。

反義字 **sis·ter** *n.* 姐；妹；修女；尼姑

---

un·cle [ˋʌŋk!] *n.* 叔叔；伯父；舅舅

My uncle died young, and my aunt has been raising my cousin by herself in the past few years.

叔叔早逝，嬸嬸過去幾年來一直獨力撫養我堂弟。

反義字 **aunt** *n.* 嬸嬸；姑姑；阿姨
相關字 **cousin** *n.* 堂（表）兄弟；堂（表）姊妹；遠房親戚

---

neigh·bor [ˋnebɚ] *n.* 鄰居；鄰國

It is said that finding a good neighbor to live next to is much harder than buying a good house.

俗話說「找到一位住在隔壁的好鄰居要比買到一棟好房子要難的多。」

衍生字 **neigh·bor·ing** *adj.* 鄰近的
neigh·bor·hood *n.* 鄰近地區；街區

What does the word *family* mean to you? An American study in 2006 showed that **people** today ___(1)___. Over 99% of the **people** who were interviewed agree that a **husband**, a **wife**, and a **child** are a **family**. At the same time, 94% see a **parent** with a **child** as a **family**, 91% say a **husband** and a **wife**, without **children**, are a **family**, and 81% think a **man** and a **woman**, with a **child**, but not married, are a **family** too.

The study also found that ___(2)___ is very important in the modern thinking on **family**. Though 81% think a **man** and a **woman**, not married, with a **child**, are a **family**, the percentage(%) drops to 40% if the **couple** doesn't have a **child**. This is also true with same-sex **couples**. About 60% see two **men**, or two **women**, with a **child**, as a **family**, but only 32% think so when the **couple** doesn't have a **child**.

In the study, those who see two **men** or two **women** that live together as a **family** often find it OK for same-sex **couples** to get married. ___(3)___. However, not everyone opens their arms to same-sex **couples**: the study said 30% have no problem seeing pets as part of one's **family**, but they do not think a same-sex **couple** is a **family**.

_____1. (A) think differently about when to start a family

(B) do not find family as important as their **parents** did

(C) want many different things when they start a family

(D) have several different ideas about what makes a family

_____2. (A) whether **people** are married or not

(B) whether **people** have a child or not

(C) whether **people** live together or not

(D) whether **people** love each other or not

_____3. (A) This is not surprising

(B) This is not possible everywhere

(C) It is no good news for everyone

(D) It cannot be this way for very long

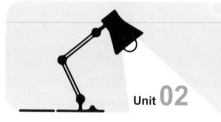

Unit 02　人物

🎧 Track 005

boss　[bɔs]　*n.* 老闆；上司

The boss wants his secretary to keep the secret.
老闆要他的秘書保守秘密。

| 聯想字 | **sec·re·ta·ry**　*n.* 秘書 |

| 衍生字 | **se·cret**　*n.* 秘密 |

記憶技巧

secretary 原意是託付秘密的人，ary 表示人。

---

clerk　[klɝk]　*n.* 店員；職員

Steve has been working as a clerk in a bank since graduating from college.
史帝夫自從大學畢業就一直在銀行擔任職員。

---

coach　[kotʃ]　*n.* 教練；長途客車／*v.* 擔任⋯⋯教練；訓練

The famous coach coached the national baseball team from 2010 to 2014.
那位知名教練從 2010 年到 2014 年擔任國家棒球隊教練。

---

guard　[ɡɑrd]　*n.* 警衛；守衛／*v.* 守衛；監視

We need to show the guard our pass when entering the main building.
我們進入大樓時必須向警衛出示通行證。

re·port·er　[rɪ`portə]　*n.* 記者

The local reporter is reporting live from the location of the accident.

那位地方記者正從事故現場實況報導。

【記憶技巧】

re + port + er = back + carry + person，port 是 carry—攜帶的意思，將消息或訊息帶回給他人的是記者。

---

en·gi·neer　[ˌɛndʒə`nɪr]　*n.* 工程師

The mechanical engineer specializes in designing cleaning robots.

那位機械工程師專精於設計打掃機器人。

【聯想字】 **ro·bot** *n.* 機器人

【記憶技巧】

engine 是指引擎，英文音譯字，黏接 eer 衍生為工程師，而字尾 eer 其字重音就在尾音節 eer。另外，engine = en + gine，en 是 in—裡面，gine 是生產、產生的意思，產生動力的機器就是 engine—引擎。單字字尾 e 黏接 e 開頭的字尾時，為避免重複，單字字尾 e 省略。

---

po·lice　[pə`lis]　*n.* 警方

The woman went to the police station and reported something to the police, and then she talked with a police officer in his office.

那位婦人去警察局向警方告發事情，然後和一名警官在他的辦公室談話。

【聯想字】 **po·lice of·fi·cer** *n.* 警官

　　　　 of·fi·cer *n.* 官員

　　　　 of·fice *n.* 辦公室；診所

　　　　 po·lice sta·tion *n.* 警察局

sol·dier [`soldʒɚ] *n.* 士兵

Dozens of soldiers were working hard to help clean up the community after the strong typhoon.
強颱過後，數十位士兵一直辛苦協助清理該社區。

king [kɪŋ] *n.* 國王

After the old king passed away, his second son ruled over the kingdom.
老邁國王辭世之後，他的次子統治王國。

衍生字 **king·dom** *n.* 王國

queen [`kwin] *n.* 女王；王后

The Queen is meeting a group of children from a village in the north today.
今天女王要接見一群來自北方村落的孩子。

記憶技巧
queen 的字源是 woman—婦人的意思。

prince [prɪns] *n.* 王子

The witch cast a spell on the prince and he turned into a butterfly.
女巫對王子下咒，他就變成一隻蝴蝶。

記憶技巧
prince = prin + ce，prin—first 首先，ce = cept，take一拿，prince 是第一位取得王位的繼承人。

prin·cess [`prɪnsɪs] *n.* 公主

The prince and princess got married and lived happily ever after.
王子和公主結婚，此後就過著幸福的日子。

記憶技巧
princess = prince + ess，ess 表示女性或雌性，單字字尾 e 黏接 e 開頭的字尾時，為避免重複，字尾 e 省略。

A·mer·i·can [ə`mɛrɪkən] *n.* 美國人 ／ *adj.* 美國的；美洲的

The writer moved to America and became an American citizen seven years later.

那位作家移居美國，七年後成為美國公民。

聯想字 **A·mer·i·ca** *n.* 美國；美洲

記憶技巧

American = America + an，an 通常表示國家或地區的人，母音結尾的單字黏接字尾 an 時，為避免母音重複，單字字尾的母音字母 a 省略。

Tai·wan·ese [͵taɪwə`niz] *n.* 臺灣人 ／ *adj.* 臺灣的

The Smith family tasted a variety of Taiwanese food during their stay in Taiwan.

史密斯一家人停留臺灣期間品嚐了各式各樣臺灣食物。

聯想字 **Tai·wan** *n.* 臺灣

記憶技巧

Taiwanese = Taiwan + ese，字尾 ese 是屬於、起源於的意思，字重音的位置。

Chi·nese [`tʃaɪ`niz] *n.* 中國人；中文 ／ *adj.* 中國的

The Chinese language is used in China, Taiwan and Hong Kong.

中文使用於中國、臺灣和香港。

聯想字 **Chi·na** *n.* 中國

記憶技巧

Chinese = China + ese，為避免母音重複，China 省略字尾母音字母 a。

Bill and Jill were going to visit Da-wei and Li-hua Wu in Taiwan for several days. Before they left **America**, Bill and Jill tried to learn about **Chinese** food and **Taiwanese** ways of doing things. They wanted to be polite. They learned that most **people** in **Taiwan** eat rice, drink tea, and take off ther shoes when they go into a **friend's** apartment. Bill and Jill even learned to use chopsticks.

At the same time, Da-wei and Li-hua learned about **American** food and **American** ways of doing things. <u>They</u> wanted to be **friendly**. When Bill and Jill came to the Wu's house, Da-wei and Li-hua told them to keep their shoes on. Later they went out for dinner. They ate pizza and drank Coke. The next few days, they had breakfast in a coffee shop and ate hamburgers in a fast-food restaurant.

On their way back to **America**, Bill and Jill were thinking about why they never ate rice or drank tea or ate with chopsticks. They never took off their shoes when they visited the Wu **family**. They thought that living in **Taiwan** was just like living in **America**.

_____1. How did Bill and Jill prepare for their trip to **Taiwan**?

(A) They learned to speak **Chinese**.

(B) They prepared a new pair of shoes.

(C) They bought a lot **American** food.

(D) They learned to do things the way **Taiwanese people** do.

_____2. Which made Bill and Jill think that **Taiwan** was just like **America**?

(A) The Wu **family** often ate fast food.

(B) The Wu **family** drank tea after dinner.

(C) The Wu **family** could speak good English.

(D) The Wu **family** took off their shoes in the house.

_____3. What does <u>They</u> mean in the reading?

(A) Bill and Jill.

(B) Da-wei and Li-hua.

(C) Most **people** in Taiwan.

(D) **American** ways of doing things.

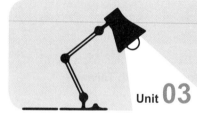

Unit 03　動作

🎧 Track 009

act　[ækt]　*n.* 行為；（戲）幕 ／ *v.* 舉止；表現

In the second act, actors and actresses will do some funny actions.

第二幕，男女演員會做一些好笑的動作。

衍生字　**ac·tor**　*n.* 男演員
　　　　ac·tress　*n.* 女演員
　　　　actress = act + or + ess，ess 表示女性或雌性。
　　　　ac·tion　*n.* 行動；動作，字母 t 黏接字尾 ion，t 唸較易發音的 /ʃ/。

- -

bake　[bek]　*v.* 烘烤

In the bakery, one baker is making bread, and the other two are baking buns and toast.

麵包店裡，一位糕點師傅在做麵包，其他二位在烘烤小圓麵包和吐司。

聯想字　**bread**　*n.* 麵包
　　　　bun　*n.* 小圓麵包
　　　　toast　*n.* 吐司

衍生字　**bak·er**　*n.* 糕點師傅
　　　　bak·er·y　*n.* 麵包店

記憶技巧

1. 字尾 er 表示產生動作的人或器具，ery 表示場所。
2. e 結尾的單字黏接 er、ery 等 e 開頭的字尾時，為避免 e 字母相鄰，字尾的首字母 e 省略，僅標示 r 或 ry，以維持單字的拼字完整。
3. 劃分音節時，音節應包含母音字母或 y，因此分別劃分為 bak·er 及 bak·er·y。

lead　　[lɛd]　*n.* 鉛 ／ [lid]　*v.* 領導

We need a good leader to lead us to overcome the difficulty.

我們需要一位合適的領導者帶領我們克服困境。

衍生字　**lead·er**　　*n.* 領導者，leader = lead + er

- -

cheer　　[tʃɪr]　*n.* 歡呼聲；歡樂 ／ *v.* 歡呼；鼓舞

The cheerleaders are cheering for their school soccer team.

啦啦隊員正在為她們的足球校隊歡呼。

衍生字　**cheer·lead·er**　　*n.* 啦啦隊員

- -

win　　[wɪn]　*n.* 贏 ／ *v.* 贏；贏得

If you win the game, you will be a winner; if you lose it, you will be a loser.

如果你贏得比賽，你將是一位獲勝者；如果輸了，你就是魯蛇一枚。

聯想字　**game**　*n.* 遊戲；比賽

衍生字　**win·ner**　*n.* 獲勝者

反義字　**lose**　*v.* 失敗；失去；輸掉

　　　　los·er　*n.* 失敗者

記憶技巧

win 是封閉音節，i 唸短母音 /ɪ/，黏接母音為首的字尾時，重複字尾字母 n，字尾取得音節首子音而不影響單字 win 的唸音。

car·ry [`kærɪ] *v.* 攜帶;傳輸;傳播

Dengue fever is a disease carried by mosquitoes.

登革熱是一種藉由蚊子傳播的疾病。

複合字 **mail car·ri·er** *n.* 郵差

mail·man *n.* 郵差

mail *n.* 郵件 ／ *v.* 寄信

e-mail *n.* 電子郵件

記憶技巧

1. carry 是字根 car 黏接字尾 y 構成的,car 是 run 的意思,畢竟古時候沒有 car—汽車。

2. car 是封閉音節,a 唸短母音 /ɑ/,黏接字尾 y 時,重複字尾字母 r,y 取得音節首子音而不影響字根 car 的唸音。

own [on] *n.* 自己 ／ *v.* 擁有 ／ *adj.* 自己的

The owner of this company also owns two factories. He has a lot of money, but he never believes what he gets really belongs to him.

這家公司的所有人也擁有二家工廠。他很有錢,但從不相信他得到的真的都屬於他的。

聯想字 **have** *v.* 有

be·long *v.* 屬於

get *v.* 得到;拿到

衍生字 **own·er** *n.* 擁有者;所有人

play   [ple]   *n.* 戲劇／ *v.* 玩；演奏

Players were playing dodge ball on the playground and
cheerleaders were sitting on the ground around the players.

選手正在操場打躲避球，啦啦隊員則坐在選手周圍的地上。

| 衍生字 | **play·er**   *n.* 運動員；選手 |

| 複合字 | **play·ground**   *n.* 遊樂場；操場 |
| | **ground**   *n.* 地面；場地；根據 |

記憶技巧

play 的字尾 y 與 a 一起唸母音 /e/，黏接字尾 er 時，y 不變化。

- -

save   [sev]   *v.* 拯救；儲存；節省

A brave man saved the kid from danger, and for his safety, he
was set down in a safe place.

一位勇敢的男子從危險中救了那名孩童，為了他的安全，他被安置在一處安全
的地方。

| 同源字 | **safe**   *n.* 保險箱／ *adj.* 安全的；萬無一失的 |
| | **safe·ty**   *n.* 安全 |

| 反義字 | **dan·ger**   *n.* 危險 |
| | **dan·ger·ous**   *adj.* 危險的 |

記憶技巧

1. safe 與 save 同源，子音 /f/、/v/ 同發音部位。

2. safety = safe + ty，ty 是名詞字尾。

sing [sɪŋ] v. 唱歌；演唱

The popular singer sang two Taiwanese songs during the concert.

那位人氣歌手在演唱會唱了兩首臺語歌曲。

衍生字 sing·er n. 歌手

同源字 song n. 歌曲

記憶技巧

sing、sang、sung 及名詞 song 都是同源，母音通轉。

---

in·vite [ɪnˋvaɪt] v. 邀請

Many of my friends will be invited to experience a special treat. Join us!

我的許多朋友將受邀體驗一頓特別款待，加入我們吧！

聯想字 join v. 參加；加入
treat n. 特別款待 ／ v. 款待；對待；治癒

---

speak [spik] v. 說；講

The speaker gave a speech in Japanese because he is good at speaking the language.

演講者用日語演講，因為他擅長說該語言。

衍生字 speak·er n. 演講者；喇叭，speaker = speak + er
speech n. 演講；口語；說話

記憶技巧

speak、spoke、spoken 及名詞 speech 都是同源。

swim [swɪm] *n. / v.* 游泳

Tom wants to be a good swimmer, and he goes swimming in the swimming pool in his neighborhood every day.

湯姆想要成為一位出色的泳者,他每天都去他家附近的游泳池游泳。

聯想字 **pool** *n.* 水池;撞球
swim·ming pool *n.* 游泳池

衍生字 **swim·mer** *n.* 游泳者

記憶技巧

swim 是封閉音節,i 唸短母音 /ɪ/,黏接母音字母為首的字尾時,為維持唸音,重複字尾子音字母 m。

----

vis·it [ˋvɪzɪt] *n. / v.* 參觀;拜訪

Some visitors see the entire museum in just one visit.

有些訪客只在一次的參觀便看了整座博物館。

衍生字 **vis·it·or** *n.* 訪客;觀光客;參觀者,visitor = visit + or

----

wait [wet] *n. / v.* 等待

The waiters and waitresses are waiting for their first customers at the door.

男女服務生正在門口等待他們的首批客人。

衍生字 **wait·er** *n.* 男服務生
wait·ress *n.* 女服務生

記憶技巧

1. waiter = wait + er,站在餐桌旁等待客人招喚的侍者。

2. waitress = waiter + ess,非重音節字尾 ter 黏接母音字母為首的字尾時,ter /tɚ/ 分析為 /tər/,「子音＋短母音＋子音」結構,黏接母音字母為首字尾的 er 時,省略字母 e。

3. 為了維持詞素完整,waiter、waitress 的音節分別劃分為 wait·er、wait·ress。

小試身手 ★出自 90 年第二次基測

Playing computer games is fun. It has **become** very popular. Young people **like** to **do** it in their free time. Here are some important things you have to **know** when you **play** computer games.

First, you should **learn** English well. If your English is good enough, you can **understand** the computer games more clearly. Then you will **play** the games better than your friends.

Second, you should not **buy** illegal software. The fake copies are much cheaper, but they will easily **hurt** your computers.

Third, you should not **spend** too much time **playing** the games. That will **make** your eyes **become** weaker. **Take** a 10-minute rest after you **play** 50 minutes every time.

Follow these things and you can be a happy computer game player.

_____1. According to the **reading**, how can you **become** a good computer game player?

    (A) **Buy** a lot of software.

    (B) **Follow** the game rules.

    (C) **Spend** a long time **playing** computer games.

    (D) **Learn** English to **understand** the games better.

_____2. What is the best title for the **reading**?

    (A) The Most Popular Computer Games.

    (B) News About Illegal Computer Game Software.

    (C) Tips for **Playing** Computer Games Well and Safely.

    (D) Ways to **Find** Cheap and Fashionable Computer Games.

Unit **04**　　**學校**

🎧 Track 015

school　　[skul]　　*n.* 學校；上學時間；學院

School begins on October 30th.
學校在十月三十日開學。

---

el·e·men·ta·ry school　　[ˌɛləˈmɛntərɪ] [skul]　　*n.* 小學

Children in elementary school are learning some elementary lessons.
小學階段的孩童學習一些基礎課程。

聯想字　**el·e·men·ta·ry**　　*adj.* 基本的；基礎的

記憶技巧

elementary = element + ary，element 是指元素，ary 是形容詞字尾，
elementary 原意是屬於元素的。

---

ju·ni·or high school　　[ˈdʒunjɚ] [haɪ] [skul]　　*n.* 國中

David is junior to his sister by two years and he will become a
junior high school student this summer.
大衛比他姐姐小兩歲，他今年夏天將成為一名國中生。

聯想字　**ju·ni·or**　　*n.* 晚輩；年資較淺者 ／ *adj.* 年紀較輕的；資淺的

記憶技巧

junior 與年輕的—young 同源，原意是較年輕的。

se·ni·or high school [`sinjɚ] [haɪ] [skul] *n.* 高級中學

My grandfather is a senior teacher in a senior high school.
我祖父是一所高級中學的資深老師。

聯想字 **se·ni·or** *n.* 上司；年長者 ／ *adj.* 年紀較大的；資深的

記憶技巧
senior 的 sen 是老的—old 的意思，sir—先生的尊稱也是 old 的意思。

teach·er [`titʃɚ] *n.* 教師

Teachers can learn from teaching students.
老師可從教導學生中學習。

聯想字 **teach** *v.* 教導

stu·dent [`stjudnt] *n.* 學生

All the students will be studying hard for the final exam.
所有學生即將為期末考用功讀書。

聯想字 **stud·y** *n.* 書房 ／ *v.* 學習；用功

記憶技巧
student 的原意是 "one who is studying" ——位讀書的人。

grade [gred] *n.* 年級；成績

My cousin is a 9th grader, and he usually gets good grades on tests.
我堂哥是國三學生，考試常得到好的成績。

衍生字 **gra·der** *n.* ……年級學生

class [klæs] *n.* 班級；一節課

Some of my classmates have to go to another classroom for their own class.

我一些同學必須到另一教室上他們自己的課。

複合字 **class·room** *n.* 教室

class·mate *n.* 同班同學，mate 有夥伴、配偶的意思。

---

black·board [`blæk͵bord] *n.* 黑板

Davis drew a picture on the blackboard with chalk of different colors.

Davis 用不同顏色的粉筆在黑板上畫一幅圖。

聯想字 **board** *n.* 木板；板

chalk *n.* 粉筆

---

les·son [`lɛsn] *n.* 課程；教科書中的一課；教訓

The student has never taken any acting lessons.

那位學生從未上過任何表演課程。

記憶技巧

lesson 的原意是大聲朗讀聖經或學生學習的事物，與蒐集—collect 的字根 lect 同源。

---

u·ni·form [`junə͵fɔrm] *n.* 制服 ／ *adj.* 一致的

The newcomer filled in the form and put on his uniform.

那位新來的人填好表格，隨後穿上他的制服。

聯想字 **form** *n.* 形式；表格 ／ *v.* 形成

記憶技巧

uniform = uni + form，字首 uni 是 one 的意思，形式一致的衣服是制服。

test [tɛst] *n.* / *v.* 測驗；檢查；檢測

With the midterm tests coming up, there will be many quizzes and assignments for students.

期中考即將來臨，學生將有許多小考和作業。

聯想字 **quiz** *n.* 小考

---

li·bra·ry [ˋlaɪ͵brɛrɪ] *n.* 圖書館

My aunt has been working as a librarian in a public library for ten years.

十年來，我阿姨一直在一所公立圖書館擔任圖書館管理員。

衍生字 **li·brar·i·an** *n.* 圖書館員

記憶技巧
1. library = libr + ary，libr 是書—book 的意思，字尾 ary 表示場所。
2. librarian = library + an，輕音節的字尾 y 不黏接字尾綴詞，變換為字母 i 才黏接字尾綴詞。

---

pub·lic [ˋpʌblɪk] *n.* 民眾 / *adj.* 公開的；民眾的；公立的

The secret only became public after the factory owner's death.

工廠老闆過世之後，那個秘密才公開。

衍生字 **pub·lic·ly** *adv.* 公開地；當眾

記憶技巧
1. public = publ + ic，字根 publ 與受歡迎的—popular 的字根 popul 同源，都是人—people 的意思，單字語意都與人有關。
2. 字尾 ic、ive、y 都表示狀態。

spe·cial ［`spɛʃəl］ *n.* 特價商品／*adj.* 特別的；額外的；專門的

It's quite common to see couples who dress alike. It's nothing special.

看到裝扮相似的情侶是蠻常見的，一點也不特別。

反義字 **com·mon** *adj.* 普通的；常見的；共同的

記憶技巧
1. special = spec + i + al，字根 spec 是觀察—to observe 的意思，因明顯特質而從其他事物標示出來，且被人觀察到的是特別的。
2. al 是形容詞字尾，i 是填補字母，字母 c 黏接 ial 形成 cial 字母串，唸音是 /ʃəl/。

 小試身手 ★ 出自 93 年第二次基測

　　Kelly is a very special **student** in my **class**. Her father is an American, and her mother is a Chinese from Hong Kong. Kelly was born in New York and finished **elementary school** there. Then the family decided to move to Taiwan because Kelly's father found a new job in Taipei. Kelly could speak only English, but her parents did not send her to a **special school** for foreign children. <u>They</u> wanted her to study in a **regular junior high school** and to make friends with the local students.

　　Kelly has to work very hard at **school**. English is easy for her, of course. **Math** is OK, too. But **Chinese** and **History** are <u>big headaches</u> for her because she cannot **read** the **books** in **Chinese**. She often comes to me, her **English teacher**, to **ask questions** about **Chinese** and **History**. She is trying very hard, and I believe she will do well in Taiwan.

_____1. Who wrote the two paragraphs?

(A) Kelly herself.

(B) Kelly's mother.

(C) Kelly's **teacher**.

(D) Kelly's **classmate**.

_____2. Why did Kelly's family move to Taiwan?

(A) Kelly's father changed his job.

(B) Kelly wanted to **study** in a foreign country.

(C) Kelly's parents had many friends in Taiwan.

(D) Kelly's mother needed to **learn Chinese** to do business.

_____3. Who are <u>They</u> in the first paragraph?

(A) Kelly's parents.

(B) Kelly's **teachers**.

(C) Foreign children.

(D) Kelly's American friends.

_____4. What does <u>big headaches</u> mean in the second paragraph?

(A) Useful tips.

(B) Strict rules.

(C) Expensive **books**.

(D) Difficult **subjects**.

Unit 05 動物一

🎧 Track 020

an·i·mal [`ænəml̩] *n.* 動物

Both of my cousins really are animal lovers.
我的兩位表弟都是十足的動物熱愛者。

---

zoo [zu] *n.* 動物園

The cages in the zoo will be left open during the night.
動物園的獸籠在夜間都會是保持開著。

聯想字 **cage** *n.* 籠子；獸籠／*v.* 關進籠子

---

cat [kæt] *n.* 貓；貓科動物

Lions and tigers both belong to the cat family.
獅子和老虎都屬於貓科動物家族。

聯想字 **li·on** *n.* 獅子
ti·ger *n.* 老虎

---

dog [dɔg] *n.* 狗；犬

Red foxes are in the dog family. They look like puppies when they are young.
火狐屬犬科家族。牠們幼小時看起來像小狗。

衍生字 **dog·gy** *n.* 狗／*adj.* 狗的
聯想字 **pup·py** *n.* 小狗；幼犬
fox *n.* 狐狸

ox [ɑks] *n.* 公牛　複數形：ox·en

On this farm, there are three times as many cows as there are oxen.

這處農場，母牛的數量是公牛的三倍。

聯想字 **cow** *n.* 母牛

---

horse [hɔrs] *n.* 馬

Zebras and hippos are found in Africa, but horses are not.

斑馬及河馬能在非洲被發現，但是馬卻不能。

聯想字 **ze·bra** *n.* 斑馬
　　　 hip·po *n.* 河馬

記憶技巧

字源上，horse 與汽車—car、跑—run 等單字同源。

---

goat [got] *n.* 山羊

Goats are kept on farms for their skin and meat, and sheep are kept to provide milk, meat and wool.

山羊是為了牠們的羊皮和肉而被飼養在農場，綿羊則是為了提供羊奶、肉和羊毛而被飼養。

聯想字 **sheep** *n.* 綿羊

---

ko·a·la [koˋɑlə] *n.* 無尾熊

Koalas live in eucalyptus trees and eat their leaves.

無尾熊住在尤加利樹上並且吃它們的樹葉。

聯想字 **bear** *n.* 熊

---

el·e·phant [ˋɛləfənt] *n.* 大象

In the past few years, the elephant population in Africa has been halved.

在過去幾年中，非洲大象的數量已經變成一半。

mon·key [ˋmʌŋki] *n.* 猴子

The monkeys are riding a unicycle one after another.
那些猴子正接二連三地騎著單輪車。

- -

pig [pɪg] *n.* 豬

The farmer will build a pig pen behind the cow barn.
那位農夫將要在牛舍後面蓋一座豬圈。

衍生字 **pig·let** *n.* 小豬

- -

drag·on [ˋdrægən] *n.* 龍

Dragons appear in the folklore of many cultures around the world.
龍出現在世界各地許多文化的民間傳說中。

複合字 **drag·on·fly** *n.* 蜻蜓

- -

mouse [maʊs] *n.* 老鼠　複數形：mice

This morning, I found the glue trap in my garage had caught a mouse.
今天早上我發現車庫的黏鼠板抓到一隻老鼠。

聯想字 **rat** *n.* 老鼠
kan·ga·roo *n.* 袋鼠

記憶技巧
字尾是 oo 的單字，重音節在最後一音節。

- -

rab·bit [ˋræbɪt] *n.* 兔子

I saw a rabbit hopping across the grass in the park.
我看到有隻兔子在公園草坪上到處跳來跳去。

bird [bɝd] *n.* 鳥;禽

Geese are a large water bird similar to ducks.
鵝是一種與鴨子相似的大型水禽。

聯想字 **goose** *n.* 鵝;鵝肉　複數形:geese

★出自 94 年第二次基測

Susan was a woman who hated **animals**. She never wanted to keep any **pets** at home. To her, all **animals** were dirty and boring. Susan could never understand why people would like to have **cats** or **dogs** in the house. It was so stupid!

Last month Susan's daughter, Penny, came home from school with a **mouse** in a box. Susan was very angry. But Penny said that it was <u>her</u> homework. Her teacher asked each student to take care of an **animal** and learn to get along with it. Susan had to say yes.

It was fun for Penny at the beginning, but then she got lazy and forgot to do her homework. It became Susan's homework. She gave it food and water every day and found that the **mouse** was in fact not dirty. She even talked to it! It was not boring or stupid! Now Susan is having a good time with "her" **mouse**. She named it Nini. And she is going to buy another one to make a pair.

Track 023

Unit 05 動物一

小試身手

_____1. Why was Susan so angry when she first saw the mouse?

    (A) The **mouse** bit her.

    (B) She liked **cats** better.

    (C) She did not want any **animals** in her house.

    (D) The **mouse** was the **animal** she hated most.

_____2. What happened to the **mouse** in the end?

    (A) It got sick.

    (B) It had a baby.

    (C) It became Susan's **pet**.

    (D) It was sent to a **pet** shop.

_____3. What does <u>her</u> mean in the second paragraph?

    (A) Susan's.

    (B) Penny's.

    (C) Penny's teacher's.

    (D) Penny's classmate's.

答案：1. (C)；2. (C)；3. (B)

Unit 06　動物二

bat　[bæt]　*n.* 蝙蝠；球棒 ／ *v.* 用球棒擊球

A bat is a small mammal with wings that flies at night.
蝙蝠是一種有翅膀且夜間飛行的小型哺乳動物。

- -

frog　[frɑg]　*n.* 青蛙

Most frogs can jump up to twenty times their own height.
大部分的青蛙能跳至自己高度的二十倍。

- -

snake　[snek]　*n.* 蛇

The farmer is afraid of being bitten by a snake.
那位農夫怕被蛇咬。

- -

tur·tle　[`tɝtl]　*n.* 烏龜

Turtles are reptiles with protective shells, which live on land, in the ocean and in lakes and rivers.
烏龜是有保護殼的爬蟲類動物，住在陸地、海洋和湖泊及河流中。

- -

fish　[fɪʃ]　*n.* 魚；魚肉 ／ *v.* 釣魚

The fisherman knows sharks are fish, but he doesn't know whales are actually marine mammals.
那位漁夫知道鯊魚是魚類，但是不知道鯨魚實際上是海洋哺乳動物。

聯想字	**shark**　*n.* 鯊魚
	whale　*n.* 鯨魚
衍生字	**fish·er·man**　*n.* 漁夫

spi·der ['spaɪdɚ] *n.* 蜘蛛

Those children are watching a spider spinning its web.

那些孩子正看著一隻蜘蛛在結網。

記憶技巧

字源上，spider 與紡紗—spin 同源，拖拉—draw、延伸—stretch 的意思，都與蜘蛛吐絲編織蜘蛛網的動作有關。

---

pet [pɛt] *n.* 寵物／*v.* 輕撫

There used to be a fashion for keeping insects as pets.

以前有一種時尚，就是飼養昆蟲當作寵物。

---

in·sect ['ɪnsɛkt] *n.* 昆蟲

Ants, bugs, flies and butterflies are all insects.

螞蟻、小蟲、蒼蠅和蝴蝶都是昆蟲。

記憶技巧

insect = in + sect，in 是進入—into，sect 是切—cut，古代認為 insect 是一種分成幾部分的動物。

---

bug [bʌg] *n.* 小蟲

The gardener lifted the stone to see if there were any bugs underneath.

園丁抬起石頭看看底下是否有任何小蟲。

---

ant [ænt] *n.* 螞蟻

The ant is a small insect which lives under the ground in large social groups.

螞蟻是一種以大社群住在地底下的小昆蟲。

bee [bi] *n.* 蜜蜂

Bees turn nectar into honey.
蜜蜂將花粉變成蜂蜜。

聯想字 **hon·ey** *n.* 蜂蜜；心愛的人

---

but·ter·fly [ˋbʌtɚˌflaɪ] *n.* 蝴蝶

It is fun to watch butterflies flying from flower to flower.
看著蝴蝶在花叢間飛舞真是有趣。

記憶技巧

butter + fly，奶油—butter、飛—fly 與蝴蝶有甚麼關聯呢？蝴蝶會飛，所以重點在 butter，一説是蝴蝶攝取奶油為食，一説是蝴蝶翅膀的顏色看似奶油，另一説則是蝴蝶排泄物的顏色。

---

chick·en [ˋtʃɪkɪn] *n.* 雞；雞肉 ╱ *adj.* 膽小的

Chickens and hens are traditionally raised indoors, and so are turkeys.
傳統上小雞和母雞都養在室內，火雞也是。

聯想字 **hen** *n.* 母雞
　　　　tur·key *n.* 火雞；火雞肉

記憶技巧

字源上，chicken 源自公雞—cock，鳥叫的擬聲字，en 是小的意思，hen 則是指為著日出而唱歌的鳥。

---

duck [dʌk] *n.* 鴨；鴨肉；雁

Building a pond would bring the ducks in so we could watch them.
蓋一座池塘會引來雁鴨到裡面，這樣我們就可以觀察他們。

gi·raffe [dʒəˋræf]   *n.* 長頸鹿

A full-grown giraffe can be six times heavier than a full-grown lion.
一頭完全長大的長頸鹿可以是一頭成獅的六倍重。

小試身手 ★ 出自 98 年第二次基測

Last month Jim brought a baby **cat** home from the **pet** shop. She is beautiful with gray and white hair. Jim gave her the name Popo. He and his family love her very much and often talk to her. Popo is very shy and afraid of strangers. Every time Jim brings his friends home, she will hide herself. It takes time to make friends with Popo. But when she sees you as a friend, she will be happy to be with you all the time. Popo often lies quietly next to Jim when he is home. Sometimes she sits by the window looking at the flowers in the garden.

The family is always busy, and it is not easy for them to get together. But since they got Popo, they have tried to spend time together playing with their <u>little girl</u>, who has become the center of their family life.

_____1. What can we learn from the reading?

    (A) Flowers make a house more beautiful.

    (B) Keeping a **pet** helps a family get together.

    (C) We should be friendly to people who visit us.

    (D) It takes time to make friends with people who love **cats**.

_____2. Which is true about the <u>little girl</u> in the reading?

    (A) She loves to hide herself when playing

    (B) She cannot be quiet when Jim is around.

    (C) She does not feel comfortable with strangers.

    (D) She was found by Jim when she got lost on the street.

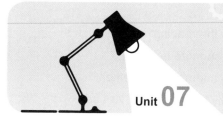

Unit 07　食物

🎧 Track 028

food　[fud]　n. 食物

My family usually does our weekly shopping at a local fresh food market.

我的家人經常在一處當地的鮮食市場採購一週的食物。

| 聯想字 | **fresh** | adj. 新鮮的 |
| 同源字 | **feed** | v. 餵養；提供食物 |

【記憶技巧】

food 與 feed、過去式 fed、過去分詞 fed 都是同源，母音通轉。

---

meal　[mil]　n. 餐

I agree personally with the idea of eating only two meals a day, breakfast and lunch, while avoiding dinner.

我個人贊同一天只吃兩餐的想法，就是早餐和午餐，避開晚餐。

聯想字	**break·fast**	n. 早餐
	lunch	n. 午餐
	din·ner	n. 晚餐

【記憶技巧】

1. breakfast = break + fast，break 是打破，fast 是禁食，早餐是指打破自前一天晚餐之後未進食—禁食的一餐。

2. dinner 原意是 "first big meal of the day"，一天的第一頓大餐，也就是 breakfast 的意思，後來表示 "main meal of the day"，一天主要的一餐，也就是晚餐。唸音方面，dinner 字中重複 n 各分二音節，前面音節 din 是封閉音節，i 唸短母音 /ɪ/。另外，dinner 與進食—dine 同源，但不是 dine 黏接 er 所衍生的，diner—進食者才是 dine + er。

rice [raɪs] *n.* 稻米；飯

Bamboo rice is a type of rice especially popular in Asia.
竹筒飯是一種在亞洲特別受歡迎的米食。

記憶技巧

rice 有幾個中文對應的詞一種在田裡的是稻、收割之後的是米、烹煮之後
則是飯，種稻、碾米、吃飯呈現中文動詞與 rice 的搭配對應。

noo·dle [`nudl̩] *n.* 麵

Cincinnati-style spaghetti is a dish of noodles served with chili
on top.
辛辛那提風味的義大利麵是一種上層搭配辣椒的麵食。

聯想字 **spa·ghet·ti** *n.* 義大利麵條

piz·za [`pitsə] *n.* 披薩

I am trying to create a handmade pizza with a pie sheet.
我一直嘗試創出一種有派皮的手工披薩。

聯想字 **pie** *n.* 派

dump·ling [`dʌmplɪŋ] *n.* 餃子

We've been making this vegetarian dumpling recipe for a long
time.
我們編寫這款素食水餃食譜很久了。

ham·burg·er [`hæmbɝɡɚ] *n.* 漢堡

I ordered a hamburger with ham and egg for my breakfast.
我點了一份火腿蛋漢堡當早餐。

聯想字 **ham** *n.* 火腿

egg *n.* 蛋；蛋狀物；卵

French fries   [frɛntʃ] [fraɪz]   *n.* 薯條

I would like a hamburger, an order of French fries and a small Coke.

我要一個漢堡，一份薯條和一杯小可。

---

hot dog   [hɑt] [dɔg]   *n.* 熱狗

My friend, Mark, planned to start a hot dog stand business.

我的朋友馬克打算開創一番熱狗攤的事業。

---

sand·wich   [`sændwɪtʃ]   *n.* 三明治

I usually eat a tuna sandwich as a light lunch.

我經常吃一份鮪魚三明治當輕便午餐。

---

sal·ad   [`sæləd]   *n.* 沙拉

Add olive oil, black pepper and some salt in the salad mixture.

把橄欖油、黑胡椒和一些鹽巴加入沙拉。

同源字 salt   *n.* 鹽

---

meat   [mit]   *n.* 肉類

Red meat such as beef and pork can form part of a healthy diet, but eating too much steak will be unhealthy.

例如牛肉和豬肉等紅肉可形成健康飲食的一部分，但是吃太多牛排就不健康。

聯想字 beef   *n.* 牛肉
　　　　steak   *n.* 牛排
　　　　pork   *n.* 豬肉

記憶技巧

1. meat 原意是 food—食物的項目。

2. 字源上，pork 是指年輕的豬—young pig，與 pig 同源。

3. steak 與筷子—chopstick 的 stick—木條、刺入同源，母音通轉。
   steak 是條狀的肉，與削成條狀的 stick 相似。

soup　[sup]　*n.* 湯

Actually, I am not a big soup person.
事實上，我不是一個喝很多湯的人。

---

sug·ar　[`ʃʊgɚ]　*n.* 糖

Don't add too much sugar in my coffee, or it will be too sweet for my liking.
不要放太多糖到我的咖啡，不然就著我的口味來說就太甜了。

聯想字　**sweet**　*adj.* 甜的；悅耳的；可愛的
衍生字　**sug·ar·y**　*adj.* 含糖的

---

but·ter　[`bʌtɚ]　*n.* 奶油

A very small percentage of butter is oil.
奶油中的油脂只占很小的比例。

聯想字　**oil**　*n.* 食用油；石油

記憶技巧
1. oil 原意是指 olive oil—橄欖油，而 oil 也源自橄欖—olive，字母 i 調換拼字順序。
2. butter 原意是牛奶的油脂部分—the fatty part of milk，與母牛—cow、牛肉—beef 等與牛有關的單字同源。

In 2005, three **rice** farmers in Tainan, Taiwan, became famous because of the movie *Let It Be*. The movie shows how the three farmers live and work on the land. People are surprised by their stories and by their love for the land they live on.

For the farmers, the land is the only hope they see in life. They stay happy in the light of hope, whether the light is strong or weak. Even in hard times, the farmers still give thanks to the land and keep working happily on their farms. When their farms grow very little **rice**, they just laugh and say, "It's OK. Don't worry! We're still living a happy life!"

That is the way many Taiwanese farmers live with their problems. They work hard and never ask for much from the land. All they want is to love and live for <u>it</u>. Because of the movie, the world can remember the farmers in Taiwan for their hard work and their "let-it-be" idea about life.

_____ 1. What can we learn from the reading?

    (A) Taiwanese farmers need help from foreign countries.

    (B) The farmland in Taiwan is getting worse for growing rice.

    (C) Many farmers in Taiwan are happy in good and bad times.

    (D) Some Taiwanese farmers are trying new ways of growing rice.

_____ 2. Which is NOT said about Taiwanese farmers in the reading?

    (A) They do more but do not ask for much.

    (B) They thank the land for what they have

    (C) They often look on the bright side of life.

    (D) They work hard and are paid back with lots of rice.

_____ 3. What does it mean?

    (A) The rice.

    (B) The land.

    (C) The movie.

    (D) The money.

答案：1. (C)；2. (D)；3. (B)

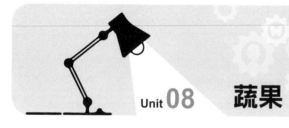

🎧 Track 032

vege·ta·ble [ˈvɛdʒtəbl̩] *n.* 蔬菜

The potato is the most popular vegetable in England.
馬鈴薯在英國是最受歡迎的蔬菜。

衍生字 **veg·e·tar·i·an** *n.* 素食者 ／ *adj.* 素食的
vegetarian = vegetable + arian

----

bean [bin] *n.* 豆莢；豆子

I've loved BBQ baked beans since my childhood.
我從小就喜愛烘烤的豆子。

----

let·tuce [ˈlɛtɪs] *n.* 萵苣

A serving of French fries and a lettuce leaf, I don't call it a meal!
我不會把一份薯條和一片萵苣葉稱為一餐。

----

pump·kin [ˈpʌmpkɪn] *n.* 南瓜

This is the traditional handmade pumpkin pie, and it's perfect for holidays!
這是傳統手工南瓜派，假日的完美食物。

----

to·ma·to [təˈmeto] *n.* 番茄　複數形：tomatoes

You need to cut the tomato in half and scoop out the seeds.
你得把番茄切成兩半，然後挖出裡面的籽。

fruit [frut] *n.* 水果

Would you like some fruit for dessert?

你要一些水果當作飯後甜點嗎？

記憶技巧

字源上，fruit 的意思是享受─to enjoy，水果是供人類或動物享用的植物果實。

ap·ple [ˈæpl̩] *n.* 蘋果

The apple trees in their garden are bearing fruit.

他們花園裡的蘋果樹正在結果子。

ba·na·na [bəˈnænə] *n.* 香蕉

Could you chop up a banana for the fruit salad?

麻煩你將一根水果沙拉用的香蕉切片好嗎？

grape [grep] *n.* 葡萄

It is reported that seedless grapes are unnatural.

報導說無籽葡萄是不天然的。

gua·va [ˈgwɑvə] *n.* 番石榴

Some people prefer to drink guava juice than to eat guava directly.

比起直接吃番石榴，一些人較喜歡喝番石榴果汁。

lem·on [ˈlɛmən] *n.* 檸檬

Would you like a slice of fresh lemon in your tea?

你的茶裡要放一片新鮮檸檬嗎？

or·ange   [ˋɔrɪndʒ]   *n.* 柳橙;橙色 ／ *adj.* 橙色的

Tom was thirsty and he drank two whole glassfuls of orange juice.

Tom 很渴,他喝了兩杯滿滿的柳橙汁。

聯想字 **tan·ge·rine**   *n.* 柑橘 ／ *adj.* 橘紅色

---

pa·pa·ya   [pəˋpaɪə]   *n.* 木瓜

Papaya milk has long been a popular Taiwanese drink.

長遠以來,木瓜牛奶一直是人氣臺灣飲品。

---

peach   [pitʃ]   *n.* 桃子

These pears are still too firm to eat, but those peaches are not.

這些梨子還太硬而無法食用,但是那些桃子不會。

聯想字 **pear**   *n.* 梨子

---

straw·ber·ry   [ˋstrɔbɛrɪ]   *n.* 草莓

They picked some strawberries and placed them in a box with straw.

他們挑了一些草莓,然後放在一個鋪著稻草的盒子裡。

記憶技巧

strawberry 是複合字,straw   *n.* 稻草;吸管,ber·ry   *n.* 醬果

小試身手　★ 出自 94 年第一次基測

Heartland is a beautiful town in which cars and motorcycles are not allowed. The town is famous for its blue sky and fresh air. The weather there is nice and warm all the year, so trees and flowers grow well in all seasons.

I went to Heartland last month and stayed there for five days. Every morning I woke up to the songs of birds. Then I would take a walk or ride a bicycle along the country roads. **Orchards** and **gardens** were everywhere. **Flower** shops and **coffee** houses were also on the way. Every night from my window I could see bright stars in the sky, and I would go to sleep with the smell of **grass**.

The five-day holiday in Heartland gave me a lot of surprises. I hope I can go there again some day and spend more time there.

_____1. Why did the writer go to Heartland?

    (A) To build a house.

    (B) To spend a vacation.

    (C) To work as a farmer.

    (D) To give a surprise party.

_____2. If the writer is talking to friends about Heartland, what will she/he say?

    (A) The sky in Heartland is very clear.

    (B) Life in Heartland is fast and modern.

    (C) Taxis in Heartland are very convenient.

    (D) The Christmas snow in Heartland is beautiful.

_____3. Which is most UNLIKELY to be found in Heartland?

    (A) A shop that fixes bicycles.

    (B) A market that sells fresh **fruit**.

    (C) A factory that makes motorcycles.

    (D) A **coffee** shop that also sells **flowers.**

答案：1. (B)；2. (A)；3. (C)

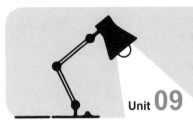

Unit 09　點心和飲料

 Track 035

snack　[snæk]　*n.* 點心

Most snack foods are high in fat, salt and sugar.
大部份點心食品都含有大量脂肪、鹽及糖。

- -

can·dy　[`kændɪ]　*n.* 糖果

Too much candy is really bad for your teeth and health.
太多糖果對你的牙齒和健康很不好。

- -

choc·o·late　[`tʃɑkəlɪt]　*n.* 巧克力

More than 50 percent of people prefer dark chocolate to milk chocolate.
比起牛奶巧克力，超過百分之五十的人較喜歡黑巧克力。

- -

ice cream　[aɪs] [krim]　*n.* 冰淇淋

Can I have a lick of your chocolate ice cream?
我可以舔一口你的巧克力冰淇淋嗎？

衍生字　**iced**　*adj.* 加冰的
　　　　ic·y　*adj.* 結冰的
　　　　cream·y　*adj.* 含鮮奶油的
　　　　cream·e·ry　*n.* 乳品商店

記憶技巧
ice cream 是複合字，ice　*n.* 冰，cream　*n.* 鮮奶油

pop·corn [`pɑpˌkɔrn] n. 爆米花

How much is a tub of popcorn and two large drinks?

一桶爆米花和二杯大杯飲料是多少錢呢？

記憶技巧

popcorn 是複合字，pop v. 發出砰的一聲，corn n. 玉米

cheese [tʃiz] n. 起司；乳酪

Would you like a slice of cheese with your toast?

你的吐司要夾一片起司嗎？

cake [kek] n. 蛋糕

We need to bake a chocolate cake and some cookies for the party.

我們需要為派對烘烤一個巧克力蛋糕和一些餅乾。

同源字 cook·ie n. 餅乾

drink [drɪŋk] n. 飲料／v. 喝

For Mongolians, milk tea is an important daily drink.

對蒙古人而言，奶茶是一種重要的日常飲料。

衍生字 drink·er n. 飲酒者

milk [mɪlk] n. 牛奶／v. 擠奶

Milking a cow by hand isn't hard to do at all once you get the hang of it.

一旦你掌握了用手擠牛奶的技巧，它一點也不難。

tea [ti] n. 茶；茶葉

How do you like your tea, strong or weak?

你的茶要怎麼沖泡，濃或是淡的？

cof·fee [`kɔfɪ] *n.* 咖啡

Could I have two cups of black coffee, please?

可以麻煩給我兩杯黑咖啡嗎？

----

co·la [`kolə] *n.* 可樂

Coke and Pepsi are both types of cola.

可口可樂和百事可樂都是可樂的種類。

----

so·da [`sodə] *n.* 汽水；小蘇打

Baking soda can be used as a natural carpet cleaner.

小蘇打粉可以用來當作一種天然的地毯清潔劑。

----

juice [dʒus] *n.* 汁；液

In this online supermarket, we can find the best prices on apple juice and fruit drinks.

在這間線上超市，我們可以找到蘋果汁和果汁的最好價格。

衍生字 **juic·y** *adj.* 多汁的，juicy = juice + y

----

wa·ter [`wɔtɚ] *n.* 水；水域 ／ *v.* 澆水

After waving goodbye to the guests, villagers washed several watermelons with fresh water beside the road.

揮手向客人道別後，村民在路邊用清水洗了幾顆西瓜。

衍生字 **wa·ter·y** *adj.* 含水的、味道淡的

複合字 **wa·ter·mel·on** *n.* 西瓜

同源字 **wave** *n.* 波浪 ／ *v.* 揮舞

wash *n.* 洗滌 ／ *v.* 洗滌；沖刷

win·ter *n.* 冬天

A small town has a good chance of ___(1)___ that can bring in a lot of money, if it has something special to be proud of. One example is Gukeng town of Yunlin, Taiwan. Gukeng has long been famous for growing good **coffee**, but the town didn't start to make much money from it until some years ago. As more and more people have visited Gukeng for its **coffee**, the **coffee** farmers have begun to open their farms to the public. At these farms, people can have the fun of finding out where **coffee** comes from. ___(2)___, **coffee** shops are opened all over Gukeng, and people can take a rest and taste delicious **coffee** on the sidewalks in or after a day's visit. The new businesses make a better life possible for those who ___(3)___ the town. They don't have to leave the town to find jobs in other places.

_____1. (A) growing the best **tea**

(B) starting a new business

(C) selling old farming lands

(D) opening a shopping center

_____2. (A) First

(B) Also

(C) However

(D) For example

_____3. (A) live in

(B) hear about

(C) take a trip to

(D) are interested in

答案：1. (B)；2. (B)；3. (A)

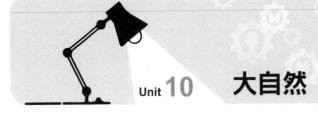

Unit **10** 大自然

🎧 Track 038

na·ture [`netʃɚ] *n.* 大自然、本質

The writer is sharing her love for nature with each of her readers.
作者一直與她的每一位讀者分享她對大自然的熱愛。

衍生字 **nat·u·ral** *adj.* 天然的；天生的
natural = nature + al，al 是形容詞字尾，表示狀態。
un·nat·u·ral *adj.* 不自然的；反常的
unnatural = un + natural，字首 un = not。

記憶技巧
nature = nat + ure，字根 nat 是出生—birth 的意思，本於出生時的特質就是本質。

---

moun·tain [`maʊntn] *n.* 山

The climber went hiking on the hill and then climbing a mountain.
該登山客去那座山丘健行，然後爬一座山。

聯想字 **hill** *n.* 山丘
climb *n.* 攀登；爬升 ／ *v.* 爬；攀登
climb·er *n.* 攀登者；登山者

記憶技巧
mountain = mount + ain，mount 意思是站出來—stand out、爬—climb、上馬—get up on a horse，ain 是名詞字尾。

---

lake [lek] *n.* 湖

We went boating on that lake on the last day of the vacation.
假期的最後一天，我們去那一座湖划船。

riv·er [ˈrɪvɚ] *n.* 河流

The tourists arrived as scheduled at the bridge that crossed the River Thames.

觀光客按照安排時間到達跨越泰晤士河的那座橋。

聯想字 **bridge** *n.* 橋;橋牌

衍生字 **ar·rive** *v.* 到達
arrive = ar + river,字首 ar 表示到—to,到達是指到達河流。

----

pond [pɑnd] *n.* 池塘

The pond was found to be alive with frogs.

那座池塘到處都是青蛙。

----

sea [si] *n.* 海 複數形:seas

I enjoyed going swimming in the sea during my stay at the fishing village.

待在漁村的時候,我喜歡去海裡游泳。

----

beach [bitʃ] *n.* 海灘

We spent the afternoon on the beach enjoying the sunshine.

我們在海灘渡過午後,享受著陽光。

----

land [lænd] *n.* 陸地;土地 ╱ *v.* 登陸

This sort of land is no good for growing watermelons.

這種土地不適合種植西瓜。

----

is·land [ˈaɪlənd] *n.* 島嶼

Madagascar is the third biggest island in the world.

馬達加斯加島是世界第三大島嶼。

衍生字 **is·land·er** *n.* 島民

farm　[fɑrm]　*n.* 農場／ *v.* 耕作；養殖

This farmer's family has farmed this land for over a century.
這位農夫的家族已在這片土地耕種超過一世紀。

衍生字 **farm·er**　*n.* 農夫，farmer = farm + er，耕作或養殖的人是農夫。

---

plant　[plænt]　*n.* 植物／ *v.* 栽種

My family will plant cherry blossoms in our new garden.
我家要在我們的新花園種植櫻花樹。

---

tree　[tri]　*n.* 樹木

These fruit trees will have to be cut down to make way for the new building.
為了騰出空間給新建築物，這些果樹將必須砍掉。

---

flow·er　[`flaʊɚ]　*n.* 花

These flowers will become fruit that will bear seeds, which we can plant to grow new trees.
這些花會變成結種子的果子，我們可以拿來種植以長出新的樹株。

聯想字 **seed**　*n.* 種子

---

grass　[græs]　*n.* 草

With the spring coming along, the grass is growing green.
隨著春天的到臨，草坪逐漸變成綠色。

衍生字 **gras·sy**　*adj.* 長滿青草的
同源字 **green**　*n.* 綠色／ *adj.* 綠色的
　　　 grow　*v.* 種植；成長

---

rock　[rɑk]　*n.* 岩石；搖滾樂／ *v.* 搖動

The rock weighs over five tons and is six-feet tall.
那塊岩石超過五噸重，六英呎高。

小試身手 ★出自 100 年第二次基測

When you hear birds singing, do you want to sing with them? When the light wind blows, can you feel its friendly touch on your face? Are you excited to see the first little **flower** in the early spring?

Nature can color our everyday lives with lovely surprises. All we have to do is get close to it and feel it from our heart. If we find some time to enjoy the simple, easy moments under the clear sky, along the quiet river, or just in the park near our houses, we can feel many wonderful things out there.

Why not get away from your busy work and take a rest in Mother **Nature**'s arms? Sing to **Nature**'s music, dance with the wind, and look for the magic of life. You'll find the gift **Nature** has prepared for you.

_____1. What is the writer trying to say about **Nature**?

　　(A) It is badly hurt by us.

　　(B) It gives us lots of joy.

　　(C) It is hard to understand.

　　(D) It gives us ideas for writing.

_____2. Which experience is NOT said in the reading?

　　(A) Singing with birds.

　　(B) Fishing in the river.

　　(C) Feeling the wind's touch.

　　(D) Seeing the first spring **flower**.

答案：1. (B)；2. (B)

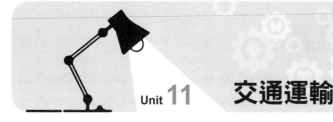

🎧 Track 041

traf·fic [`træfɪk] *n.* 交通量／*v.* 非法交易

There was heavy traffic on the highway this evening.
今晚高速公路車流量很大。

---

bike [baɪk] *n.* 腳踏車／*v.* 騎腳踏車

The boy got on his bike and rode off.
男孩跨上腳踏車，隨即騎走了。

聯想字 **ride** *n.* 搭乘；兜風／*v.* 騎；乘
同義字 **bi·cy·cle** *n.* 腳踏車

記憶技巧
bicycle = two + cycle，cycle 是輪子—wheel 的意思。

---

mo·tor·cy·cle [`motɚˌsaɪkl̩] *n.* 機車

The heavy motorcycle was speeding and hit a scooter at the intersection.
重機超速，在十字路口撞到一部輕型機車。

衍生字 **mo·tor·cy·cl·ist** *n.* 機車騎士
聯想字 **scooter** *n.* 小輪摩托車

記憶技巧
1. motorcycle = motor + cycle，motor = mot + or，mot 與移動—move 同源，產生動力的機械是 motor，中文「馬達」是 motor 的音譯。
2. scooter = scoot + er，scoot 是疾走、飛奔的意思，與 shoot—迅速通過、投球同源，音節首子音轉音。

car [kɑr] *n.* 汽車

The truck driver drives his own sports car to work every day.

那位卡車司機每天開著自己的跑車上工。

| 聯想字 | **drive** *n.* 大道；駕車路程；磁碟機 ／ *v.* 開車；迫使 |
| 衍生字 | **driv·er** *n.* 司機；驅動程式 |

tax·i [ˋtæksɪ] *n.* 計程車

The backpacker took a taxi from the station to the museum.

那位背包客從車站搭計程車到博物館。

bus [bʌs] *n.* 公車

The bus will arrive at the bus stop in two minutes.

二分鐘之後公車將抵達車站。

| 聯想字 | **bus stop** *n.* 公車站 |
| | **stop** *n.* 車站 ／ *v.* 停止 |

train [tren] *n.* 火車 ／ *v.* 訓練

Just two kilometers away from the station, the train hit a truck trapped on the railway.

離車站僅二公里，火車撞到一輛困在鐵道上的卡車。

| 聯想字 | **rail·way** *n.* 鐵路 |
| | **sta·tion** *n.* 車站 |

記憶技巧

1. 字源上，train 是拖拉—draw、pull 的意思。

2. station = stat + ion，stat 是 stand—站的意思，station 是人們站立候車的地方。

truck [trʌk] *n.* 卡車；貨運車箱

There was a truck full of vegetables and fruit parked on a private road.

有一輛載滿蔬果的卡車停在私人道路上。

---

ship [ʃɪp] *n.* 輪船 ／ *v.* 運輸

The ship sailed along the coast, with two boats following.

那艘船沿著海岸航行，二艘小船跟隨在後。

聯想字	**boat** *n.* 小船
	sail *n.* 航程 ／ *v.* 航行
衍生字	**ship·ment** *n.* 運輸；運輸的貨物

---

air·plane [`ɛr͵plen] *n.* 飛機

The foreign guest arrived at the airport just in time to catch the airplane.

那位外國旅客剛好及時抵達機場趕上飛機。

聯想字	**air·port** *n.* 飛機場
	air *n.* 空氣
同義字	**plane** *n.* 飛機

---

road [rod] *n.* 道路

There's a coffee shop on the corner of the main street and the new road. It is just two blocks away from my office, and I always stop in to get a cup of coffee on my way to work.

在主街和新路的轉角處有一家咖啡店，離我的辦公室僅二個街區，我總是在上班途中順道停下來買杯咖啡。

| 聯想字 | **street** *n.* 街道 |
| | **way** *n.* 路；方法 |

衍生字 **a·way** *adv.* 離開；不在

al·ways *adv.* 總是；一直

記憶技巧

1. road 與騎乘—ride 同源，road 是騎乘交通工具的地方。

2. away = on + way，上了路就表示離開。

3. always = all + way + s。

---

side·walk [`saɪd͵wɔk] *n.* 人行道

When Dave was walking on the sidewalk, a big mouse suddenly ran out from his right side.

戴夫走在人行道時，一隻大老鼠突然從他的右邊跑出來。

聯想字 **side** *n.* 邊

walk *n.* 步行 ／ *v.* 步行；遛

pave·ment *n.* 人行道（BE）

---

block [blɑk] *n.* 街區 ／ *v.* 阻塞；封鎖

The National Museum of History is just six blocks away from here.

國立歷史博物館離這裡只有六個街區遠。

---

sign [saɪn] *n.* 記號；號誌 ／ *v.* 簽字；做手勢

The woman signed to the waitress to bring her another drink.

那位女士做手勢要女服務生再給她一杯飲料。

複合字 **sign language** 肢體語言

---

tick·et [`tɪkɪt] *n.* 票；罰單

How much is a one-way ticket to London?

到倫敦的單程票一張多少錢？

In 1999, there were about 2,482 **traffic** accidents in Taiwan. Most of the **accidents** happened because ___(1)___. For example, some **drivers drove** too fast. Some **drivers drank** too much wine or beer before they got into the **car**. And some **drivers** never tried to stop when ___(2)___.

It is convenient to **drive a car**. But it also can be dangerous. Accidents can be avoided only when people **drive** carefully. Everyone should remember ___(3)___.

_____1. (A) **motorcyclists** were **riding** too fast

(B) the **MRT system** was not built yet

(C) **drivers** didn't **follow the traffic rules**

(D) there were too many **traffic lights on the road**

_____2. (A) it started to rain

(B) they **drove** near a police station

(C) there were too many **cars** on the **road**

(D) the **traffic** light went from yellow to red

_____3. (A) driving in a **traffic** jam is terrible

(B) learning to drive well is very difficult

(C) finding a parking space is always a problem

(D) being safe is more important than anything else

答案：1. (C)；2. (D)；3. (D)

Unit **12** 身體部位

bo·dy [`bɑdɪ]　*n.* 身體；團體；機身

The human body is made up of about 60% water.
人體有百分之六十是水所組成。

---

head [hɛd]　*n.* 頭部；頭腦 ／ *v.* 前往

The man nodded his head and said "go ahead."
那位男士點了頭，説「請便」。

聯想字 **nod** *n.* 點頭 ／ *v.* 點頭

衍生字 **a·head** *adv.* 在前；向前；預先；事前

記憶技巧

ahead = a + head，a 是 on 的意思，在頭上就表示往前。

---

hair [hɛr]　*n.* 頭髮；毛髮

My brother is starting to get a few grey hairs now.
我哥哥現在開始冒出一些白頭髮。

衍生字 **hair·y** *adj.* 毛茸茸的，hairy = hair + y

---

face [fes]　*n.* 臉；臉部表情 ／ *v.* 面對；正視

The man was making funny faces to get his baby to laugh.
那位男子做出可笑的臉部表情讓他的嬰兒開懷大笑。

---

eye [aɪ]　*n.* 眼睛 ／ *v.* 注視

The street vendor has no sight in her right eye.
那位街頭小販的右眼沒有視力。

ear [ɪr] *n.* 耳朵

The man put his hands over his ears because of the noise.
那位男子因為噪音而用手摀住他的耳朵。

---

nose [noz] *n.* 鼻子

The boy took out tissue and blew his nose loudly.
男孩拿出衛生紙，大聲擤鼻涕。

---

mouth [maʊθ] *n.* 嘴巴；口腔；入海口

Tom covered his mouth with his hands because his lower teeth bit his upper lip.
Tom 雙手摀住嘴巴，因為他的下排牙齒咬到上唇。

聯想字 **lip** *n.* 嘴唇
　　　 tooth *n.* 牙齒　複數形：teeth

衍生字 **mouth·ful** *n.* 一口的量

記憶技巧
tooth 與複數形 teeth 同源，母音通轉，也與動詞 teethe一長牙同源。字源關聯上，同源名詞字尾子音通常唸無聲，動詞則是有聲。

---

neck [nɛk] *n.* 脖子；衣領

The guy carried a live snake around his neck.
那個人扛著一條活蛇繞在脖子上。

---

hand [hænd] *n.* 手；指針；幫忙 / *v.* 遞交

My aunt held my hands and then put her arm around my shoulder.
我的阿姨握著我的手，然後用手臂摟著我的肩膀。

聯想字 **shoul·der** *n.* 肩膀
　　　 arm *n.* 手臂；扶手 / *v.* 武裝

衍生字 **hand·y** *adj.* 有用的；方便的

fin·ger　[ˋfɪŋgɚ]　*n.* 手指；撫摸

The woman cut her kid's nails on his fingers when he was asleep.

婦人在她孩子睡著時修剪他手指上的指甲。

聯想字　**nail**　*n.* 指甲；釘子

記憶技巧

字源上，finger 可能與五—five 同源——一隻手有五隻手指。

---

foot　[fʊt]　*n.* 腳；英尺　複數形：feet

Tom kicked the ball with his right foot, and then sat on the bench with his legs crossed. He touched his knees and looked at his toes.

Tom 右腳踢球，然後盤腿坐在長椅上，摸摸膝蓋，看著腳趾頭。

聯想字　**leg**　*n.* 腿；小腿

　　　　knee　*n.* 膝蓋

　　　　toe　*n.* 腳趾

　　　　kick　*n.* ／ *v.* 踢

---

heart　[hɑrt]　*n.* 心臟；心腸；中心

My grandfather has got a weak heart.

我爺爺的心臟一向無力。

---

stom·ach　[ˋstʌmək]　*n.* 胃部

The little boy has got a pain in his stomach.

小男孩的胃部疼痛。

---

tail　[tel]　*n.* 尾巴

The peacock is standing on the branch with its beautiful tail hanging down.

那隻孔雀站在樹枝上，漂亮的尾巴往下垂。

In the art world, many artists with "weak" **bodies** have shown us a "strong" power in their great works of art. Take Frida Kahlo for example. She was a healthy girl until she was knocked down by a bus at the age of twelve. Much of her **body** was seriously hurt, but her **mind** wasn't. In her paintings, we can feel her strong love of art and life. Another example is Christy Brown. He was born in bad health, and the only part of his **body** that could move was his left **foot**. However, using his only **foot**, he still was able to write and draw wonderfully. In his autobiography, Brown wrote what happened in his life and how he began to draw pictures with his left **foot**. And don't forget Stevie Wonder. He became blind soon after he was born, but he is now a popular singer and songwriter.

These artists with "weak" **bodies** bring us many good things and much hope with their "strong" **minds**. Their stories tell us that the most important thing in life is not what we have, but what we make of it.

_____1. What is the writer trying to say?

    (A) History always repeats itself.

    (B) Art is the best medicine for a weak **mind**.

    (C) We should try to make the best use of our lives.

    (D) It takes more than hard work to make a great artist.

_____2. What does <u>autobiography</u> mean?

    (A) A movie about great writers' lives.

    (B) A book of a person's life by that person.

    (C) A videotape that teaches how to write stories.

    (D) A picture with the painter's name on the bottom.

_____3. Which is true about the three artists in the reading?

    (A) They all died at a young age.

    (B) They are all famous painters.

    (C) They all had problems with their **bodies**.

    (D) They were all in bad health when they were born.

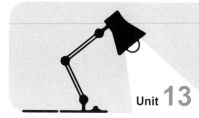

🔊 Track 048

dress [drɛs] *n.* 洋裝／*v.* 穿著；加調味料

The hostess was wearing a black and white spotted dress.
女主人穿著一件黑白圓點的洋裝。

衍生字 **dress·er** *n.* 櫥櫃；餐具櫃

---

wear [wɛr] *n.* 衣著／*v.* 穿著；戴；流露；耗損

What are you wearing to their wedding party?
你要穿搭什麼去參加他們的婚宴呢？

---

cap [kæp] *n.* 無邊便帽；蓋子

I packed a shower cap and a straw hat into the suitcase.
我把一頂浴帽和一頂草帽打包到行李箱。

聯想字 **hat** *n.* 帽子

記憶技巧
字源上，cap 與 head 同源，首子音 /k/、/h/ 轉音，都與頭部有關。

---

jack·et [`dʒækɪt] *n.* 夾克；外套

My mom bought me a jacket and a heavy winter coat during the big sale.
大拍賣時，我媽媽幫我買了一件夾克和一件冬季厚大衣。

聯想字 **coat** *n.* 外套；大衣；塗層／*v.* 塗層

coat·ing *n.* 外層；塗層

shirt [ʃɝt] *n.* 襯衫

My boss always wears jeans and a T-shirt. He never wears a shirt with a tie.
我老闆總是穿著牛仔褲搭配 T 恤，他從不穿襯衫打領帶。

聯想字 **T-shirt** *n.* 短袖圓領運動衫
　　　 tie *n.* 領帶；平手／*v.* 綁；繫；相關

---

skirt [skɝt] *n.* 裙子

This knee-length skirt looks very nice on you.
這件及膝的裙子穿在妳身上很好看。

記憶技巧
字源上，shirt 與 skirt 同源。

---

sweat·er [ˋswɛtɚ] *n.* 毛衣

A V-necked sweater may be worn under a suit jacket.
V 領毛衣可以穿在西裝外套裡面。

---

pants [pænts] *n.* 褲子

This belt will match these pants nicely. For jeans or shorts, you need to use other ones.
這條皮帶和這件長褲很搭，至於牛仔褲或短褲，你得用其它的皮帶。

聯想字 **jeans** *n.* 牛仔褲
　　　 shorts *n.* 短褲
　　　 belt *n.* 腰帶

---

shoe [ʃu] *n.* 鞋子

The boy's tennis shoes left muddy marks on the floor.
男孩的網球鞋在地板上留下泥巴印。

socks [sɑks] *n.* 一雙襪子

My mother always wears a pair of toe socks during yoga class.

瑜伽課時，我媽媽總是穿著一雙五趾襪。

---

vest [vɛst] *n.* 背心；內衣

My brother usually wears a vest on cold winter days.

我哥哥經常在寒冬天穿著一件背心。

記憶技巧

字源上，vest 與 wear 同源，都與穿著有關。

---

glass·es [`glæsɪz] *n.* 眼鏡

My father has recently started to wear reading glasses.

我爸爸最近開始戴老花眼鏡。

聯想字 **glass** *n.* 玻璃；玻璃杯

---

mask [mæsk] *n.* 面具；口罩 ／ *v.* 掩蓋

Wear a mask when sick, so you don't get others sick.

生病時戴上口罩，這樣你才不會使他人生病。

---

glove [glʌv] *n.* 手套

The worker wore a pair of gloves to protect his hands from newspaper ink.

為了防止手沾到報紙油墨，那名工人戴著一雙手套。

---

pock·et [`pɑkɪt] *n.* 口袋

The customer took some coins from his jacket pocket.

那位顧客從他的外套口袋掏出一些銅板。

Dear Sir,

I ordered a **shirt** from you last month. But there are some problems with it. First, the color is not as red as it is shown in the catalogue. I understand that the picture does not always show the real color, but it should not be that different. Second, I asked for a medium size because it is the size I usually **wear**. But your medium is so small that I have to give it to my younger brother.

I think you should be more serious about your business.

Truly,
Adam Rosen

Dear Mr. Rosen,

Thank you for telling us the problems with your order. We hope we can give you better service. We are sending you another **shirt** with this letter. It is size large, and its red color is brighter than the one you had. We hope you like it.

Our office hours are 9:00 a.m.-5:00 p.m. Please call us if you have any more questions.

Yours truly,
Victor Smith

_____1. Why does Adam Rosen write the letter?

    (A) To say sorry to his brother.

    (B) To talk about his problems with a friend.

    (C) To show how he feels about what he bought.

    (D) To find out the business hours of a new store.

_____2. What does Victor Smith do for Adam Rosen?

    (A) He finds a job for him.

    (B) He mails him a new shirt.

    (C) He gives him a camera.

    (D) He draws a picture for him.

答案：1. (C)；2. (B)

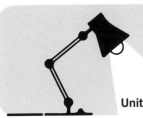

Unit **14** 運動與休閒

 Track 051

sport [sport] *n.* 運動

My classmate, Peter, is good at sports like tennis and badminton.
我的同學彼得擅長運動，像是網球或羽毛球。

聯想字 **bad·min·ton** *n.* 羽毛球
ten·nis *n.* 網球

記憶技巧
sport = away + carry，字源上，sport 是取悅、娛樂自己，就是將心思帶離開嚴重的事情而去尋求歡樂。

----

ex·er·cise [`ɛksəˌsaɪz] *n.* 運動；習題／*v.* 運動；行使

My PE teacher usually exercises at the gym in the early morning.
我的體育老師經常清晨在健身房運動。

聯想字 **gym** *n.* 體育館；健身房；體操

----

ball [bɔl] *n.* 球；球狀物

Soccer, football and dodge ball are all team sports.
足球、美式足球和躲避球都是團隊運動。

聯想字 **base·ball** *n.* 棒球
bas·ket·ball *n.* 籃球
dodge ball *n.* 躲避球
foot·ball *n.* 美式足球
soc·cer *n.* 足球

記憶技巧
字源上，ball 與 blow 同源，ball 是吹氣而成的物體。

 089

skate　[sket]　*n.* 溜冰鞋 ／ *v.* 溜冰

The ice on the lake is thick enough to skate on.
湖上的冰夠厚，可以在上面溜冰。

---

race　[res]　*n.* 賽跑；種族；民族 ／ *v.* 與……賽跑

The school's track and field team won the race yesterday.
昨天田徑校隊贏得比賽。

---

hike　[haɪk]　*n.* 遠足 ／ *v.* 徒步旅行；健行

After a long hike, we reached the top of the waterfall.
長途健行後，我們到達了瀑布頂端。

---

swim　[swɪm]　*n.* ／ *v.* 游泳

Let's go for a swim tomorrow morning.
我們明天早上去游泳吧！

---

surf　[sɝf]　*n.* 浪花 ／ *v.* 衝浪；在網路或頻道上搜尋資料

We usually go surfing at the beach at dawn.
我們經常黎明時在海邊衝浪。

---

hunt　[hʌnt]　*n.* ／ *v.* 打獵；搜尋

To hunt for a barking deer, the hunter hid himself behind a tree, with his body covered with leaves.
為了獵捕一隻山羌，獵人把自己隱藏在樹後面，用樹葉覆蓋身體。

聯想字	**hide**　*v.* 躲藏；把……藏起來
	cov·er　*n.* 封面 ／ *v.* 蓋住

---

camp　[kæmp]　*n.* 營地 ／ *v.* 露營

Last weekend, I went camping in the mountains with my family.
上週末我和家人一起去山上露營。

fris·bee [ˋfrɪzbi] *n.* 飛盤

I enjoyed playing frisbee with my dogs in the park.
我喜歡和我的狗兒們在公園玩飛盤。

kite [kaɪt] *n.* 風箏

Let's go fly a kite at the park this afternoon.
我們今天下午去公園放風箏吧！

fes·ti·val [ˋfɛstəv!] *n.* 節日；節期

We will celebrate the traditional festival in style.
我們將盛大慶祝這個傳統節日。

聯想字 cel·e·brate *v.* 慶祝

va·ca·tion [veˋkeʃən] *n.* 假期；休假／*v.* 渡假

They planned to take a trip to Europe during summer vacation.
他們計劃暑假期間去歐洲旅行。

聯想字 trip *n.* 旅行

記憶技巧
vacation = vac + ation，字根 vac 是空的—empty、自由—free 的意思，原意是從義務中得到釋放、不受佔有的狀態。

hol·i·day [ˋhɑləˌde] *n.* 假日

We will go on a picnic during Christmas holiday.
我們將在聖誕假期去野餐。

聯想字 Christ·mas *n.* 耶誕節
pic·nic *n.*／*v.* 野餐

記憶技巧
字源上，picnic 與挑選—pick 有關。

Weight-training has become very popular all over the world in the past few years. Many years ago, **Weight-training** classes were usually for men only, but today ___(1)___. **Weight-training** is now a fashionable **sport** for people who are interested in becoming stronger and healthier. Books and videos about **Weight-training** ___(2)___. Any **sports** fan can get copies of them easily.

Before you start a **Weight-training** class, you should remember two important things: first, you have to wear the right size clothes. It's impossible for you to enjoy **Weight-training** if your clothes are too big or too small. ___(3)___, never show off, even to yourself. Start with a weight that is not too heavy for you. Showing off is the easiest way to get hurt. Remember, you want to be stronger and healthier. You don't want to ___(4)___ after your **Weight-training** class.

_____1. (A) many women can also be seen in these classes

     (B) both men and women have given up the **sport**

     (C) only married women spend their time on the **sport**

     (D) more and more men are attending **weight-training** classes

_____2. (A) do not sell well in big cities

     (B) sell like cold drinks on a hot summer day

     (C) are sold only to people older than eighteen

     (D) can be found only in those bookstores next to a **gym**

_____3. (A) So

     (B) In fact

     (C) After all

     (D) Second

_____4. (A) gain weight

     (B) become dangerous

     (C) be proud of yourself

     (D) be taken to the hospital

Unit 15　音樂與藝術

🎧 Track 054

art [ɑrt] *n.* 藝術；文科

Mark took a course in the performing arts last semester.
Mark 上學期修了一門表演藝術課。

衍生字　**art·ist** *n.* 藝術家
　　　ar·ti·fi·cial *adj.* 人工的；人造的

------

mu·sic [`mjuzɪk] *n.* 音樂

The artist has created a lot of music in the last few years.
過去幾年中那名藝術家創作了很多音樂。

衍生字　**musi·cian** *n.* 音樂家

------

band [bænd] *n.* 樂團；細繩 ∕ *v.* 戴上環套

The cheerleader is also the lead singer in a rock 'n' roll band.
那位啦啦隊員也是一名搖滾樂團主唱。

衍生字　**band·age** *n.* 繃帶

------

drum [drʌm] *n.* 鼓 ∕ *v.* 敲打

The children danced beautifully to the beat of the drums.
孩子們隨著鼓聲的節拍美妙地跳著舞。

衍生字　**drum·mer** *n.* 鼓手

flute [flut] *n.* 長笛；橫笛

The cowboy usually blows the flute to calm down the animals on the farm.

那位牛仔經常吹長笛以使農場裡的動物平靜下來。

記憶技巧

字源上，flute 與吹—blow 同源，/f/、/b/ 轉音，flute 是吹奏的樂器。

----

gui·tar [gɪˋtɑr] *n.* 吉他

At the year-end party, the manager sang a Japanese song while playing the guitar.

尾牙宴中，經理彈著吉他唱了一首日文歌。

衍生字 **gui·tar·ist** *n.* 吉他手

----

pi·an·o [pɪˋæno] *n.* 鋼琴 複數形：pianos

My uncle used to play the piano in a jazz band.

我叔叔曾在一個爵士樂團演奏鋼琴。

衍生字 **pi·a·nist** *n.* 鋼琴家
piano + ist，為避免母音相鄰而不易唸音，piano 的尾字母 o 省略。

----

vi·o·lin [ˌvaɪəˋlɪn] *n.* 小提琴

During summer vacation, Leo practiced the violin three hours every day.

暑假期間，李歐每天練小提琴三個小時。

衍生字 **vi·o·lin·ist** *n.* 小提琴家

sing [sɪŋ] v. 唱歌

The well-known singer sang two popular songs in the concert.
那位知名歌手在演唱會唱了二首很夯的歌曲。

衍生字 sing·er n. 歌手
同源字 song n. 歌曲

dance [dæns] n. 舞蹈；舞會／v. 跳舞

The Russian dancers are dancing to a beautiful piece of Spanish music.
俄羅斯舞者正隨著一首美妙的西班牙音樂翩翩起舞。

衍生字 danc·er n. 舞者

mov·ie [`muvɪ] n. 電影

I don't like action movies very much.
我不是很喜歡動作片。

記憶技巧
movie = moving picture + ie，與移動─move 同源。

chess [tʃɛs] n. 西洋棋

My teacher is good at playing game of Go, a Japanese chess game.
我的老師擅長圍棋，一種日本的棋盤遊戲。

記憶技巧
字源上，chess 與下棋的將軍─check 同源。

pic·ture [`pɪktʃɚ] *n.* 圖畫；照片 ／ *v.* 想像

The backpacker took a picture of the old tree with his digital camera.

背包客用他的數位相機拍了一張那棵老樹的照片。

衍生字 **pic·tur·esque** *adj.* 美麗的；古色古香的

聯想字 **cam·e·ra** *n.* 照相機

記憶技巧

字源上，picture 是作畫—to paint 的意思。

---

draw [drɔ] *v.* 畫；吸引；拖拉

The artist was drawing a picture and then painting it with oil paints.

那位藝術家畫一幅圖，然後用油性塗料著色。

聯想字 **paint** *n.* 油漆；塗料 ／ *v.* 繪畫；油漆

衍生字 **draw·er** *n.* 抽屜

draw·ing *n.* 繪畫；圖畫

---

col·or [`kʌlɚ] *n.* 顏色 ／ *v.* 著色

When we mix black with white, we will get the color gray.

黑色和白色混合時，我們會得到灰色。

聯想字 **black** *n.* 黑色 ／ *adj.* 黑色的

blue *n.* 藍色 ／ *adj.* 藍色的

brown *n.* 棕色 ／ *adj.* 棕色的

gray *n.* 灰色 ／ *adj.* 灰色的

pink *n.* 粉紅色 ／ *adj.* 粉紅色的

pur·ple *n.* 紫色 ／ *adj.* 紫色的

red *n.* 紅色 ／ *adj.* 紅色的

white *n.* 白色 ／ *adj.* 白色的

yel·low *n.* 黃色 ／ *adj.* 黃色的

衍生字 **color·ful** *adj.* 彩色的

color·less *adj.* 無色的

Isadora Duncan was born in America in 1877. She was a great **dance** teacher who enjoyed **dancing** at an early age, and even began teaching other children to **dance** when she was only six. Although Duncan herself stopped going to school at ten, she later had students from all over the world.

Duncan was called the mother of **modern dance** because she brought lots of new ideas into the **dancing** of her time. She believed that **dance** is life itself and comes from the heart. Duncan also said that **dance** belongs to everyone, rich and poor young and old. That was why one time she did not agree to **dance** in a **theater** where the tickets were very expensive.

Duncan also surprised the people of her time by **dancing** in comfortable clothes and without shoes on. She broke the rules in many ways and gave **dance** <u>a new language</u>. Now people who are interested in **modern dance** are still getting new ideas from this great teacher.

_____1. What is the reading mainly about?

    (A) The history of American **modern dance**.

    (B) The **dancing** life of an American **dancer**.

    (C) The **dance** group Isadora Duncan started

    (D) The way of lit in Isadora Duncan's time.

_____2. What did Duncan think of **dance**?

    (A) It shows how people feel.

    (B) It should be learned at an early age.

    (C) It is a hobby that needs strong shoes.

    (D) It could be enjoyed more in a **theater**.

_____3. What does a new language mean in the reading?

    (A) A new word for **dancing**.

    (B) New ideas about **dancing**.

    (C) A new kind of **dance music**.

    (D) New rules for selling **dance** tickets.

🎧 Track 058

a·part·ment [əˋpɑrtmənt] *n.* 公寓

The three-bedroom apartment is for sale at an unbelievable price.
那套三房的公寓以不可置信的價格求售。

記憶技巧

apartment = a + part + ment，a = ad，to 的意思，到建築物的一部分作為住處的是公寓。

----

room [rum] *n.* 房間；空間

The manager is waiting for you in the meeting room upstairs.
經理正在樓上的會議室等你。

----

liv·ing room [ˋlɪvɪŋ] [rum] *n.* 客廳

To enjoy a relaxing life, the couple live in an apartment with a big living room.
為了享受輕鬆的生活，那對夫婦住在一套擁有大客廳的公寓。

記憶技巧

living = live + ing，live *v.* 居住，live 與 life 同源，life *n.* 人生；生命。

----

bed·room [ˋbɛd͵rʊm] *n.* 臥房

There's a king size bed in the main bedroom.
主臥室有一張特大號的床。

聯想字 **bed** *n.* 床
bed·ding *n.* 寢具

di·ning room [`daɪnɪŋ] [rum] *n.* 飯廳

The couple are dining by candlelight in the dining room.

那對夫婦在飯廳享用燭光晚餐。

記憶技巧

dining = dine + ing，dine *v.* 用餐；din·er *n.* 用餐者

kitch·en [`kɪtʃɪn] *n.* 廚房

Mom is cooking in the kitchen. Especially for me, she will fry an egg, instead of boiling it.

媽媽正在廚房做菜，尤其為了我，她要煎一顆蛋，而不是用水煮的。

聯想字 **fry** *n.* 炸薯條 ／ *v.* 油炸
　　　 boil *v.* 沸騰；煮沸

同源字 **cook** *n.* 廚師 ／ *v.* 煮

bath·room [`bæθˌrum] *n.* 廁所；浴室

I took a long hot bath in the wooden tub in the bathroom.

我在浴室裡的木頭浴缸泡熱水澡泡很久。

聯想字 **bath** *n.* 洗澡
　　　 bathe *v.* 浸泡、壟罩
　　　 tub *n.* 浴缸

記憶技巧

字源上，tub 可能與 two 同源，取自 tub 原意是有二手把的容器。

rest·room [rɛstˌrum] *n.* 廁所

We can take a rest or use the restroom free of charge at the convenience store.

我們可以在便利商店歇息或是免費使用廁所。

聯想字 **rest** *n.* 其餘；休息；支架 ／ *v.* 休息；暫停

door [dor] *n.* 門

The back door is far away from the main gate, but there is a bell on it that visitors can ring.

後門離大門很遠，不過上面有訪客可以按的門鈴。

聯想字 **gate** *n.* 大門；登機門

bell *n.* 鈴；鐘

ring *n.* 指環；鈴聲 ╱ *v.* 鳴；響

衍生字 **indoor** 戶內的

indoors 在戶內

outdoor 戶外的

outdoors 在戶外

---

win·dow [`wɪndo] *n.* 窗戶

There are two windows on the back wall.

後面的牆上有二扇窗戶。

聯想字 **wall** *n.* 牆壁；圍牆

記憶技巧

window = wind + ow，wind 就是風，與吹—blow 同源，ow 是指eye—眼睛，window 是風吹入室內的洞口。window 與 wind—風，wing—翅膀等字同源。

---

floor [flor] *n.* 地板；樓

The balcony floor needs cleaning.

陽臺地板需要清潔。

stair　[stɛr]　*n.* 樓梯

When you go up the stairs, the principal's office is on the left.
你若爬上樓梯，校長室就在左手邊。

衍生字 **upstairs**　*adj.* ／ *adv.* 上樓；在樓上
　　　 downstairs　*adj.* ／ *adv.* 下樓；在樓下

聯想字 **lad·der**　*n.* 梯子

---

bal·co·ny　[`bælkənɪ]　*n.* 陽臺；廂房

We chatted over tea on the hotel balcony.
我們在飯店陽臺泡茶聊天。

---

cor·ner　[`kɔrnɚ]　*n.* 街角；角落

Kevin hit his leg on the corner of the table during his break time.
下課時，Kevin 的腿撞到桌角。

記憶技巧
corner 是指街道與牆壁交會處，字源上與 horn一角同源。

---

gar·den　[`gɑrdn̩]　*n.* 花園

There is a vegetable garden beside the barn.
穀倉旁邊有一個菜園。

聯想字 **yard**　*n.* 庭院；碼
　　　 court　*n.* 庭院；法庭；球場

衍生字 **gar·den·ing**　*n.* 園藝
　　　 gar·den·er　*n.* 園丁

Stanley was a person who loved singing to himself in the **bath**. One cold winter night, he went into the **bathroom** to have a hot **bath**. He took off his clothes and turned on the tap, but there was no hot water — the water from the tap was cold!

Stanley didn't know what was wrong, but he finally decided to take a **bath** without hot water. He started to sing as usual, one song after another. Stanley was surprised that the water felt warm <u>this way</u>. So he kept singing, louder and louder, until he finished his **bath**.

The next morning when Stanley was going to work, he saw a piece of paper on his door.

> Please do not sing so loud! Every time you sing, I get headache, and my baby cries.
>
> the poor mother next door

_____1. What does the mother think of Stanley?

(A) He gets up too early.

(B) He is a helpful person

(C) He should see a doctor

(D) He makes too much noise.

_____2. What does <u>this way</u> mean?

(A) Singing to a crying baby.

(B) Singing when taking a cold **bath**.

(C) Taking a cold **bath** in the morning.

(D) Taking a **bath** before going to bed.

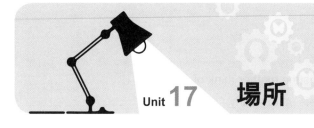

Track 062

place [ples] *n.* 地方／*v.* 放置

There are a couple of places of interest to visit in the area.
這個地區有二、三處值得參觀的地方。

----

cit·y [`sɪtɪ] *n.* 城市

Taichung is really a livable city. It is not only convenient but it is comfortable to live there.
臺中真是個宜居城市，住在那裡不只方便，而且舒適。

聯想字 **con·ve·ni·ent** *adj.* 方便的
con·ve·ni·ence *n.* 便利；便利設施

記憶技巧

convenient = con + ven + ient，字首 con 表示 together，字根 ven 表示去—go，ient 是形容詞字尾，大家可以一起來的是方便的。

----

coun·try [`kʌntrɪ] *n.* 國家；鄉下

Christmas is not a national holiday in this country.
在這國家，聖誕節不是國定假日。

聯想字 **na·tion** *n.* 國家
na·tion·al *adj.* 國家的；國立的

記憶技巧

national = nation + al，nation = nat + ion，字根 nat 是出生—birth 的意思，出生的地方就是自己的國家。

store [stor] *n.* 商店 ／ *v.* 儲存

There are two big bookstores in this department store.

這家百貨公司裡有二間大型書店。

聯想字	**book·store** *n.* 書店
	de·part·ment store *n.* 百貨公司
衍生字	**stor·age** *n.* 儲存；存放
	re·store *v.* 修復；使復原

記憶技巧

1. 字源上，store 的名詞―商店可能源自動詞―儲存，儲存以為著將來使用，儲存有使貨物站立―stand 的意思，因此，store 源自站立―stand，二字同源。

2. department = de + part + ment，字首 de 是分離的意思，分離出來的部分就是部門。

---

shop [ʃɑp] *n.* 商店 ／ *v.* 購物

A shopkeeper is a person who owns and manages a small shop.

店主是擁有並管理一家小型店鋪的人。

衍生字	**shop·ping** *n.* 購物；購買的物品
複合字	**shop·keep·er** *n.* 店主

---

su·per·mar·ket [`supɚ͵mɑrkɪt] *n.* 超級市場

The manager of the local supermarket is good at marketing and sales.

這家當地超級市場的經理很會行銷及販售。

記憶技巧

字首 super 是 over 的意思，表示超越、在……之上，超越一般市場―market 的是 supermarket，mar·ket *n.* 市場 ／ *v.* 銷售。

res·tau·rant [ˈrɛstərənt] *n.* 餐廳

The seafood restaurant has a long menu of about 60 items.
那家海鮮餐廳有一份約六十樣菜色的長菜單。

聯想字 **me·nu** *n.* 菜單

記憶技巧
1. restaurant 是修復、更新的食物—food that restores 的意思，後來衍生為烹調食物的餐廳。
2. menu 是小的—small 的意思，也就是餐桌上說明菜餚的小張表格。

ho·tel [hoˋtɛl] *n.* 旅館；飯店

My family stayed at a hotel on the beach on our last vacation to Kenting.
我全家人上次到墾丁渡假時，入住在一家海濱飯店。

聯想字 **mo·tel** *n.* 汽車旅館，汽車—motor 與 hotel 形成的混成字。

post of·fice [post] [ˋɔfɪs] *n.* 郵局

I bought several postcards and stamps in the post office.
我在郵局買了幾張明信片和郵票。

聯想字 **post·card** *n.* 明信片
　　　 card *n.* 卡片
　　　 stamp *n.* 郵票；戳記
　　　 en·ve·lope *n.* 信封

gal·le·ry [ˋgælərɪ] *n.* 畫廊；美術館

We will visit a few galleries during our stay in Prague.
我們停留布拉格的期間將參觀幾家畫廊。

fac·to·ry　[ˋfæktəri]　*n.* 工廠

The entire production happens in this factory from start to finish.
整個生產從開始到完成都是在這間工廠進行。

記憶技巧

factory = fact + ory，字根 fact 是 make—製造、做的意思，字尾 ory 表示場所，製造產品的場所是工廠。

---

church　[tʃɝtʃ]　*n.* 教堂；教會

The believers all fell to their knees and began to pray in the church.
信徒在教堂全都屈膝跪下，開始禱告。

聯想字　**pray**　*v.* 禱告
　　　　prayer　*n.* 禱告，pray + er

---

tem·ple　[ˋtɛmpl]　*n.* 廟宇；神殿；寺院

I hope I can go to the temple and make a wish this weekend.
我希望這個週末我可以去廟裡許願。

聯想字　**wish**　*n.* 心願／*v.* 祈願
　　　　hope　*n.*／*v.* 希望

---

park　[pɑrk]　*n.* 公園／*v.* 停車

In the park, some children are playing on the seesaw, some are playing on the slide, and others are playing on the swings.
公園裡，有些小孩在玩蹺蹺板，有些在溜滑梯，其他的在盪鞦韆。

聯想字　**see·saw**　*n.* 蹺蹺板
　　　　slide　*n.* 滑梯；土崩／*v.* 滑動；滑落
　　　　swing　*n.* 鞦韆／*v.* 搖擺；揮動

cas·tle [`kæs!] *n.* 城堡

The castle was built in around the 13th century.
這座城堡大約在十三世紀建造。

聯想字 **build** *n.* 體形;身材 / *v.* 建造;蓋

 小試身手

★ 出自 92 年第一次基測

　　When I was a little girl, my family lived in a small **village**. There was a very beautiful **river** near my home. The **water** was clean and cool. I liked to go fishing there with my mom. We would catch fish, look for clams and play in the **water**. There were also a lot of birds near the **river**. We would spend all day watching the birds. Life was beautiful and wonderful in the old days.

　　Now my family lives in the **city**. Last Sunday my daughter asked me to take her to see the beautiful **river** I was always talking about. "I want so much to go fishing there with you and Grandma," she said.

　　When we went to the **river**, we only saw a factory and a mountain of garbage. My mom was surprised, my daughter was disappointed , and I was sad — the **river** was my best friend; I grew up with it. Now there are no fish in it; the birds are gone, too. I hear it crying for help. But what can I do?

_____1. When the writer went back to see the **river**, what did she find?

    (A) The pollution in the **river** was very serious.

    (B) The river was a good **place** for children to play.

    (C) Bird-watching was more and more popular along the **river**.

    (D) There were no fish in the **river** because too many people went fishing.

_____2. Who is the <u>Grandma</u> in the reading?

    (A) The writer.

    (B) The writer's mom.

    (C) The writer's daughter.

    (D) The writer's grandmother.

_____3. What did the writer mean when she said, "<u>I grew up with it.</u>"?

    (A) She helped clean the garbage out of the **river**.

    (B) She spent much time playing around the **river**.

    (C) She had many friends who lived near the **river**.

    (D) She grew well by eating fish and clams from the **river**.

地球、太空與方位

space [spes] *n.* 太空;空間

The driver found a parking space close to the post office.
那位駕駛人找到一個郵局旁邊的停車位。

- -

earth [ɝθ] *n.* 地球;陸地;泥土

Earth, Mars, Venus, Mercury are called "rocky planets."
地球、火星、金星、水星稱為岩石行星。

- -

moon [mun] *n.* 月亮

There will be a full moon next Monday.
下星期一將有滿月。

衍生字 **Monday** *n.* 星期一,Monday = moon + day,moon 縮簡。

- -

sun [sʌn] *n.* 太陽

Last Sunday, it was a sunny day and the sun was shining brightly.
上星期日天氣晴朗,陽光明亮地照耀。

聯想字 **shine** *v.* 發光;照耀

衍生字 **sun·ny** *adj.* 晴朗的
Sun·day *n.* 星期日

- -

star [stɑr] *n.* 星星;星狀物;明星

These bright stars make the shape of a large rectangle.
這些明亮的星星構成一個巨大的長方形形狀。

plan·et [`plænɪt] *n.* 行星

Last Saturday, they launched a rocket to the planet Mars.
上星期六,他們發射一枚火箭到火星。

聯想字 **Sat·ur·day** *n.* 星期六,Satur 是 Saturn—土星的意思。

- -

world [wɝld] *n.* 世界

This vacation spot is a great place for meeting people from all around the world.
這個旅遊景點是個很棒的地方,可以遇見來自世界各地的人。

- -

cen·ter [`sɛntɚ] *n.* 中心

The art gallery is located in the center of the city.
畫廊位在市中心。

衍生字 **cen·tral** *adj.* 中心的;中央的
center + al,center 的第二音節 ter 是輕音節,黏接字尾 al 時,縮簡為 tral。

- -

east [ist] *n.* 東方 / *adj.* 東方的 / *adv.* 向東方

The sun rises in the east and sets in the west.
太陽在東邊升起,西邊落下。

反義字 **west** *n.* 西方 / *adj.* 西方的 / *adv.* 向西方
衍生字 **east·ern** *adj.* 東部的
　　　 west·ern *adj.* 西部的

記憶技巧
字源上,**east** 是照耀—shine 的意思,旭日東昇,朝陽照耀大地;**west** 則是晚上—evening 的縮減,夕陽西下,夜幕低垂的方向。

north [nɔrθ] *n.* 北方 ╱ *adj.* 北方的 ╱ *adv.* 向北方

The new station will be built in the north of the city, but not in the south.

新車站將蓋在城市的北邊，不是南邊。

反義字 **south** *n.* 南方 ╱ *adj.* 南方的 ╱ *adv.* 向南方

衍生字 **north·ern** *adj.* 北部的
　　　 south·ern *adj.* 南部的

記憶技巧
字源上，south 與 sun 同源。

- -

right [raɪt] *n.* 權利 ╱ *adj.* 右邊的；對的 ╱ *adv.* 向右地；馬上

In London, drivers drive on the right, not on the left.

在倫敦，駕駛人是右邊駕駛，不是左邊。

反義字 **left** *n.* 左邊 ╱ *adj.* 左邊的；剩下的 ╱ *adv.* 向左地

- -

front [frʌnt] *n.* 前面；正面 ╱ *adj.* 前面的；前部的

Sign your name in the blank space at the bottom on the front of the form.

在表格正面的下方空白處簽名。

反義字 **back** *n.* 後面；背面；背部 ╱ *v.* 支持；援助 ╱ *adj.* 後面的；背部的 ╱ *adv.* 回原處；向後

- -

top [tɑp] *n.* 頂部；陀螺 ╱ *adj.* 最高的

The name list will be found at the bottom of the page, not at the top.

那份名單會在頁面底部找到，不是在頂部。

反義字 **bot·tom** *n.* 底部；臀部

up [ʌp] *adv.* 向上；在上面；完全地 ／ *pre.* 在……上面；沿著

The kids were riding a seesaw up and down at the playground.
小朋友在遊樂場上下地玩著蹺蹺板。

反義字 **down** *adv.* 向下；在遠方 ／ *prep.* 向下；在下面；沿著

- -

map [mæp] *n.* 地圖

I was trying to read the road map and direct my brother to the farm.
我一直盡力看著地圖，指引我哥哥到達農場。

複合字 **mind mapping** 心智圖

Siena is an old city in the **north** of Italy. It began with a group of people living on its **hills** over 2,900 years ago. Around the year 1100, Siena became an important business **center** in Italy. In 1472, the first bank of the **world** was built in this city and has been doing business ever since.

Today Siena is famous for keeping its "old face." For example, its **city** walls, which helped keep the city safe in the past, are hundreds of years old now and look almost the same as before. Also, many old **buildings** are seen at the Piazza del Campo, the most important meeting **place** of the **city**. Few things have really changed in this **center** of public life for hundreds of years. Now people still go to the open **space** for sharing news, shopping, or playing sports. There is one more thing that helps keep Siena's old face: cars cannot enter the **city** most of the time.

True, Siena is old, but it is beautifully old. People are welcome to visit this beautiful **city** and walk into the past.

_____1. What is the best title for the reading?

(A) A **City** of Love.

(B) A **City** of Festival.

(C) A Forgotten Old **City**.

(D) A **City** Living in History.

_____2. What can we learn from the reading?

(A) The oldest **bank** in the **world** is in Italy.

(B) A good way to get around Siena is by car.

(C) Italy is making its **cities** beautiful with trees.

(D) Walls that were built around Siena are not there now.

_____3. Which is NOT true about the Piazza del Campo?

(A) It is in Siena.

(B) It is a public **space**.

(C) It is a new business **center**.

(D) It is kept almost as it was before.

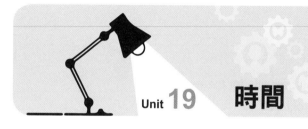

時間

🎧 Track 071

time [taɪm] n. 時間；一段時間；次數 ／ v. 計時

Peter sometimes came to class early, and sometimes late. He has no sense of time.

Peter 上課有時會早到，有時會遲到，他沒有時間觀念。

衍生字 **tim·er** 定時器
聯想字 **ear·ly** adj. 早的 ／ adv. 早
late adj. 晚的；遲的 ／ adv. 晚

複合字 **some·times** adv. 有時候；偶爾

---

year [jɪr] n. 年

My family went to North Korea on holiday last year.

去年我們全家到北韓渡假。

衍生字 **year·ly** adj. ／ adv. 每年；一年一次

---

sea·son [`sizn] n. 季節；演出季 ／ v. 加調味料

Autumn is the season when leaves fall from trees.

秋天是葉子從樹上掉落的季節。

衍生字 **sea·son·al** adj. 季節的；季節性的
聯想字 **spring** n. 春天　　**sum·mer** n. 夏天
au·tumn n. 秋天　　**fall** n. 秋天 ／ v. 掉下
win·ter n. 冬天　　**drop** n. 滴 ／ v. 使滴下；掉下

記憶技巧
1. 字源上，season 決定播種—sow 的時機，二字同源，母音通轉。
2. winter 是濕冷的季節，與 wet、water 都是同源字。

month [mʌnθ] *n.* 月份

January and February are the first two months of the year, and November and December are the last two.

一月和二月是一年的前二個月，十一月和十二月是最後二個月。

聯想字	Jan·u·a·ry *n.* 一月	Feb·ru·a·ry *n.* 二月
	March *n.* 三月	A·pril *n.* 四月
	May *n.* 五月	June *n.* 六月
	Ju·ly *n.* 七月	Au·gust *n.* 八月
	Sep·tem·ber *n.* 九月	Oc·to·ber *n.* 十月
	No·vem·ber *n.* 十一月	De·cem·ber *n.* 十二月

衍生字	month·ly *n.* 月刊 / *adj.* / *adv.* 每月；一月一次

記憶技巧

1. month—月份與月亮—moon 有關，二字同源。

2. October 的字根 octo 是八的意思，古代一年原本只有十個月，October 是第八個月，後來凱薩大帝以自己的名字加入了七月—July，而他兒子奧古斯都仿效父親，也以自己的名字加入了八月—August，因此 October 變成了十月，原本十月的 December 變成了十二月，December 的字根 dec 是十的意思。

---

week [wik] *n.* 星期

Tom has been working hard for weeks. Their work will be done by the end of this week.

Tom 一直努力工作了幾個星期，這個週末前他們的工作會完成。

聯想字	o·ver *adj.* 結束 / *adv.* 在上方；超過；越過 / *prep.* 在⋯⋯正上方

衍生字	week·ly *n.* 週刊 / *adj.* / *adv.* 每週

複合字	week·end *n.* 週末
	end *n.* 盡頭；結局 / *v.* 結束

date [det] *n.* 日期；約會 ／ *v.* 註明日期；約會

Hank will ask Gina out on a date the day after tomorrow.

Hank 邀請 Gina 後天和他約會。

同源字 **day** *n.* 白天；日

Tues·day [`tjuzde] *n.* 星期二

My sister goes to math class on Tuesdays, Wednesdays and Fridays.

我姐姐星期二、星期三和星期五上數學課。

聯想字 **Wednes·day** *n.* 星期三
Thurs·day *n.* 星期四
Fri·day *n.* 星期五

---

to·day [tə`de] *n.* 今天 ／ *adv.* 現今

Today is my birthday, but I got a lot of gifts yesterday. Tomorrow, I will eat out with several of my friends.

今天是我的生日，但是昨天就收到很多禮物，而明天要和幾位朋友出去用餐。

聯想字 **yes·ter·day** *n.* 昨天 ／ *adv.* 昨天
to·mor·row *n.* 明天 ／ *adv.* 明天
birth·day *n.* 生日

記憶技巧
1. today = to + day，今天正是到了所指的一天，有現代的意思。
2. tomorrow = to + morning（morrow），到了天明之時，便是明天的開始。

---

morn·ing [`mɔrnɪŋ] *n.* 早晨

The Lin family go to church on Sunday mornings.

林家星期日早上都去教堂做禮拜。

noon [nun] *n.* 中午

It was sunny at noon, but cold in the late afternoon.
中午天氣晴朗，傍晚的時候就變冷了。

複合字 af·ter·noon *n.* 下午

記憶技巧

noon 源自古英文 non，午後三時，太陽清晨六時升起後的第九小時，與 nine 同源。

eve·ning [`ivnɪŋ] *n.* 傍晚；晚上

On the evening of Halloween, even my grandparents went trick-or-treating with a group of children.
萬聖節晚上，甚至我祖父母都會跟一群孩子去玩「不給糖就搗蛋」。

同源字 eve *n.* 前夕；前夜

e·ven *adj.* 偶數的；平手的 ／ *adv.* 甚至

night [naɪt] *n.* 夜晚

The young guy works at night and sleeps by day, but he is off to-night.
那位年輕人夜晚工作，白天睡覺，而今晚休假。

衍生字 to·night *n.* ／ *adv.* 今夜；今晚

tonight 是指 in the night after the persent day─這一天過後的夜晚。

hour [aʊr] *n.* 小時

It is ten o'clock, and we have been waiting at the second gate for one hour and twenty minutes.
現在是十點鐘，我們已在第二大門等了一小時又二十分鐘。

聯想字 o'clock *adv.* ⋯⋯點鐘

min·ute *n.* 分鐘；片刻

sec·ond *n.* 秒鐘 ／ *adj.* 第二的

now　[naʊ]　*n.* 現在；此刻／*adv.* 現在；立刻

From now on, I want to save money for future needs.

從現在起，我要為將來的需求存錢。

聯想字 **fu·ture**　*n.* 未來

----

mo·ment　[ˋmomənt]　*n.* 時刻；瞬間；片刻

I happened to see that stranger the moment I entered the meeting room.

我一進到會議室碰巧見到那位陌生人。

記憶技巧

moment 包含字根 mov—移動，每一片刻都是時間的挪移。

Dad left us several **months** ago. He ___(1)___ a man who loved his family and his life a lot. He liked to help others, and everyone around him liked him very much.

Last **year**, Dad got very sick and had to stay in the hospital. Mom ___(2)___ very busy running between the house and the hospital. Six **months** later, Dad died. I couldn't believe I ___(3)___ him again.

Today is Dad's 50th **birthday**. I really want to tell him how much I miss him....

_____1. (A) was

　　　(B) is

　　　(C) has been

　　　(D) will be

_____2. (A) became

　　　(B) becomes

　　　(C) has become

　　　(D) is becoming

_____3. (A) did not see

　　　(B) have not seen

　　　(C) am not seeing

　　　(D) would not see

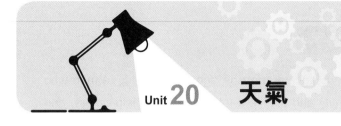

weath·er　[ˋwɛðɚ]　*n.* 天氣

Driving in bad weather is a major cause of accidents.

惡劣天候時開車是意外的一個主要原因。

記憶技巧

字源上，weather 與風—wind、窗戶—window 同源，都有吹拂—blow 的意思。

---

wind　[wɪnd]　*n.* 風

It was a windy night, and the wind had begun to get stronger since nine o'clock.

那是一個刮風的夜晚，風從九點就開始逐漸變強。

衍生字　**wind·y**　*adj.* 風大的

---

rain　[ren]　*n.* 雨／*v.* 下雨

The rain stopped, and a rainbow appeared in the sky.

雨停了，一道彩虹出現在天空。

衍生字　**rain·y**　*adj.* 下雨的；多雨的

複合字　**rain·bow**　*n.* 彩虹，**bow**　*n.* 弓

---

cloud　[klaʊd]　*n.* 雲

On a cloudy day, the sun disappeared behind heavy clouds.

在一個多雲的日子，太陽消失在厚重的雲層後方。

衍生字　**cloud·y**　*adj.* 多雲的；陰天的

snow [sno] *n.* 雪 ／ *v.* 下雪

On a winter afternoon full of snow, children had fun building a lovely snowman in the yard.
在冬天裡的一個雪花紛飛的午後，孩子們在院子堆可愛的雪人，玩得很開心。

衍生字 **snow·y** *adj.* 下雪的；多雪的
複合字 **snow·man** *n.* 雪人

hot [hɑt] *adj.* 熱的；辛辣的

The heat of the sun made the railroad workers feel hot and thirsty.
太陽的熱氣令鐵路工人感到又熱又渴。

同源字 **heat** *n.* 熱 ／ *v.* 加熱
heat·er *n.* 暖氣機

warm [wɔrm] *v.* 使暖和 ／ *adj.* 溫暖的

Mom ordered a warm winter coat online for me.
媽媽在線上幫我訂購一件溫暖的冬季大衣。

衍生字 **warmth** *n.* 暖和；溫暖

cool [kul] *n.* 從容 ／ *v.* 使涼爽 ／ *adj.* 涼快的；很棒的；酷

Taking a cold shower has cooled me down.
沖冷水澡使我涼爽一下。

衍生字 **cool·er** 冷藏箱

記憶技巧
字源上，cool 與 cold（*n.* 感冒 ／ *adj.* 寒冷的）同源，都有 freeze—凍結的意思。

Unit

20
天氣

dry [draɪ] *v.* 烘乾；晾乾 ∕ *adj.* 乾的

This towel is still wet. Hang it up to dry now.
這條毛巾還是濕的，現在把它掛起來晾乾。

衍生字 **dry·er** 烘乾機
反義字 **wet** *adj.* 潮溼的

ty·phoon [taɪ`fun] *n.* 颱風

A ship went down two miles off the shore during the typhoon.
有艘船颱風期間在離海岸二英哩處沉沒。

記憶技巧
字尾 oon 的單字其字重音在尾音節，例如：af·ter·noon *n.* 下午、car·toon *n.* 卡通、co·coon *n.* 繭

cli·mate [`klaɪmɪt] *n.* 氣候；風氣

The climate is warmer in the south of the island.
這座島的南部氣候比較溫暖。

fog [fɑg] *n.* 霧；霧氣

On the cold foggy morning, there was thick fog everywhere.
在那個寒冷多霧的早晨，到處都是厚重的霧氣。

衍生字 **fog·gy** *adj.* 有霧的；多霧的

storm [stɔrm] *n.* 暴風雨

A row of trees fell down in the storm two days ago.
一整排的樹木在二天前的暴風雨中倒塌了。

衍生字 **storm·y** *adj.* 暴風雨的

show·er　[`ʃaʊɚ]　*n.* 陣雨；淋浴

There will be wintry showers over many parts of this island.

這座島上許多地方將有冬天特有的陣雨。

- -

thun·der　[`θʌndɚ]　*n.* 雷；雷聲／*v.* 打雷

After a loud clap of thunder, heavy rain started to pour.

一聲震耳雷鳴後開始下起傾盆大雨。

複合字　**thunderstorm**　*n.* 雷雨

Could it be possible to live in a house made of ice? What is it like to sleep on an ice bed? North Hotel is the magic place that brings people from all over the world to __(1)__ in the **cold**. Here you can have dinner at an ice table, watch movies in an ice chair, and even take a bath in a large ice box. Worried about catching a **cold**? __(2)__! North Hotel keeps you **warm** and makes you feel comfortable all the time. You can live in this dreamland for a few days and enjoy many special experiences in the **snow**. It is not easy to tell you about everything here at North Hotel; you must __(3)__. Pack now and get ready to be **COOL**!

_____1. (A) have fun

(B) is

(C) start a new life

(D) learn to make friends

_____2. (A) Good idea

(B) You don't have to be

(C) Take care of yourself

(D) Don't forget your heavy coat

_____3. (A) think about it carefully

(B) come to see it for yourself

(C) check out the **weather** first

(D) wait and see what will happen

答案：1. (A)；2. (B)；3. (B)

Unit 21 數字

🎧 Track 080

num·ber [`nʌmbɚ] *n.* 數字;號碼 / *v.* 共計

There used to be a number of fruit trees on both sides of the road.

以前道路兩旁有許多果樹。

| 衍生字 | **nu·me·rous** *adj.* 許多的;大量的 |
| | **out·num·ber** *v.* 數量上超過 |

---

ze·ro [`zɪro] *n.* 零

The number one thousand is written with a one and three zeros.

數字一千的寫法是一個一和三個零。

---

one [wʌn] *n.* 一;一個人 / *det.* 一個的

In one of the high schools in town, every girl and every boy has a vegetarian lunch only once a week.

在鎮上的一所中學,每個女孩和男孩一星期只吃一次素食午餐。

聯想字	**each** *det.* 每個的 / *pron.* 每個
	ev·ery *det.* 每個的
	on·ly *adj.* 唯一的 / *adv.* 只;僅僅
同源字	**once** *adv.* 一次;曾經

記憶技巧

only 是 one 黏接字尾 ly 而形成,ly 的意思是 like一像。

129

e·lev·en [ɪˋlɛvn] *n.* 十一 / *det.* 十一的

The cub has grown eleven kilograms this year.

那隻小熊今年已長到 11 公斤。

衍生字 **e·lev·enth** *det.* 第十一的

記憶技巧

字源上，eleven 是 one + leave—以十為基準，離開十再加一的數字是
十一，twelve 則是 two + leave。

---

two [tu] *n.* 二 / *det.* 二的

The couple has two children, both of whom are living abroad.
They come back to Taiwan just twice a year.

那對夫婦育有二名子女，目前都旅居國外，一年只回臺灣二次。

聯想字 **both** *det.* 兩者 / *pron.* 兩者
ei·ther *adv.* 也不 / *det.* 兩者之一 / *pron.* 兩者之一

衍生字 **twelve** *n.* 十二 / *det.* 十二的
twen·ty *n.* 二十 / *det.* 二十的
ty 是十的倍數的意思，二的十倍是二十。

同源字 **twice** *adv.* 二次

---

three [θri] *n.* 三 / *det.* 三的

Around three thirty this afternoon, three cars crashed into each
other at the third road after city hall.

今天下午大約三點三十分，三輛汽車在市政府之後第三條路相撞。

衍生字 **thir·teen** *n.* 十三 / *det.* 十三的
thirteen = three + ten，三加上十就是十三
thir·ty *n.* 三十 / *det.* 三十的
thirty = three + ty，三的十倍是三十

同源字 **third** *det.* 第三的

記憶技巧

three 與 third 同源，r 字母移位。

four [for] *n.* 四 / *det.* 四的

It is a quarter past four, so there will be forty passengers coming from gate fourteen.

現在是四點一刻，將有四十位旅客從十四號登機門進來。

聯想字 **quar·ter** *n.* 四分之一；美金 25 分；一刻鐘

衍生字 **four·teen** *n.* 十四 / *det.* 十四的

fourteen = four + ten，四加上十是十四

for·ty *n.* 四十 / *det.* 四十的，四的十倍是四十

fourth *det.* 第四的

- -

five [faɪv] *n.* 五 / *det.* 五的

Fifteen times three is forty-five, and this plus five is fifty.

十五乘三等於四十五，再加五等於五十。

衍生字 **fif·teen** *n.* 十五 / *det.* 十五的

fifteen = five + teen

fif·ty *n.* 五十 / *det.* 五十的

fifty = five + ty，五的十倍是五十

fifth *det.* 第五的

- -

six [sɪks] *n.* 六 / *det.* 六的

Player number sixteen is one hundred and sixty-six centimeters tall.

16 號球員是 166 公分高。

衍生字 **six·teen** *n.* 十六 / *det.* 十六的

sixteen = six + teen

six·ty *n.* 六十 / *det.* 六十的

sixty = six + ty

sixth *det.* 第六的

seven [ˋsɛvn] *n.* 七 ╱ *det.* 七的

These seventeen colored sunglasses cost seventy-seven US dollars in total.

這 17 副有色太陽眼鏡共值 77 美元。

衍生字 **sev·en·teen** *n.* 十七 ╱ *det.* 十七的
seventeen = seven + teen
sev·en·ty *n.* 七十 ╱ *det.* 七十的
seventy = seven + ty
sev·enth *det.* 第七的

---

eight [et] *n.* 八 ╱ *det.* 八的

Each stone weighs between eight and ten kilograms.

每塊石頭重八到十公斤之間。

衍生字 **eigh·teen** *n.* 十八 ╱ *det.* 十八的
eighteen = eight + teen
eigh·ty *n.* 八十 ╱ *det.* 八十的
eighty = eight + ty
eighth *det.* 第八的

---

nine [naɪn] *n.* 九 ╱ *det.* 九的

Nine subtracted from nineteen equals ten.

19 減 9 等於 10。

衍生字 **nine·teen** *n.* 十九 ╱ *det.* 十九的
nineteen = nine + teen
nine·ty *n.* 九十 ╱ *det.* 九十的
ninety = nine + ty
ninth *det.* 第九的

ten [tɛn] *n.* 十 ╱ *det.* 十的

Mrs. Lin bought a dozen eggs and ten hot dogs for the picnic.
林太太買了一打雞蛋和十根熱狗供野餐時食用。

衍生字 **tenth** *det.* 第十的

聯想字 **doz·en** *n.* 一打

記憶技巧
構詞上，dozen 是 two 及 ten 等二字根（dou + dec）的混成。

hun·dred [`hʌndrəd] *n.* 一百 ╱ *det.* 一百的

The snake is one hundred centimeters long, and its head is as big as a ten-cent coin.
那條蛇有一百公分長，牠的頭有十分硬幣那麼大。

衍生字 **hun·dredth** *det.* 第一百的

聯想字 **cen·ti·me·ter** *n.* 公分
cent + i + meter，i 是填補字母，為了形成 CV一子音連接母音的唸音形式。字義方面，基數與序數的字根通常同源，也就是說，cent 可表示一百或是百分之一，meter 是公尺，百分之一公尺等於一公分。

同源字 **cent** *n.* 分
字源上，cent 的首字母 c 在拉丁文唸 /k/ 音，與 hundred 的首子音 /h/ 轉音。

thou·sand [`θaʊznd] *n.* 千 ╱ *det.* 千的

One kilogram equals one thousand grams.
1 公斤等於 1000 公克。

聯想字 **mil·lion** *n.* 百萬 ╱ *det.* 百萬的
kil·o·gram *n.* 公斤
gram *n.* 公克

If you cannot live without your car, Zurich might be the last city you would like to visit. In Zurich, people are welcome, but cars are not! Over the past **twenty** years, this city has used smart ways ___(1)___. One is to keep the same **total number** of parking spaces. For example, if **fifty** new parking spaces are built in **one** part of the city, then **fifty** old spaces in other parts are taken away for other uses. So the **total number** does not change. Some are unhappy that there are never enough spaces. That is just what the city has in mind: If people find parking more difficult, they will drive less.

___(2)___, the **total number** of cars in the city is counted. Over **three thousand** and **five hundred** little computers are put under Zurich roads to check the **number** of cars that enter the city. If the **number** is higher than the city can deal with, the traffic lights on the roads that enter the city will be kept red. So drivers who are traveling into Zurich have to stop and wait until there are fewer cars in the city. Now, you may wonder ___(3)___. The answer is simple: The city wants to make more space for its people.

_____1. (A) to make traffic lighter

(B) to invite people to visit

(C) to make itself a famous city

(D) to build more parking spaces

_____2. (A) This way

(B) However

(C) For example

(D) Also

_____3. (A) why Zurich is doing this

(B) what all this has cost Zurich

(C) if Zurich should try other ways

(D) if Zurich can deal with angry drivers

Unit **22**　度量衡

🎧 Track 085

first [fɝst]　*adv.* 首先／*det.* 第一的

Tom won first place in the race, and Jack was second to last.
Tom 贏得賽跑第一名，Jack 則是倒數第二。

反義字　**last**　*v.* 持續／*adj.* 最後的／*adv.* 最後地
　　　　last·ing　*adj.* 持續的；持久的

----

half [hæf]　*n.* 一半／*det.* 一半的

The well-known poet was born in the latter half of the 18th century.
該位知名詩人出生於十八世紀中葉以後。

記憶技巧
字源上，half 是切—cut 的意思，一刀切兩半。

----

li·ter [`litɚ]　*n.* 公升

A liter is equal to 1,000 c.c.
1 公升等於 1000 毫升。

----

vol·ume [`vɑljəm]　*n.* 體積；音量；冊

Ice has a larger volume than water.
冰的體積比水大。

記憶技巧
字源上，volume 是轉動—turm、捲—roll 的意思，古時候，書冊是寫在捲起的羊皮紙上，後來又將一本書的大小視為約略的體積量，因此 volume 又有體積的意思。

pound [paʊnd] *n.* 磅；英鎊

There are one hundred pence in a pound.

1 英鎊等於 100 便士。

---

mile [maɪl] *n.* 英里

A mile equals 1.609 kilometers.

1 英哩等於 1.609 公里。

衍生字	**mile·age** *n.* 英里數
聯想字	**kil·o·me·ter** *n.* 公里

kilo = thousand，一千公尺等於一公里

mile·stone *n.* 里程碑

---

inch [ɪntʃ] *n.* 英吋

The boy has a cut an inch long above his right eye.

男孩的右眼上方有一道 1 英吋長的割傷。

---

size [saɪz] *n.* 尺寸

These avocado trees will grow to a large size.

這些酪梨樹會長到巨大的尺寸。

聯想字	**gi·ant** *n.* 巨人／ *adj.* 巨大的
	large *adj.* 大的
	big *adj.* 大的
	me·di·um *adj.* 中等的
	small *adj.* 小的

high　[haɪ]　*adj.* 高的 ／ *adv.* 高

The woman has placed cookies on a high shelf where her dog cannot get at them.
婦人把餅乾放在她的狗搆不到的高架上。

衍生字　**high·ly**　*adv.* 在高處；非常
同源字　**height**　*n.* 高度
　　　　height·en　*v.* 增強
反義字　**low**　*adj.* 低的；矮的 ／ *adv.* 低

---

tall　[tɔl]　*adj.* 高的

The girl with short hair is about six feet two inches tall.
那位短髮女孩大約 6 呎 2 吋高。

反義字　**short**　*adj.* 矮的；短的

---

long　[lɔŋ]　*v.* 渴望 ／ *adj.* 長的；長久的 ／ *adv.* 長久地

It's a long time since my uncle worked in that glass factory.
我叔叔在那家玻璃工廠工作一段長時間了。

衍生字　**a·long**　*v.* 向前 ／ *pre.* 沿著
相關字　**length**　*n.* 長度
　　　　length·en　*v.* 延長；延期

---

heav·y　[`hɛvɪ]　*adj.* 重的；大量的

This lamp is really heavy, and we need to put it down for a while.
這盞燈很重，我們得把它放下來一會兒。

反義字　**light**　*n.* 光線；燈 ／ *v.* 點燃；照亮 ／ *adj.* 輕的；明亮的；淺色的

thick [θɪk] *adj.* 厚的；濃的

The slim dancer has thick dark hair and fair skin.
那位纖細的舞者擁有濃密烏黑的秀髮及白皙的皮膚。

| 反義字 | thin *adj.* 薄的；瘦的 |
| | slim *adj.* 苗條的；纖細的 |

---

fast [fæst] *n.* 禁食；禁食期 ／ *v.* 禁食 ／ *adj.* 快的；迅速的 ／
adv. 快；迅速地

The high-speed train is very fast, and therefore the visitors will arrive soon.
高鐵列車速度很快，因此訪客很快就會到達。

聯想字	quick *adj.* 快的；敏捷的
	soon *adv.* 不久；很快地
	quick·ly *adv.* 迅速地
反義字	slow *v.* 減速 ／ *adj.* 慢的；遲緩的 ／ *adv.* 緩慢地
	slow·ly *adv.* 緩慢地

---

count [kaʊnt] *n.* 計數；計算 ／ *v.* 計算；數

There will be ten for lunch, counting ourselves.
連我們算在內，有十個人要吃午餐。

衍生字	ac·count *n.* 帳戶；說明
	ac·count·ant *n.* 會計
	count·er *n.* 櫃檯

Billy is one of my classmates in junior high school. Three years ago, he was very **heavy**, but he looks wonderful now. Here is his story about how he lost **weight**.

Billy ___(1)___ a lot of snacks and **fast** food in his elementary school days. Besides, he did not do **much** exercise. So he kept putting on **weight**. He became so **heavy** that one day he broke the chair he was sitting on when he was in class.

After this experience, Billy decided to lose some **kilos**. **First**, he went to see a doctor and ___(2)___ to avoid **fast** food. Also, the doctor said he should start exercising. Billy followed the doctor's advice: he ___(3)___ away from **fast** food and snacks for one year, and **most** important of all, he jogged every day.

That is how Billy lost 20 **kilos** before he entered junior high school.

_____1. (A) eats

      (B) has eaten

      (C) ate

      (D) was going to eat

_____2. (A) is asked

      (B) was asked

      (C) will be asked

      (D) would be asked

_____3. (A) has stayed

      (B) is staying

      (C) will stay

      (D) stayed

🔊 Track 089

bag　[bæg]　*n.* 袋子 ／ *v.* 裝入袋子

This afternoon, my parents took me shopping with our own shopping bags.
今天下午，我父母帶我去購物，帶著我們自己的購物袋。

衍生字 **bag·gage**　*n.* 行李

---

bas·ket　[`bæskɪt]　*n.* 籃子

Mom helped me pack my picnic basket before I went on the picnic.
我去野餐之前，媽媽幫我打包野餐籃子。

---

bot·tle　[`bɑtl̩]　*n.* 瓶子 ／ *v.* 裝瓶

Glass bottles are heavier than plastic ones.
玻璃瓶比塑膠瓶來得重。

衍生字 **bot·tled**　*adj.* 瓶裝的

---

bowl　[bol]　*n.* 碗

I ate a bowl of beef noodles for lunch today.
今天我吃一碗牛肉麵當作午餐。

記憶技巧
字源上，bowl 也與吹—blow 同源，圓形的碗如同吹脹的器皿。

box　[bɑks]　*n.* 箱子；盒子

My cousin should not have eaten the whole box of chocolates.
我堂妹原本不該吃掉那整盒的巧克力。

衍生字 **box·ing**　*n.* 拳擊
　　　 box·er　*n.* 拳擊手

---

case　[kes]　*n.* 箱子；案件

Harry's uncle brought a case of wine to his wedding.
Harry 的叔叔帶了一箱酒到他的婚禮。

---

cup　[kʌp]　*n.* 杯子／ *v.* 以手做成杯狀

I drank a cup of black coffee, and Tina drank a glass of guava juice.
我喝了一杯黑咖啡，Tina 喝了一杯芭樂汁。

聯想字 **glass**　*n.* 玻璃杯；玻璃

記憶技巧
字源上，glass 有照耀—to shine 的意思，一些 gl 為首的單字與光有關。

---

plate　[plet]　*n.* 盤子；碟子

The salad plate should be placed on top of the dinner plate.
沙拉盤應該放在晚餐盤的上方。

記憶技巧
字源上，plate 與扁的—flat 同源，盤子是扁平狀的器皿。

---

dish　[dɪʃ]　*n.* 盤子；一盤菜

There's a little butter left on the butter dish.
奶油盤裡剩下一些奶油。

記憶技巧
字源上，dish 與磁碟—disk 同源，都是扁平狀的物體。

pot [pɑt] *n.* 陶罐;壺;鍋子

Fill a medium pot with clean water and bring it to a boil.
用清水裝滿中型鍋,然後將水燒開。

---

lid [lɪd] *n.* 蓋子

Could you please get the lid off this bottle?
麻煩您將這瓶子的蓋子弄掉,好嗎?

---

fork [fɔrk] *n.* 叉子

Miss Lin taught us how to hold a knife and fork correctly.
林老師教我們如何正確握住刀叉。

---

spoon [spun] *n.* 湯匙

Mrs. Chen added a couple of spoons of sauce over the fried fish.
陳太太在整條油炸的魚上面淋了二湯匙的醬汁。

衍生字 **spoon·ful** *n.* 一匙的量

---

chop·sticks [`tʃɑpˌstɪks] *n.* 筷子

Do not use chopsticks to gesture while talking during a meal.
用餐時不要用筷子邊講話邊比劃。

記憶技巧

chopstick = chop + stick,chop 是削的動作,stick 是棍子,筷子是削成的細小棍子。

---

o·ven [`ʌvən] *n.* 烤箱

Microwave ovens and gas stoves are both cooking appliances.
微波爐和瓦斯爐都是烹調器具。

聯想字 **stove** *n.* 火爐

If you sail between Hawaii and California, you'll find a big part of the ocean, as big as Africa, covered with garbage. Most of the trash comes from the land, by wind or by water, and some is thrown straight into the sea. Most of the trash is plastic: plastic **bags**, plastic **cups**, plastic **cans**, and a lot more.

___(1)___? Some just stays in the sea, some is washed onto the beaches, and, worst of all, some ___(2)___. Many seabirds and sea animals that eat the trash in the sea die. Those that are lucky enough to live on may someday arrive on our dinner **plate**. What we throw away will all ___(3)___ one way or another.

Keep in mind what happens to trash, and you may think twice before you throw anything away.

_____1. (A) Where does the trash go

      (B) How do we deal with the trash

      (C) Where does the trash come from

      (D) How does the trash arrive in the sea

_____2. (A) enters seabirds' and sea animals' stomachs

      (B) stops seabirds and sea animals from growing up

      (C) fills the living space of seabirds and sea animals

      (D) goes down to the bottom of the sea and never comes up

_____3. (A) be cleared up

      (B) come back to us

      (C) be useful to others

      (D) get out of our sight

Unit 24　情緒、感覺

🎧 Track 092

feel　[fil]　*n.* 觸覺；氣氛／*v.* 感覺；認為；觸

I felt so touched when I touched the scarf my mom made for me.
我摸著媽媽為我編織的圍巾，深受感動。

衍生字　**feel·ing**　*n.* 感覺；感情
聯想字　**touch**　*v.* 觸摸；感動
　　　　touched　*adj.* 受感動的

---

glad　[glæd]　*adj.* 高興的

I would be only too glad to help out.
我會很樂意幫忙。

記憶技巧
字源上，glad 意思是照耀—to shine，gl 首字母的單字多有光、亮的意涵，高興時常容光煥發，閃耀愉悅的神采。

---

hap·py　[ˋhæpɪ]　*adj.* 快樂的；滿意的

The customer seems to be happy with the service.
那位顧客對服務似乎感到滿意。

衍生字　**hap·pi·ness**　*n.* 快樂
　　　　hap·pi·ly　*adv.* 快樂地
反義字　**un·hap·py**　*adj.* 不快樂的，字首 un 是 not 的意思。

a·fraid　　[ə`fred]　　*adj.* 害怕的；擔憂的；發愁的

My wife has always been afraid of heights.

我太太一向懼高。

記憶技巧

字源上，afraid 是 "take out of peace" 一從平和中出來的意思，字首 a =
ex，out，字根 fraid 是平和一peace 的意思。

scared　　[skɛrd]　　*adj.* 害怕的

Joe was scared to tell his mother what really happened to him at
school.

Joe 害怕告訴他媽媽他在學校真實發生的事。

衍生字　**scare**　*n.* 驚恐 ／ *v.* 使驚恐
　　　　scar·y　*adj.* 駭人的；恐怖的

an·gry　　[`æŋgrɪ]　　*adj.* 生氣的；紅腫的

The coach got really angry with the player who got mad in the
game.

教練對那位比賽中動怒的選手感到非常生氣。

衍生字　**an·gri·ly**　*adv.* 憤怒地
聯想字　**mad**　*adj.* 發怒的；發瘋的；狂熱的

記憶技巧

angry = an·ger + y，an·ger　*n.* 憤怒

bored　　[bord]　　*adj.* 感到無聊的；感到厭煩的

We were getting bored with the boring movie.

我們對那部無聊的電影漸漸感到厭倦。

聯想字　**bore**　*v.* 使厭煩；使討厭
　　　　bor·ing　*adj.* 令人厭倦的；令人生厭的
　　　　bor·dom　*n.* 厭煩；乏味

ex·cit·ed　[ɪk`saɪtɪd]　*adj.* 感到興奮的

The crazy man got excited about the exciting game.

那位瘋狂的男子對刺激的比賽感到興奮。

聯想字　**ex·cit·ing**　*adj.* 令人興奮的
　　　　cra·zy　*adj.* 瘋狂的；著迷的
　　　　craze　*n.* 時尚；風行一時的事物

記憶技巧

excited = ex + cite + ed，ex = out，cite = call，感到興奮時大聲叫出來。

----

in·ter·est·ed　[`ɪntərɪstɪd]　*adj.* 感興趣的

My brother is interested in that interesting comic book.

我哥哥對那本有趣的漫畫書興趣勃勃。

聯想字　**in·ter·est·ing**　*adj.* 有趣的
　　　　interest　*n.* 興趣；利益／*v.* 使感到興趣

記憶技巧

inter + est，inter = between, among，est = to be，存在的意思，利益是存在於二者之間的糾葛。

----

sur·prised　[sə`praɪzd]　*adj.* 感到驚訝的

We were surprised at the new and surprising information that the secretary revealed.

我們對秘書走漏的那個又新又令人訝異的消息感到驚訝。

聯想字　**sur·prise**　*n.* 意想不到的事物；驚訝／*v.* 使驚奇
　　　　sur·pris·ing　*adj.* 令人驚訝的

記憶技巧

surprise = sur + prise，sur = over—超越，prise = seize—抓奪，原意是某地遭受意料之外的奪取或軍隊遭受突襲。

de·pressed　[dɪ`prɛst]　*adj.* 沮喪的

The man became deeply depressed when he got laid off.
男子遭到解僱時變得非常沮喪。

記憶技巧

depress = de + press，字首 de 是往下—down 的意思，有事往下壓著心頭
當然就會沮喪。

---

lone·ly　[`lonlɪ]　*adj.* 寂寞的

The woman got lonely after her husband passed away.
婦人在丈夫過世之後變得寂寞。

記憶技巧

lonely = lone + ly，lone 是單獨的、獨自的意思，ly 是形容詞字尾，
alone—「單獨的、僅有的」的縮減，lone 黏接字尾 er 衍生成 loner，指的
是孤僻的人、不合群的人。

---

wor·ry　[`wɝɪ]　*n.* 擔憂；令人擔憂的事 ／ *v.* 擔心；使焦慮

The student worried that he might not be able to pass the test.
那位學生擔心他可能無法通過測驗。

---

sad　[sæd]　*adj.* 令人難過的；悽慘的

Actually, I didn't feel angry so much as sad when hearing the news.
事實上，我聽到消息時，不是氣憤，而是難過。

衍生字　**sadly**　*adv.* 傷心地；令人遺憾地

🎧 Track 096

shy [ʃaɪ] *v.* 畏縮／*adj.* 害羞的；靦腆的

Tom was too shy to ask Ruby out on a date.
Tom 太害羞，未能邀 Ruby 出去約會。

衍生字 **shy·ness** *n.* 害羞；羞澀
shy·ly *adv.* 害羞地

小試身手 ★出自 94 年第一次基測

　　There are some popular singers these days. Many of their fans enjoy getting together to share their love for the stars. My younger sister, Mei-ling, is one of these fans.

　　Mei-ling is **crazy** about Rye Kim. She has been in one of his fan clubs since last year. Mei-ling did not have any **close** friends before, and she always felt **lost** and **lonely**. But she has made many friends with the same **interests** since she joined the club. Now Mei-ling and her friends are planning a big party for Kim's birthday. Mei-ling is **happy**, but my dad is not. In fact, he is very **worried**. Rye Kim is a total stranger to him, and he cannot understand why a man who sings **crazy** songs can be so important to his daughter. He really hopes that Mei-ling can love her family as much as she loves Rye Kim.

_____1. Who is <u>Rye Kim</u>?

      (A) A singer.

      (B) A crazy fan.

      (C) Mei-ling's father.

      (D) Mei-ling's brother.

_____2. Which is true about Mei-ling?

      (A) She is **proud** of her beautiful voice.

      (B) She always wants to be a movie star.

      (C) She is going to have a party on her birthday.

      (D) She has changed a lot since she joined a fan club.

_____3. Why is Mei-ling's father NOT **happy**?

      (A) Mei-ling does not have any friends.

      (B) Mei-ling is not doing well at school.

      (C) Mei-ling is **crazy** about playing computer games.

      (D) Mei-ling is spending too much time on a stranger.

Unit 25　特質一

🎧 Track 097

hand·some　[`hænsəm]　*adj.* 英俊的；漂亮的

The new member is tall, dark, and handsome.
那位新成員長得高，皮膚黝黑又英俊。

【記憶技巧】

handsome = hand + some，形容詞字尾 some 表示「有……的傾向」或「有相當程度的」，handsome 原意是容易處理、預備好的，後來衍生為美貌的、看起來愉悅的。

---

beau·ti·ful　[`bjutəfəl]　*adj.* 美麗的；美好的；極好的

The beautiful girl can play the flute pretty well.
那位美麗的女孩能夠十分美妙地吹奏長笛。

【聯想字】　**pret·ty**　*adj.* 漂亮的 ／ *adv.* 十分地
　　　　　beau·ty　*n.* 美；美人
　　　　　beau·ti·ful·ly　*adv.* 美麗地；完美地
　　　　　beau·ti·fy　*v.* 美化

---

cute　[kjut]　*adj.* 可愛的；精明的

Peter looks very smart in his new jacket, but his hat makes him look cute.
Peter 穿上新外套看起來很時髦，但他的帽子讓他看起來可愛。

【衍生字】　**cute·ness**　*n.* 嬌小可愛
【聯想字】　**smart**　*adj.* 聰明的；時髦的

wise [waɪz]   *adj.* 有智慧的；明智的

Mr. Lin is a wise man, and he will never do such a stupid thing.

林先生是個有智慧的人，他絕不會做這麼愚蠢的事。

衍生字	**wis·dom** *n.* 智慧，wisdom = wise + dom
	wise·ly *adv.* 明智地
反義字	**stu·pid** *adj.* 愚蠢的；笨的

記憶技巧

字源上，wise 是看—to see 的意思，看見就明白—to know，變得有智慧—wise。

- -

ex·cel·lent [`ɛkslənt]   *adj.* 卓越的；非常好的

Cycling is an excellent way of keeping fit. It is also a great way to enjoy wonderful scenery.

騎腳踏車是保持身材的絕佳方式，也是享受美好風景的好方法。

聯想字	**ex·cel·lent·ly** *adv.* 優異地；極好地
	great *adj.* 巨大的；偉大的；優秀的
	won·der·ful *adj.* 極好的；奇妙的
	won·der *n.* 奇觀；疑惑

記憶技巧

1. excellent = excel + ent，ex·cel   *v.* 擅長於，黏接形容詞字尾 ent，字重音雖移至第一音節，不是尾音節，但仍插入字尾子音字母 l，不同於尾音節為字重音，黏接母音為首的字尾綴詞時才插入尾子音字母，以維持字幹的重音節唸音。excellent 重複字母 l 的拼字算是英語字彙的任性。

2. ex·cel·lence   *n.* 卓越；優秀，excellence = excel + ence，重複字母 l 同樣是任性的表現。另外，黏接形容詞字尾 ent 的單字，常具有黏接名詞字尾 ence 的衍生字，形成字彙的對稱，另外，ent、ence 二者同源。

suc·cess·ful [sək`sɛsfəl]   *adj.* 成功的；達到目的的

The man failed many times before he became successful in his business.

那名男子事業成功之前，失敗過很多次。

反義字 fail   *n.* 失敗；不及格 ／ *v.* 失敗；不及格；未能做到

▶ successful = success + ful，suc·cess   *n.* 成功，字首 suc 是 under—在……下面的意思，字根 cess 是 go—去的意思，從下往上而去就是成功。

---

nice   [naɪs]   *adj.* 好的；美好的；友善的

The weather was nice and we all had a good time enjoying a picnic.

天氣很好，我們都在享受野餐中渡過一段愉快的時光。

衍生字 nice·ly   *adv.* 精確地；出色地

聯想字 fine   *adj.* 好的；健康的；優秀的
　　　good   *adj.* 好的；擅長的；樂於助人的

反義字 bad   *adj.* 壞的；劣質的；道德敗壞的

---

kind   [kaɪnd]   *n.* 種類 ／ *adj.* 親切的；和藹的

It's very kind of you to help me out.

您人真好，對我伸出援手。

衍生字 kind·ness   *n.* 好意；友好的行為
　　　kind·ly   *adj.* 親切的 ／ *adv.* 親切地
　　　un·kind   *adj.* 不和善的

hon·est [`ɑnɪst] *adj.* 誠實的；可信的

To be honest, I'm afraid the student wasn't very polite to his teacher at that time.

老實說，我擔心那位學生當時對他的老師不是很有禮貌。

衍生字 **hon·est·ly** *adv.* 誠實地；公正地
dis·hon·est *adj.* 不誠實的

聯想字 **po·lite** *adj.* 有禮貌的；斯文的
bow *n.* 蝴蝶結；弓 ／ *v.* 鞠躬

---

hard-work·ing [ˌhɑrd`wɜˑkɪŋ] *adj.* 努力工作的；勤勉的

Hank is not lazy at all. On the contrary, he is always hard-working.

Hank 一點也不懶惰，相反的，他一直都很勤勉。

聯想字 **hard** *adj.* 困難的；硬的 ／ *adv.* 辛苦地；猛烈地；牢固地
反義字 **la·zy** *adj.* 懶惰的

---

fa·vo·rite [`fevərɪt] *n.* 特別喜愛的人、物 ／ *adj.* 最喜愛的

My current favorite board game is Blood Bowl, which is popular with a lot of young students.

我目前最喜愛的桌遊是 Blood Bowl，它受到很多年輕學生的歡迎。

聯想字 **pop·u·lar** *adj.* 受歡迎的；流行的

記憶技巧

popular = popul + ar，字根 popul 是 people一人的意思，二者同源；字尾 ar 是 al 的變化形，al 黏接 l 字母時，為避免二 /l/ 音相鄰而唸音不易，因此 變形為 ar，這是相對於同化的異化現象。

bus·y [ˋbɪzɪ] *adj.* 忙碌的

The businessman is always busy with his own business.
那位商人總是忙著他自己的事業。

衍生字 | **busi·ness** *n.* 商業；事
business = busy + ness，字尾 y 字母不黏接字尾綴詞，因此變換為同唸音的 i 字母。

busi·ness·man *n.* 商人，businessman = business + man

---

luck·y [ˋlʌkɪ] *adj.* 幸運的

Eight is my lucky number.
「八」是我的幸運數字。

相關字 | **luck** *n.* 運氣；成功
luck·ly *adv.* 幸運地

---

care·ful [ˋkɛrfəl] *adj.* 小心的；認真的

Be careful when taking care of a newborn baby.
照顧新生兒時要小心。

衍生字 | **care·ful·ly** *adv.* 小心地；仔細地

記憶技巧
careful = care + ful，care *n.* 照料；關懷／ *v.* 關心；照顧

---

help·ful [ˋhɛlpfəl] *adj.* 有益的；願意幫助的

Fred is such a pleasant, helpful guy! He is ready to help some-one whenever possible.
Fred 是個多麼親切又願意幫忙的人，只要有可能，他隨時都要幫助別人。

記憶技巧
helpful = help + ful，help *n.* ／ *v.* 幫助

Reading is an activity people enjoy a lot in their free time. Some like reading newspapers, and others enjoy novels or comic books. I like reading about the lives of **great** people. <u>This</u> always gives me a lot of ideas on how to make my own life better.

Great people are remembered not because they were **handsome** or **beautiful**, but because they did not give up when their lives were **difficult**. They used every opportunity to change their lives and make the world **better**.

One **good** example is Orville and Wilbur Wright, the two brothers who invented the airplane. The plane has made the world into a **small** village. **Hard** work, not **good** luck, is the reason why the Wright Brothers could invent this **convenient** machine and become <u>remarkable</u> people. Today we still remember them when we see planes in the sky.

When I feel **sad**, stories of **great** people always help me feel **better**. This is why I enjoy reading about **great** people's life.

_____ 1. What does "This" mean in the first paragraph?

   (A) Being a **great** person.

   (B) Living in a **special** way.

   (C) Reading about the lives of **great** people.

   (D) Reading newspapers, novels, or comic books.

_____ 2. Which book might the writer be most interested in?

   (A) *How to Build a Strong Plane*

   (B) *Ten Books That Have Made Our World Better*

   (C) *Use Every Opportunity to Read in Your Free Time*

   (D) *Michael Jordan: The Man Who Changed Basketball History*

_____ 3. What does "remarkable" mean in the third paragraph?

   (A) **Nice** and **polite**.

   (B) **Tall** and **handsome**.

   (C) **Special** and **famous**.

   (D) **Lucky** and **interesting**.

Track 102

hu·mor·ous　　[`hjumərəs]　　*adj.* 幽默的；詼諧的

My boss has a good sense of humor, and he is making the office a humorous workplace.

我老闆幽默感很好，他總是讓辦公室成為幽默的職場。

相關字　**hu·mor**　　*n.* 幽默；幽默感

記憶技巧

造字上，中文的「幽默」源自英文 "humor" 的音譯。

---

old　　[old]　　*adj.* 老的；舊的

The new member is a twenty-year-old student. He is really young.

那位新成員是個二十歲的學生，非常年輕。

反義字　**young**　　*adj.* 年輕的；幼小的
　　　　　new　　*adj.* 新的；生疏的

---

rich　　[rɪtʃ]　　*adj.* 富有的；富饒的

In Finland, the gap between the rich and the poor has been narrowing in recent years.

在芬蘭，貧富差距在這幾年一直在縮小。

衍生字　**en·rich**　　*v.* 使富含；使富裕
反義字　**poor**　　*adj.* 貧窮的；可憐的

strong [strɔŋ] *adj.* 強壯的；堅定的；強烈的；擅長的

Could you please talk about your strong points and weak points?

可以請您談一下您擅長的及不夠好的特質嗎？

衍生字 **strength** *n.* 力量

反義字 **weak** *adj.* 虛弱的；稀的；不夠好的

---

loud [laʊd] *adj.* 大聲的；響亮的

You are so loud. Please be quiet!

你太大聲了，請安靜。

反義字 **qui·et** *adj.* 安靜的；寧靜的

qui·et·ly *adv.* 安靜地

---

bright [braɪt] *adj.* 明亮的；晴朗的

The room was dark before, but now it is bright and airy.

這個房間以前很暗，但現在明亮又通風。

衍生字 **bright·ness** *n.* 明亮；亮度

反義字 **dark** *adj.* 黑暗的；深色的

dark·ness *n.* 黑暗

---

dif·fi·cult [ˋdɪfəˌkəlt] *adj.* 困難的；費力的

Take it easy. This question is simple, and not difficult for you.

別著急，這問題簡單，對你來說不困難。

反義字 **eas·y** *adj.* 容易的；舒適的

相關字 **ease** *n.* 舒適 ／ *v.* 緩解

sim·ple *adj.* 簡單的；樸素的

記憶技巧

造字上，difficult 是 difficulty—困難的逆向構詞，也就是 difficulty 略去字尾 y 才形成 difficult，而不是 difficult 黏接 y 而形成 difficulty。另外，difficult 的字首 dif 表示分離—apart，字根 fic 是 easy to do—容易去做的意思，與容易去做的狀況分離就是遇上困難。

same [sem] *adj.* 相同的 ／ *adv.* 同樣地 ／ *pron.* 同樣的事物

The twins do not want to look the same, so they usually wear different clothing.

那對雙胞胎不要看起來一樣，因此他們經常穿著不同的服飾。

反義字 **dif·fe·rent** *adj.* 不同的

記憶技巧

different = dif + fer + ent，字首 dif 表示分離—apart，字根 fer 表示攜帶—carry，被帶離開的就是不同的。ent 是形容詞字尾，常與名詞字尾 ence 形成對稱的衍生字，difference 是「不同」的意思。

---

ti·dy [`taɪdi] *v.* 使整潔 ／ *adj.* 整潔的

Your bedroom is a little messy. Let me help you make it neat and tidy.

你的臥室有點凌亂，讓我幫忙弄整潔。

反義字 **mess·y** *adj.* 凌亂的；雜亂的
　　　mess *n.* 骯髒；雜亂；混亂局面

---

clean [klin] *v.* 打掃 ／ *adj.* 乾淨的；空白的 ／ *adv.* 完全地

The water in the bottle looks so clear. I am sure it is clean, not dirty.

瓶子裡的水看起來好清澈，我確定它是乾淨的，不是髒的。

聯想字 **clear** *v.* 清除 ／ *adj.* 清楚的；晴朗的；清澈的

衍生字 **clean·er** *n.* 清潔工；清潔劑
　　　un·clean *adj.* 骯髒的；不潔淨的

反義字 **dirt·y** *adj.* 骯髒的
　　　dirt *n.* 灰塵

cor·rect [kəˋrɛkt] *v.* 訂正;糾正 / *adj.* 正確的

The student was asked to correct all the wrong sentences.

那位學生被要求訂正所有的錯誤句子。

反義字	**wrong** *adj.* 錯誤的
	wrong·ly *adv.* 錯誤地

記憶技巧

correct = cor + rect,字首 cor = com,表示強調,字根 rect 是引導、規範的意思,加強引導、規範就是訂正、糾正,使成為正確的。

----

use·ful [ˋjusfəl] *adj.* 有用的

The tool can be used to make fire to survive in the wild. It is quite useful.

這工具可以用來野外生火求生,相當好用。

▶ use *n.* 用途 / *v.* 使用;利用

----

far [fɑr] *adj.* 遠的 / *adv.* 遠

Is the bus station far away? Not really. It is nearby.

公車站遠嗎?不會,就在附近。

反義字 **near** *adj.* 近的 / *adv.* 近 / *prep.* 在……附近

----

proud [praʊd] *adj.* 自豪的;驕傲的

The couple must be very proud of their daughter.

那對夫妻一定以他們的女兒感到非常自豪。

同源字 **pride** *n.* 驕傲;獅群

----

fun [fʌn] *n.* 樂趣 / *adj.* 有趣的

It is fun to watch that funny movie.

觀賞那些搞笑的電影很有趣。

衍生字 **fun·ny** *adj.* 可笑的;滑稽的;搞笑的

October 25, 2000

Dear Hong-min,

How have you been? It's been a long time since you wrote me a letter. I miss you a lot.

I started going to ___(1)___ in September. My classes begin at 7:00 every evening from Monday to Friday. So far I have studied very **hard** in every subject. Of all the subjects, math is the most **useful** to me. Other subjects, like History and Chinese Art, are **difficult**. ___(2)___ is much **easier**. I'm having a lot of fun with the **new** language. Maybe I can talk to your American friends some day.

I enjoy my life so much! I almost forget that I am a 60-year-old woman. I feel that I am ___(3)___ than before.

Best wishes

_____1. (A) church

       (B) night school

       (C) a birthday party

       (D) a computer class

_____2. (A) Math

       (B) English

       (C) History

       (D) Chinese Art

_____3. (A) **lazier**

       (B) **quieter**

       (C) **thinner**

       (D) **younger**

感官及心理

look [lʊk] *n.* 注視；神情 ／ *v.* 看；看起來；朝向

I saw Tom watching films on his cellphone at his desk. He looked excited.
我看見 Tom 在書桌那裡用手機觀看影片，看起來很興奮。

聯想字 **see** *v.* 看見；觀看；知道；認為
watch *n.* 手錶 ／ *v.* 觀看；注視；留神觀察

---

ap·pear [ə`pɪr] *v.* 似乎；出現

The police could not find the wanted man until he appeared on the talk show.
警方直到該名通緝男子出現在脫口秀才能找到他。

聯想字 **show** *n.* 表演；節目；秀 ／ *v.* 表演；顯示
find *v.* 找到；發現

衍生字 **ap·pear·ance** *n.* 出現；外觀
ap·par·ent *adj.* 明顯的
ap·par·ent·ly *adv.* 顯然地

記憶技巧
appear = ap + pear，ap = ad，to 的意思，pear 的意思是往前—come forth。

---

smell [smɛl] *n.* 氣味 ／ *v.* 聞起來

Can you smell something burning in the kitchen?
你可以聞到廚房裡有東西燒焦嗎？

衍生字 **smell·y** *adj.* 難聞的

taste [test] *n.* 味道；品味 ／ *v.* 嚐起來；嚐一嚐

The steak tasted so delicious. It was really yummy.

牛排嚐起來很美味，非常好吃。

| 聯想字 | **de·li·cious** *adj.* 美味的；好吃的 |
| | **yum·my** *adj.* 美味的；好吃的 |

| 衍生字 | **tast·y** *adj.* 美味的；有魅力的 |

eat [it] *v.* 吃

The girl usually bites her fingernails after eating food.

那個女孩經常在吃完食物後咬手指甲。

| 聯想字 | **bite** *n.* 咬；螫傷 ／ *v.* 咬 |

say [se] *v.* 說；陳述；說明

It is said that the principal will give a talk about the plan soon.

聽說校長很快就會談到那個計劃。

| 聯想字 | **talk** *n.* 談話；交談 ／ *v.* 講話 |
| 衍生字 | **say·ing** *n.* 格言；諺語 |

hear [hɪr] *v.* 聽見；聽說

Listen! You'll have to speak up because I can't hear you.

注意聽，你要大聲說，因為我無法聽見你的聲音。

| 聯想字 | **listen** *v.* 留神聽；聆聽 |
| 衍生字 | **hear·ing** *n.* 聽力；聽證會 |

記憶技巧

字源上，hear 與 listen、loud 同源，都是 hear 的意思。

sound [saʊnd] *n.* 聲音／*v.* 聽起來

My wife's voice sounds like a beautiful music when she talks to me.

我太太跟我說話時，她的聲音聽起像是一首美好的音樂。

聯想字　**noise** *n.* 噪音；聲響
　　　　nois·y *adj.* 吵鬧的
　　　　voice *n.* 聲音

記憶技巧
字源上，voice 是講一speak 的意思，通常指人發出的聲音。

laugh [læf] *n.* 笑聲／*v.* 笑；嘲笑

The crying girl turned tears to smiles and then laughed.

哭泣的女孩破涕為笑，然後大笑。

聯想字　**smile** *n.* 微笑／*v.* 微笑
衍生字　**laugh·ter** *n.* 笑；笑聲
反義字　**cry** *n.* 呼喊；一陣哭泣／*v.* 哭；叫喊
　　　　shout *v.* 呼喊；大聲叫

love [lʌv] *n.* 愛／*v.* 愛好；喜愛

I love my loving dog very much, and I usually kiss him good night.

我非常喜愛我可愛的小狗，經常和牠親吻道晚安。

聯想字　**like** *v.* 喜歡／*prep.* 像
　　　　kiss *n.* 吻／*v.* 親吻
衍生字　**love·ly** *adj.* 動人的，可愛的；美好的
反義字　**hate** *n.* 憎恨；厭惡／*v.* 不喜歡；憎恨

en·joy [ɪn`dʒɔɪ] _v._ 喜歡;享受

Playing online games is one of my greatest joys. I enjoy it so much.

玩線上遊戲是我最大的樂趣之一,我非常喜歡。

記憶技巧

enjoy = en + joy,字首 en 是使—make,字根 joy 是歡喜、樂趣的意思,使人處於 joy 的狀態就是喜歡、享受。

---

plea·sure [plɛʒɚ] _n._ 愉快;滿意;樂事

The boring boy seems to take great pleasure in annoying me.

那個令人討厭的男孩似乎以把我惹火為一大樂事。

衍生字 **please** _v._ 取悅;使高興 ／ _int._ 請
pleas·ant _adj._ 令人愉快的

---

thank [θæŋk] _n._ 感謝 ／ _v._ 感謝

I'm so grateful for all that you've done. Thanks so much.

我好感激您所做的一切,非常謝謝。

聯想字 **grate·ful** _adj._ 感謝的;感激的
grateful = grate + ful,字根 grate 是贊同—favor 的意思。

---

a·gree [ə`gri] _v._ 同意;贊同

My stepfather and I don't agree on very much.

我和我繼父難以意見一致。

記憶技巧

agree = a + gree,a = ad,to 的意思,字根 gree 也是 favor—贊同的意思。

praise [prez] *n.* / *v.* 讚美；表揚

The teacher praised the student for his honesty and courage.
老師表揚那位學生的誠實和勇氣。

記憶技巧

字源上，praise 與 price、prize 同源，都有價值—value 的意思。

★ 出自 96 年第一次基測

What comes to your mind when you **hear** the world "twins"? Born on the same day? **Looking** almost the same? Or having the same hobbies? Well, I have a twin brother who was born on a different day from me. We do not **look** very much **alike** and we are always interested in different things.

Twelve years ago, my brother, Wayne, was born at eleven fifty-eight on the night of May 28. Five minutes later, I was born — on May 29. Since the time we were born, I have always been heavier and stronger than Wayne, so people usually think I am the older brother.

But Wayne is always smarter than I. He **loves** reading and learns many things quickly. He **knows** a lot about animals, although he does not spend much time with our dogs and birds. He **knows** a lot about bicycles, but never **likes** to ride bikes as much as I do.

Though we are very different, I **love** my brother very much. I **hope** both of us can have a happy life in the future.

_____1. Which is most likely the picture of the twins in the reading?

 (A)

 (B)

 (C)

 (D)

_____2. What do we **know** about the twins?

(A) They are twelve years old.

(B) They have the same interests.

(C) They were born on the same day.

(D) They both want to be teachers in the future.

_____3. Which is true about the writer?

(A) He has several pets.

(B) He is the older one of the twins.

(C) He does not enjoy riding a bicycle.

(D) He does not like to stay with his brother.

健康

🎧 Track 111

health·y　[ˋhɛlθɪ]　*adj.* 健康的；有益健康的

For health reasons, I choose to eat healthy foods all the time.
為了健康原因，我總是選擇吃健康的食物。

衍生字　**health**　*n.* 健康

- -

sick　[sɪk]　*adj.* 生病的；噁心的；惱怒的

The reporter has been off sick for a long while.
那位記者已經請病假很長一陣子了。

- -

fe·ver　[ˋfivɚ]　*n.* 發燒；狂熱

The patient has a high fever and a sore throat.
那位病人發高燒以及喉嚨痛。

- -

head·ache　[ˋhɛd͵ek]　*n.* 頭痛；令人頭痛的事

I had a serious headache last night.
我昨晚頭痛得很厲害。

- -

sore　[sor]　*adj.* 疼痛的

I am sorry to hear that you have a sore throat.
我對於聽到您喉嚨疼痛的事情感到遺憾。

衍生字　**sor·ry**　*adj.* 感到抱歉的；感到遺憾的
聯想字　**throat**　*n.* 喉嚨

tired [taɪrd] *adj.* 累的;疲倦的

The doctor spoke in a tired voice after a long tiring day.
那位醫生在漫長且累人的一天之後,用疲倦的聲音說話。

相關字 **tir·ing** *adj.* 令人疲憊的

---

thirst·y [`θɝˌstɪ] *adj.* 口渴的;渴望的

The players felt hot and thirsty after the football game.
選手們在美式足球賽後,感到又熱又渴。

相關字 **thirst** *n.* 渴;渴望

---

hun·gry [`hʌŋgrɪ] *adj.* 飢餓的;渴求的

My roommate is always hungry when he gets back from his part-time job.
我室友打工回來時總是飢餓的。

---

sleep [slip] *n.* 睡眠 / *v.* 睡覺

Last night, I had a strange dream about my late grandfather in sleep.
昨晚我睡覺時做了一個關於我往生爺爺的奇怪的夢。

衍生字 **sleep·y** *adj.* 想睡覺的
　　　　a·sleep *adj.* 睡著的
聯想字 **dream** *n.* 夢;夢想 / *v.* 做夢;夢見

---

hurt [hɝt] *n.* 傷害;疼痛 / *v.* 傷害;使……疼痛
　　　　　　　　adj. 受傷的;疼痛的

Several foreign workers were seriously hurt in the explosion.
幾位外籍工人在這次爆炸中嚴重受傷。

聯想字 **se·ri·ous** *adj.* 嚴重的;嚴肅的;認真的
　　　　ter·ri·ble *adj.* 可怕的;嚴重的

hos·pi·tal [ˋhɑspɪt!] *n.* 醫院

My daughter spent two weeks in hospital last month.

我女兒上個月在醫院住了二個星期。

---

doc·tor [ˋdɑktɚ] *n.* 醫生；博士

The doctor checked my teeth, with a nurse standing by.

醫生檢查我的牙齒，有位護士在旁待命。

> 聯想字 **den·tist** *n.* 牙醫，dent + ist，dent = tooth
> **tooth** *n.* 牙齒
> **nurse** *n.* 護士 ／ *v.* 照顧；培育

---

med·i·cine [ˋmɛdəsn] *n.* 藥；醫學

The doctor has been practicing medicine for over 20 years.

二十多年來，那位醫師一直在行醫。

---

well [wɛl] *adj.* 健康的；安好的 ／ *adv.* 很好地；成功地 ／ *int.* 嗯；啊

My aunt hasn't been very well lately. She really needs a comfortable space to take a long rest.

我姑媽近來身體一直不是很健康，她真的需要一個舒適的空間長期休息。

> 聯想字 **com·fort·a·ble** *adj.* 使人舒服的；舒適的

---

dead [dɛd] *adj.* 死的；失效的

My grandfather has been dead for two years. He died of skin cancer.

我爺爺過世二年了，他死於皮膚癌。

> 聯想字 **kill** *n.* 捕殺 ／ *v.* 殺死；使非常痛苦
> **dy·ing** *adj.* 垂死的
> 同源字 **die** *v.* 死；（機器）突然停轉
> **death** *n.* 死亡

小試身手

★ 出自 93 年第一次基測

It was late. I was too **hungry** to **sleep**, so I put on my jacket and went downstairs to a coffee shop to get some food. A cute little dog was standing at the door. It looked friendly. I stopped to play with it and I thought it liked me. "Does it have a home?" I wondered. So I decided to ask the clerk whose dog it was. I thought if the dog didn't have an owner, I might take it home and take care of it. "It's my dog," said <u>the young girl</u>. "She's waiting for me to finish my work. She worries and barks a lot if she doesn't see me at night, so I let her stay here with me."

_____1. Which is true about the cute littie dog?

    (A) It felt cold and hungry.

    (B) It liked to be with its owner.

    (C) It needed a quiet place to sleep.

    (D) It would go home with the writer.

_____2. What was <u>the young girl</u> doing in the coffee shop?

    (A) She was working.

    (B) She was buying food.

    (C) She was waiting for friends.

    (D) She was looking for her dog.

心智

🎧 Track 114

mind [maɪnd]　n. 心智；頭腦／v. 介意；當心

My cousin has made up his mind to study medicine in college.
我表哥已經下定決心要唸醫學院。

---

think [θɪŋk]　v. 想；認為

Many people think it is important to learn English from an early age.
很多人認為從年紀小的時候開始學英文很重要。

【記憶技巧】
字源上，mind 是 think 的意思，與 music—音樂、museum—博物館等同源。

---

choose [tʃuz]　v. 選擇；挑選

Those mountain climbers choose to take a shortcut to the lake.
那些登山客選擇走捷徑去湖泊。

|同源字| choice　n. 選擇

---

de·cide [dɪˋsaɪd]　v. 決定；裁決；判決

Tom has decided to enter politics and run for office.
Tom 已經決定進入政界參選總統。

【記憶技巧】
decide = de + cide，de 是 off—分離，而 cide 是切—cut、撞擊—strike 的意思，將爭辯切割開來，使之平息就是 decide 的動作。

guess [gɛs] *n.* / *v.* 猜測；推測

The salesman guessed the total amount to be about 25,000 dollars.
銷售員猜測總金額大約二萬五千元。

【記憶技巧】

字源上，guess 與獲得—get 同源，藉由觀察、判斷、決定而形成的意見就是猜測。

---

re·mem·ber [rɪˋmɛmbɚ] *v.* 記得；紀念；緬懷

I can remember people's faces, but sometimes forget their names.
我能記得人們的容貌，但有時會忘記他們的名字。

衍生字 re·mem·brance *n.* 紀念；懷念，remember + ance
反義字 for·get *v.* 忘記

【記憶技巧】

remember = re + member，字首 re 是 again 的意思，字根 member 表示 mindful—記著的，remember 就是 bring to mind 的意思。

---

let [lɛt] *v.* 讓；允許；出租

I am letting you go out for a drink of beer, but no next time.
我會讓你出去喝個啤酒，但是沒有下次。

---

miss [mɪs] *v.* 想念；錯過

You will miss your train if you don't hurry up.
如果你不快點，你會錯過你的火車。

---

need [nid] *n.* 需要；需求 / *v.* 需要；必須

I think the machine needs fixing.
我認為這部機器需要修理。

衍生字 need·y *adj.* 貧窮的

want [wɑnt] *n.* 缺乏 ／ *v.* 想要；需要

Your daughter really wants a good brush for her hair.
你女兒真的要好好梳理一下她的頭髮。

衍生字 **want·ed** *adj.* 渴望的、通緝的

---

ex·cuse [ɪk`skjuz] *n.* 藉口 ／ *v.* 原諒

Please excuse me for arriving late. There was a lot of traffic.
請原諒我遲到，車流量很大。

記憶技巧

excuse = ex + cuse，字首 ex 是 out、away，字根 cuse 表示控告、法律行動，企圖自控告中脫身的說詞是藉口，使人免除法律追訴的動作是原諒。
cause *n.* 原因 ／ *v.* 導致

---

fol·low [`fɑlo] *v.* 跟隨；遵從；密切關注

A stray dog followed me into the restaurant.
有隻流浪狗跟著我進入餐廳。

衍生字 **fol·low·ing** *adj.* 接著的

---

be·lieve [bɪ`liv] *v.* 相信

Sam is sure he can make it, believe it or not.
信不信由你，Sam 確定他可以辦得到。

衍生字 **be·liev·er** *n.* 信徒
聯想字 **sure** *adj.* 確信的；一定的
be·lief *n.* 信念

---

cheat [tʃit] *n.* 作弊者 ／ *v.* 欺騙；作弊

The clerk cheated me by lying to me about the price.
店員欺騙我，在售價上向我說謊。

聯想字 **lie** *n.* 謊言 ／ *v.* 說謊；躺

de·sire [dɪˋzaɪr] *n.* 渴望；慾望／*v.* 渴望；要求

The manager desires to meet the latest hires soon.
經理要求很快與最近的新員工會面。

小試身手

★出自 91 年第一次基測

Ted sat next to me when we were in elementary school. He had serious problems in **communicating** with people. One always had to **guess** what he was saying. Besides, most of my classmates did not like to be with him because his hands and shirts were always dirty. I ___(1)___ **let** him know the importance of being clean by telling him several times a day to wash his hands. But he just could not **understand**.

One day, our teacher Miss Hsieh walked up to Ted. Without saying anything, she took Ted to the washroom. Slowly, Miss Hsieh washed his hands and told him that he should keep himself clean. She ___(2)___ that every day for one month. Finally, Ted understood.

Miss Hsieh's love has given me a good example to follow when I ___(3)___ my job. I always **remember** to teach my students by showing them the right ways to do things. And most important of all, I always **remember** to give them more time to learn and to grow up.

_____1. (A) tried to

(B) am trying to

(C) have tried to

(D) will try to

_____2. (A) did

(B) was doing

(C) has done

(D) was going to do

_____3. (A) did

(B) am doing

(C) have done

(D) am going to do

Unit **30** 事務

🎧 Track 118

mat·ter [`mætɚ] *n.* 事情；物質 ／ *v.* 要緊

There's a matter of some importance to deal with.
有一件相當重要的事情要處理。

記憶技巧
字源上，matter 與 mother 同源，應該取自母親對孩子的生命很重要的意思。

---

thing [θɪŋ] *n.* 事物；東西

Try not to let that stupid thing hold you back!
設法別讓那種傻事阻礙你。

---

plan [plæn] *n.* 計畫；平面圖 ／ *v.* 計劃；打算

I'm not planning to stay in town this weekend.
我沒打算這個週末要待在鎮上。

衍生字 **plan·ning** *n.* 策畫；規劃，plan + ing

記憶技巧
plan 與 plane—平面、floor—地板等同源，都是平面的意思，/p/、/f/ 轉音。

hap·pen [`hæpən]   *v.* 發生；碰巧

Something strange happened to him the night before.
前一天晚上有件奇怪的事發生在他身上。

衍生字 **hap·pen·ing**   *n.* 發生的事

記憶技巧

happen = hap + en，字根 hap 是運氣─luck 的意思，因著運氣而發生是 happen。或許；可能─per·haps（字首 per 表示 through─遍及）有靠運氣看事情的意味。

---

pre·pare [prɪ`pɛr]   *v.* 準備；防範

The special team has already prepared for any possibility.
特遣隊已經為任何可能的情況做好準備。

聯想字 **read·y**   *adj.* 準備好的
　　　　al·read·y   *adv.* 已經

衍生字 **prep·a·ra·tion**   *n.* 準備工作；預備
　　　　pre·par·a·to·ry   *adj.* 預備的

記憶技巧

prepare = pre + pare，字首 pre 是 before 的意思，字根 pare 表示 make ready，事先預備好的動作是 prepare。

---

im·por·tant [ɪm`pɔrtənt]   *adj.* 重要的；重大的；珍貴的

I have to be in Chicago next Thursday for an important meeting.
我下星期四必須在芝加哥出席一場重要會議。

衍生字 **im·por·tance**   *n.* 重要性，字尾 ance、ant 形成對稱。

記憶技巧

important = im + port + ant，im 就是 in─裡面，port 是 bring、carry─攜帶的意思， bring in from abroad─自國外攜入的是重要的。

pos·si·ble [`pɑsəbl̩] *adj.* 可能的

Perhaps the new coach is able to make it possible.

也許新的教練能夠使它成為可能。

相關字 **may·be** *adv.* 可能；也許

記憶技巧

possible = poss + ible，字根 poss 表示 be able—有能力的，字尾 ible 是
使能夠的意思。反義字 im·pos·si·ble 是不可能的意思。

----

chance [tʃæns] *n.* 機會；可能性

Mandy has missed the chance to star in that play.

Mandy 錯過在那場戲劇擔當演出的機會。

----

change [tʃendʒ] *n.* 改變；零錢 ／ *v.* 改變；交換；兌換

My cousin is going to change her hairstyle.

我表姐即將變換她的換髮型。

----

troub·le [`trʌbl̩] *n.* 麻煩；困境 ／ *v.* 使苦惱；使有麻煩

I got into trouble with the police for running through the red light.

我因為闖紅燈和警方惹上麻煩。

----

in·ter·view [`ɪntɚˌvju] *n.* ／ *v.* 面談；採訪

I had an interview for a job in the meeting room.

我在會議室有一場工作面試。

聯想字 **meet** *v.* 遇見；會面；達到；迎接

記憶技巧

interview = inter + view，字首 inter 是 between、among 的意思，字根
view 表示 see—看見，interview 表示相互地看著。

job [dʒɑb] *n.* 職業；工作

Mr. Lin is a harbor worker. He is always working hard at his job. This morning, his son was doing his homework at home.

林先生是碼頭工人，工作上一向努力打拚，今天早上他兒子在家做功課。

衍生字	job·less *n.* 失業者 ／ *adj.* 失業的
聯想字	work *n.* 工作；作品 ／ *v.* 工作；運轉
	work·er *n.* 工人
	do *v.* 做；完成 ／ *aux.* 助動詞
	home·work *n.* 家庭作業
	home *n.* 家

---

be·gin [bɪ`gɪn] *v.* 開始；著手

My sister has just begun learning to play the violin.

我姐姐剛開始學拉小提琴。

| 衍生字 | begin·ning *n.* 開始；開頭部份 |
| 同義字 | start *n.* 開始 ／ *v.* 開始；著手；動身 |

---

fin·ish [`fɪnɪʃ] *n.* 結束 ／ *v.* 完成；結束

The manager wants the job finished by the deadline.

經理要求工作在期限之前完成。

| 衍生字 | un·fin·ished *adj.* 未完成的 |

記憶技巧

finish = fin + ish，字根 fin 是 end—結束、limit—限制的意思。

---

try [traɪ] *n.* 設法；嘗試 ／ *v.* 嘗試；試圖

Maybe you should try going to bed earlier today.

也許你今天應該嘗試早點去睡覺。

My mother is always **busy**. During the day, she sits in front of the computer and writes stories for children. Mom always **says** that writing is the most **important** thing in her life. She enjoys it a lot and also gets paid for her writing. <u>That</u> makes her happy because she has three daughters to bring up.

Mom always **tries** to **finish** her writing before we get back in the evening. By **doing** so, she has more time to be with us. Mom loves **talking** and reading with us, but she hates cooking and cleaning. So we have learned how to **do housework** since we were very young.

Mom is always **busy** writing and taking care of us, but she is always smiling. To me, my mother is the most beautiful woman in the world.

_____1. What does the writer try to say in the reading?

    (A) Her mother is a busy but happy woman.

    (B) She hopes to be a writer like her mother.

    (C) She should study harder to make her mother happy.

    (D) Her mother should learn how to use the computer better.

_____2. Which is true about the writer's mother?

    (A) She is seldom at home.

    (B) She usually writes at night.

    (C) She doesn't like to do housework.

    (D) She enjoys playing computer games.

_____3. What does That mean in the reading?

    (A) Getting paid for her writing.

    (B) Sitting in front of the computer.

    (C) Having three daughters to bring up.

    (D) Being the most beautiful woman in the world.

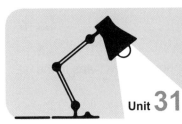

Unit **31** 家電用品

🎧 Track 122

ma·chine [mə`ʃin] *n.* 機器

I got a can of soda from a vending machine.
我從販賣機買了一罐汽水。

衍生字 **ma·chin·ry** *n.* 機械；體系

---

com·put·er [kəm`pjutɚ] *n.* 電腦

The computer program can be downloaded on the Internet through the computer.
這個電腦程式可以透過電腦在網路上下載。

衍生字 **com·put·er·ize** *v.* 電腦化
聯想字 **In·ter·net** *n.* 網際網路
　　　　pro·gram *n.* 節目；計畫；程式

記憶技巧

1. computer = compute + er，compute 是 count—計算的意思，字首 com 表示 together——起，字根 pute 就是 count—計算的意思，電腦又是計算機，計算的機器。

2. Internet = inter + net，字首 inter 是 between、among—二者或三者之間，字根 net 就是網。

3. program = pro + gram，字首 pro 表示之前—before，gram 是寫—write 的意思，寫在執行之前的是計劃。

phone [fon] *n.* 電話／*v.* 打電話

The salesman called me with his cell phone when I was in the meeting.

那位推銷員在我開會時用他的手機打電話給我。

聯想字 **call** *n.* 打電話；喊叫／*v.* 稱呼

衍生字 **cell·phone** *n.* 手機；行動電話

tel·e·phone *n.* 電話／*v.* 打電話

記憶技巧

phone 的原意是聲音—sound、voice，畢竟古代沒有電話。cellphone 是一種劃分通訊區域的電話系統，cell 是小室—small room，區域範圍的意思。telephone = tele + phone，字首 tele 是遠離—far off 的意思，傳遞遠方聲音的工具是電話。

---

tel·e·vi·sion [`tɛlə͵vɪʒən] *n.* 電視

Mom set the television to her favorite soap opera.

媽媽將電視調到她最愛的連續劇。

聯想字 **tel·e·vise** *v.* 電視播放

screen *n.* 銀幕；屏風／*v.* 測試；放映

記憶技巧

television 的字根 vis 是 see—看的意思，傳遞遠方節目以供人觀看的機器是電視。

---

vid·e·o [`vɪdɪ͵o] *n.* 錄影；音樂視頻／*v.* 錄影／*adj.* 錄影的

The children are watching a video on television screen.

孩子們正看著電視螢幕上的音樂視頻。

記憶技巧

字源上，video 是 I see—我看見的意思，錄影是供人觀看的工具。

ra·di·o [ˋredɪ‚o] *n.* 收音機；廣播節目

Many people usually listen to the radio as they work.
許多人經常工作時收聽廣播節目。

---

re·fri·ge·ra·tor [rɪˋfrɪdʒə‚retə] *n.* 冰箱

Mom stored a dozen eggs in the refrigerator.
媽媽在冰箱裡存放一打雞蛋。

> **記憶技巧**
>
> refrigerator = refrigerate + or，refrigerate 是冷凍、冷藏的意思。

---

lamp [læmp] *n.* 燈；檯燈

In art class, we made a paper lantern which was closed at the top. It looked like a lamp.
美術課，我們製作一個頂端封閉的紙燈籠，看起來像檯燈。

聯想字 **lan·tern** *n.* 燈籠

> **記憶技巧**
>
> lamp 與 lantern 同源，都是 to light—照亮的意思。

---

fan [fæn] *n.* 風扇；扇子；迷

The baker is a great fan of rock music.
那位烘焙師是一位搖滾樂鐵粉。

---

re·cord·er [rɪˋkɔrdə] *n.* 錄音機；錄影機

We can create a podcast with a voice recorder.
我們可以用錄音機創建一個播客。

> **記憶技巧**
>
> recorder = record + er，字根 record—紀錄、履歷、病歷的意思，，字首 re 是使修復—restore，字根 cord 表示心—heart，喻為記憶，紀錄就是讓人再次記憶。

clock [klɑk] *n.* 時鐘

The town-hall clock says twelve o'clock.

市政廳的時鐘顯示十二點鐘。

---

pow·er [`paʊɚ] *n.* 動力；權力；權限；力量 ／ *v.* 提供動力

It's not in the sales clerk's power to cancel the order.

取消訂單不在行銷專員的權限之內。

---

bat·ter·y [`bætərɪ] *n.* 電池

My rechargeable battery is being recharged through a new recharger.

我的充電電池正用新的充電器充電。

> 聯想字 **re·charge** *v.* 給……充電
> **re·charg·er** *n.* 充電器

記憶技巧

1. battery 的字根是 bat—打擊，引申為釋放，電池就是釋放電力的物品。
2. recharge = re + charge，字首 re 表示再次—again，字根 charge 與 car 同源，run—跑的意思，讓 battery 再次有電力就是充電，而充電的器具 就是 recharger—充電器。

---

ra·zor [`rezɚ] *n.* 刮鬍刀；剃刀

I use an electric razor for my daily shaving routine.

我用電動刮鬍刀當作每天刮鬍子的例行公事。

記憶技巧

razor = raz + or，字根 raz 是擦去的意思，擦子—eraser = e + ras +er，字 首 e = ex，out，字根 ras 也是擦去的意思，同 raz。

vac·u·um [ˋvækjʊəm] *n.* 真空；真空吸塵器 ／ *v.* 用吸塵器清掃

The maid is vacuuming up the carpet in the living room.
女侍正在客廳裡用吸塵器將地毯清掃乾淨。

記憶技巧

vacuum 的字根是 vac，空的—empty 的意思。

★ 出自 100 年第二次基測

Dear Mr. Hush,

I just learned over the **radio** that you feel as bad as I do about the way people use their **cellphones**. Very often in public places, people speak loudly on their **cellphone**, and we have to hear about other people's business. But who cares about <u>that</u>? Not me! Why should I know the life of people I don't even know? It's really nice that someone famous like you speaks out for a quiet living space.

And it's even more wonderful to know that you yourself always talk quietly when you have to use the **cellphone** in public places. <u>Thanks for NOT sharing what you are talking about</u>. We have shared too much noise already!

A Person on Your Side

_____1. What does <u>that</u> mean in the letter?

    (A) Being quiet.

    (B) The cellphone.

    (C) Others' business.

    (D) Talking with strangers.

_____2. What does the writer mean by saying "<u>Thanks for NOT sharing what you are talking about?</u>"

    (A) It is kind to forget about other people's mistakes.

    (B) It is wrong to listen to others talking on the phone.

    (C) It is polite to use a low voice when you talk on the phone in public places.

    (D) It is dangerous to say something important over the cellphone in public places.

答案：1. (C)；2. (C)

Unit 32　　居家用品

🎧 Track 127

desk　[dɛsk]　*n.* 書桌；服務臺；詢問臺

The secretary usually keeps her lunchbox in the bottom drawer of the desk.

祕書經常將她的便當盒放在書桌的底層抽屜。

聯想字	**draw·er**　*n.* 抽屜
	draw　*v.* 繪畫；拖拉
	ta·ble　*n.* 桌子；餐桌

---

chair　[tʃɛr]　*n.* 椅子；主席；系主任 ∕ *v.* 主持

On the balcony are a chair and a two-person couch.

陽臺上有一張椅子和一張兩人長沙發。

聯想字	**so·fa**　*n.* 沙發
	couch　*n.* 長沙發
複合字	**arm·chair**　*n.* 扶手椅

---

seat　[sit]　*n.* 座位 ∕ *v.* 使就座

The actor stood for a while and then sat in the seat.

那位演員站了一會，然後坐在座位上。

| 同源字 | **sit**　*v.* 坐 |
| 反義字 | **stand**　*n.* 攤位；架；立場 ∕ *v.* 站立；忍受 |

記憶技巧

sit 的動詞三態 sit、sat、sat 都是同源字，seat 也是同源。

mat　[mæt]　*n.* 蓆子；墊子

The waiter placed the hot coffee cup on the mat.
服務生把熱咖啡杯放在墊子上。

---

blan·ket　[`blæŋkɪt]　*n.* 毯子；毛毯／*v.* 厚層覆蓋

Fred covered up his puppies with towels and blankets.
Fred 用毛巾和毛毯裹住他的小狗。

聯想字　**tow·el**　*n.* 毛巾

記憶技巧
blanket 與 blank—空白處、空白的同源，blanket 原是人或馬匹睡覺時覆蓋身體保暖的大張的長方形羊毛布，羊毛是白色，因此與一些白色意涵的單字同源。

---

tool　[tul]　*n.* 工具

The technician checked and then fixed the machine with his own tools.
技術人員用自己的工具檢視那部機器，然後予以修復。

聯想字　**fix**　*v.* 修理；做飯；確定；使固定
　　　　check　*n.* 支票；帳單；方格圖案／*v.* 檢查；核定

---

glue　[glu]　*n.* 膠；膠水／*v.* 黏住；緊附

The labels are pasted with glue on the lower left-hand corner.
那些標籤被用膠水黏貼在左手邊底下的角落。

聯想字　**paste**　*n.* 漿糊；麵糰／*v.* 黏貼

記憶技巧
字源上，glue 可能與 clay—黏土同源，/k/、/g/ 轉音，而 paste 與 pasta—義大利麵同源。

tape [tep] *n.* 膠帶／*v.* 用膠布固定

We need tape and a box cutter to pack the box.

我們需要膠帶和一把紙箱刀來打包箱子。

- -

key [ki] *n.* 鑰匙；鍵／*adj.* 關鍵性的

The driver might have left his car key on the breakfast bar.

司機或許把他的車鑰匙遺留在早餐吧臺上。

- -

knife [naɪf] *n.* 刀子

The butter knife should be placed on the right edge of the bread plate.

奶油刀要放在麵包盤子的右側邊緣。

- -

pin [pɪn] *n.* 別針；大頭針；胸針／*v.* 釘住

The girl used pins to hold two flowers in her hair.

那位女孩用別針將兩朵花固定在她的頭髮上。

> **記憶技巧**
>
> 字源上，pin 原指 feather—羽毛，飛翔的意思，而羽毛可用為書寫的筆—pen，二字同源。

- -

pipe [paɪp] *n.* 管子；管道；笛

These water pipes have frozen up twice this winter.

這些水管今年冬天已經結冰二次了。

- -

rope [rop] *n.* 繩索；串

The poor dog was tied up with a rope and left with no food or water.

那隻可憐的小狗被繩子綁起來，沒有留下食物或水。

複合字 **jump rope** *n.*／*v.* 跳繩

195

um·brel·la [ʌmˋbrɛlə] *n.* 雨傘

I put my umbrella up when drops of rain began to fall on me.
雨滴開始落在我的身上時，我撐開雨傘。

---

pack [pæk] *n.* 一小包；一群／*v.* 包裝

The client's package was packed and ready to ship.
客戶的包裹包裝好了，準備要運送。

衍生字　**pack·age** *n.* 包裹，pack + age
　　　　un·pack *v.* 打開行李箱，字首 un 是 opposite of—相反的意思。

I had a <u>horrendous</u> experience last Saturday.

That day, my family went camping near a big lake. While my parents were preparing dinner, my brother and I were playing by the lake. A dirty man appeared from somewhere, and his face was half covered by his hair. He walked to us and asked for some water.

When I gave him water, the bag he carried dropped, and things inside fell out on the grass. I saw a **rope**, a **knife**, and a baseball bat. The strangest thing was that there were also a woman's shoe and a ring, and I'm sure they were not his. The man quickly put all his things back in the bag and looked at us angrily. At that moment, the picture of a man the police was looking for came to my mind. He was the crazy killer! I was so afraid that I could not move at all.

Luckily, before he could get any closer, my mom shouted from far away, and the man hurried off into the dark.

_____1. What happened in the story?

    (A) A killer was caught by the police.

    (B) The writer's family invited a stranger to dinner.

    (C) The writer's brother ran to their parents for help.

    (D) A man ran away after he heard the writer's mother's voice.

_____2. What can we learn about the writer and the man with a bag?

    (A) The man attacked the writer.

    (B) The writer followed the man into the dark.

    (C) The writer did not find out who the man was in the end.

    (D) The man did not want the writer to see things in his bag.

_____3. How do people feel when they experience something horrendous?

    (A) Angry.

    (B) Sad.

    (C) Scared.

    (D) Tired.

Unit **33** 學習

🎧 Track 131

learn [lɜ·n] *v.* 學習；得知

These children are in the habit of learning in groups.
這些孩子習慣分組學習。

聯想字 **group** *n.* 群；組 ／ *v.* 分組
hab·it *n.* 習慣

衍生字 **learn·ing** *n.* 學習
learned *adj.* 有學問的

---

knowl·edge [ˋnɑlɪdʒ] *n.* 學問；知識

I didn't know the customer had a wide knowledge of Greek history.
我不知道那位顧客擁有廣泛的希臘歷史知識。

記憶技巧
knowledge 的字根是 know—知道；認識，字尾 ledge 尚待考據。

---

fact [fækt] *n.* 事實；真相

In fact, it is a parable, not a true story.
事實上，它是一則寓言，不是真實的故事。

聯想字 **truth** *n.* 真相；真理
true *adj.* 真實的；正確的
real *adj.* 真正的；實際的
really *adv.* 真實地；非常

un·der·stand [ˌʌndɚˋstænd] v. 了解;懂得;理解;體諒

We are looking for someone who understands the French language.
我們正在尋找一位懂得法語的人。

衍生字 un·der·stand·ing n. 理解;體諒
mis·un·der·stand v. 誤解
mis·un·der·stand·ing n. 誤解;爭執

記憶技巧
understand = under + stand,站在對方立場底下思考才是真實的了解。

---

prac·tice [ˋpræktɪs] n. 練習 / v. 練習;訓練

Students practiced by repeating the movements over and over again.
學生們藉由一再重複動作來練習。

衍生字 prac·ti·cal adj. 實際的;實用的
聯想字 re·peat v. 重複

---

ex·pe·ri·ence [ɪkˋspɪrɪəns] n. 經驗 / v. 經歷;感受

From my past experience, the manager will likely treat us to a lobster dinner.
從我過去的經驗,經理可能會款待我們去吃一頓龍蝦晚餐。

衍生字 ex·pe·ri·enced adj. 有經驗的,experience + ed

記憶技巧
experience = ex + per + ience,字首 ex 表示 out of,字根 per 是 try一試驗的意思, experience 的原意就是 try。

ex·am·ple [ɪg`zæmpl̩] *n.* 例子;範例;榜樣

This oil painting is an excellent example of the teenager's work.
這幅油畫是那位青少年作品的一個傑出例子。

記憶技巧

example = ex + ample,字首 ex = out,字根 ample 是拿取─take 的意思,例子是拿出來的解說。

---

ask [æsk] *v.* 問;詢問;請求

My teacher will ask me the answer to this question tomorrow.
我的老師明天會問我這個問題的答案。

聯想字　**ques·tion** *n.* 問題 ／ *v.* 詢問
　　　　prob·lem *n.* 問題;(數學)習題

記憶技巧

question = quest + ion,字根 quest 是 ask─詢問、seek 尋求的意思;
problem = pro + blem,字首 pro 是往前─forward,字根 blem 是丟擲─throw,問題是往前丟出的議題。

---

friend [frɛnd] *n.* 朋友

Johnny has lots of friends because he is always friendly to other people.
Johnny 有很多朋友,因為他總是對其他人友善。

衍生字　**friendship** *n.* 友誼
　　　　friend·ly *adj.* 友善的 ／ *adv.* 友善地
　　　　be·friend *v.* 加好友;對……友好

mis·take [mɪ`stek] *n.* 錯誤;過失;誤認 / *v.* 誤認

This paper is full of spelling mistakes.

這份報告充滿了拼字的錯誤。

記憶技巧

mistake = mis + take,字首 mis 是 wrongly—錯誤地,mistake 有誤入歧途—take in error 的意思。

---

sub·ject [`sʌbdʒɪkt] *n.* 主題;學科 / *adj.* 臣服的

She is interested in these subjects.

她對這些科學有興趣。

衍生字 **sub·jec·tive** *adj.* 主觀的
sub·jec·tive·ly *adv.* 主觀地

聯想字 **course** *n.* 課程;科目
PE *n.* 體育,PE 是一頭字詞 "Physical Education"—生理的教育。

記憶技巧

subject = sub + ject,字首 sub = under,字根 ject 是 throw—丟擲的意思,subject 的原意是 under control—控制之下,學科是人文或科學的一主題。

---

sci·ence [`saɪəns] *n.* 科學;自然科學

It goes without saying that Math is the mother of all sciences.

不用說,數學是一切科學之母。

衍生字 **sci·en·tist** *n.* 科學家
sci·en·tif·ic *adj.* 科學的

聯想字 **math** *n.* 數學
math·e·mat·ics *n.* 數學

記憶技巧

science = sci + ence,字根 sci 是知道—know 的意思。

lan·guage [ˈlæŋgwɪdʒ] *n.* 語言

This video will lead us to take a look at the history of the English language.

這部視頻將帶我們看見英語的歷史。

聯想字 **En·glish** *n.* 英語
Chin·ese *n.* 中文
Tai·wa·nese *n.* 臺語

記憶技巧

language = langu + age，字根 langu 的意 "思是 language、tongue。

---

his·to·ry [ˈhɪstərɪ] *n.* 歷史；履歷；沿革

My teacher studied modern European history in college ten years ago.

我的老師十年前在大學研讀現代歐洲史。

衍生字 **his·tor·ic** *adj.* 歷史上的
his·tor·i·cal *adj.* 歷史的
his·to·ri·an *n.* 歷史學家

聯想字 **past** *n.* 過去 ／ *adj.* 過去的 ／ *prep.* 經過
a·go *adv.* 以前
then *adv.* 當時；之後；那麼
mod·ern *adj.* 現代的；近代的

---

story [ˈstorɪ] *n.* 故事；樓層

The writer was telling an old story to a group of children in English.

那位作家用英文向一群孩子說一則古老的故事。

聯想字 **tell** *v.* 告訴；講述；辨別
tale *n.* 故事

It is fun and exciting to visit different countries and meet different people. You can see beautiful mountains and seas. You can **learn** different ways of living and doing things. You can try many kinds of foods. You can buy special presents for yourself and your friends.

It is also a good way to **learn** a foreign **language** because you can **learn** the **language** by using it. You can **practice** speaking English when visiting America or England. Or you can **practice** speaking French in France or German in Germany.

Have you ever taken a trip to a foreign country? Think about it for your next vacation!

_____1. According to the **reading**, what is a good way to **learn** a

foreign **language**?

(A) **Studying** it in **school**.

(B) Finding a good **teacher**.

(C) Visiting a foreign country.

(D) Writing e-mails to a foreign **friend**.

_____2. According to the **reading**, what makes a trip fun?

(A) You can take a lot of pictures.

(B) You can see new ways of living.

(C) You can meet your old **friends** there.

(D) You can buy presents at better prices.

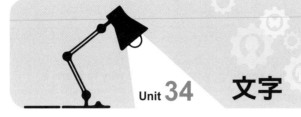

文字

🔊 Track 136

word [wɝd] *n.* 字詞；單字；談話

The student usually spelled the word wrong.
那位學生經常把字拼錯。

聯想字 **spell** *n.* 咒語；符咒 ╱ *v.* 拼字；拼寫
衍生字 **word·ing** *n.* 措辭；用語

---

let·ter [ˋlɛtɚ] *n.* 信；字母

The man slid a letter into the red envelope while no one was looking.
男子趁著無人在看，把一封信塞進紅色信封。

聯想字 **en·ve·lope** *n.* 信封
envelope = en + velope，字首 en 就是 in，字根 velope 是 wrap up—包裹的意思，信封是將信包裹進來的物品。

---

book [bʊk] *n.* 書；書本 ╱ *v.* 預訂

There is a workbook and a notebook to accompany this picture book.
這本繪本附一本作業本和一本筆記本。

衍生字 **book·let** *n.* 小書；小冊子
複合字 **work·book** *n.* 作業本

dic·tion·a·ry ［`dɪkʃənˌɛrɪ］ *n.* 字典；詞典

Why not look up what this word means in the dictionary?

何不用字典查閱這個字是什麼意思？

聯想字 **mean** *v.* 意指 ／ *adj.* 吝嗇的；卑鄙的

記憶技巧
dictionary 的字根 dict 是 say 一說，拉丁文也有 word 的意思。

---

pa·per ［`pepə］ *n.* 紙；論文；報告

The writer's new novel will be printed on recycled paper.

那位作家的新小說會用回收紙印刷。

---

pen ［pɛn］ *n.* 鋼筆；原子筆

Please write your answers in pen, not in pencil.

請用原子筆寫答案，不要用鉛筆。

聯想字 **pen·cil** *n.* 鉛筆 ／ *v.* 用鉛筆寫字

---

mark ［mɑrk］ *n.* 記號；痕跡；成績 ／ *v.* 做記號；批改

The new student scored full marks on the math test.

那位新學生數學測驗考滿分。

衍生字 **mark·er** *n.* 白板筆；馬克筆

---

e·ras·er ［ɪ`resə］ *n.* 橡皮擦；板擦

The teacher erased the blackboard with a new eraser.

老師用新板擦擦拭黑板。

相關字 **e·rase** *v.* 擦拭；抹去；刪除

rul·er   [`rulɚ]   *n.* 尺;統治者

As the longtime rulers, the tribal chiefs ruled the old town, Banvasi, for at least two centuries.

身為長期的統治者,部落首領統治舊城鎮巴納瓦西至少二世紀之久。

衍生字 **rule**   *n.* 規則;條例 / *v.* 統治

---

page   [pedʒ]   *n.* 頁;網頁

The writer's picture appeared on the front page of a local newspaper.

那位作家的照片出現在一份當地報紙的頭版。

複合字 **home page**   首頁

---

note   [not]   *n.* 筆記;音符;便條 / *v.* 注意;記下

The engineer took notes throughout the speech.

那位工程師整個演講都在做筆記。

衍生字 **not·ed**   *adj.* 著名的

複合字 **note·book**   *n.* 筆記本;筆記型電腦

---

name   [nem]   *n.* 名字;名稱 / *v.* 給……取名

Please write your full name and phone number on the form.

請將您的全名和電話號碼寫在表格上。

複合字 **family name = last name = surname** 姓
       first name   名
       middle name   中間名
       nick name   綽號
       stage name   藝名

🎧 Track 139

list [lɪst] *n.* 名單；清單 ／ *v.* 列出；上市

Tom has made a list of spots he would like to visit during his stay in London.

Tom 列了一份停留倫敦期間想去造訪的景點清單。

----

read [rid] *v.* 閱讀；朗讀

The writer has written a number of books for young readers.
They are all worth reading.

那位作家為年輕讀者寫了許多本書。它們都值得閱讀。

衍生字 | **read·er** *n.* 讀者
read·ing 閱讀；讀書會

反義字 | **write** *v.* 寫
writ·er *n.* 作家

----

cop·y [`kɑpɪ] *n.* 拷貝；副本；一冊；一份 ／ *v.* 拷貝；抄襲；模仿

The assistant will make ten copies of this handout using the new copy machine.

助理會用新影印機將這份講義列印十份。

衍生字 | **cop·i·er** *n.* 影印機

If you enjoy **reading**, don't miss Shakespeare and Company when you visit the city of Paris. It is a famous English-language **bookstore** on the left bank of the river Seine. The first Shakespeare and Company in history was opened in 1919 by an American, Sylvia Beach. Ms. Beach did more than sell **books**. Her bookstore was also a **library**, and she even prepared beds for **writers** visiting there. Ms. Beach was not only kind to people but also good at choosing books, so her bookstore was often visited by writers like Ernest Hemingway and James Joyce. But in 1941, after the Germans took power in Paris, Ms. Beach was told to close her **bookstore**.

In 1951, another American, George Whitman, opened in Paris another English-language **bookstore**, Librairie Mistral. Since then, just as Ms. Beach did, Mr. Whitman has also made his **bookstore** a **library** for people to borrow **books**, and a free hotel for **writers** to stay in. To remember Ms. Beach, Mr. Whitman changed the name of his **bookstore** to Shakespeare and Company in 1964, two years after Ms. Beach died.

Next time when you are in Paris, don't forget to visit this friendly **bookstore**, and see if you can spend a night there!

_____1. About Shakespeare and Company, which is NOT talked about in the **reading**?

(A) It sells books.

(B) It prepares beds for **writers**.

(C) It lends **books**.

(D) It **reads books** to children.

_____2. What do we know about Mr. Whitman?

(A) He was Ms. Beach's neighbor.

(B) He used to work at Ms. Beach's **bookstore**.

(C) He has followed Ms. Beach's ways of doing business.

(D) He opened a **bookstore** in 1951 to remember Ms. Beach.

_____3. Why was Ms. Beach's business closed?

(A) She was asked to leave Paris.

(B) The Germans made her give it up.

(C) Her business went from bad to worse.

(D) She died.

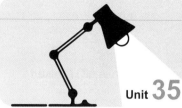

Unit **35**　**形狀**

🎧 Track 140

shape　[ʃep]　*n.* 形狀；樣貌 ／ *v.* 使成形

These cutting boards are all different shapes.
這些砧板都是不同的形狀。

聯想字 **type**　*n.* 類型 ／ *v.* 打字

---

point　[pɔɪnt]　*n.* 點；得分；意見 ／ *v.* 指向；指出

The teacher pointed at the dot, which indicated a full stop at the end of the sentence.
老師指著小圓點，就是顯示句子結尾的句點。

聯想字 **dot**　*n.* 點；小圓點 ／ *v.* 在……上面加點

---

line　[laɪn]　*n.* 線；線條；隊伍 ／ *v.* 排隊

The visitor was asked to sign his full name on the dotted line.
那名訪客被要求在虛線上簽他的全名。

---

cir·cle　[ˈsɝk!]　*n.* 圓；圓圈 ／ *v.* 圈出

The children were sitting in a circle around the round carpet.
小朋友圍著圓形地毯繞一個圓圈坐著。

聯想字 **round**　*adj.* 圓形的
　　　　a·round　*adv.* 到處；周圍；大約 ／ *prep.* 圍繞
　　　　字首 a 是 in、on 的意思。

square [skwɛr] *n.* 正方形；廣場 / *adj.* 正方形的；平方的

The concert will be held in the town square.
音樂會將在鎮上的廣場舉行。

記憶技巧

字源上，square 是由字首 ex—out 及字根 quare 所構成，quare 是 four 的
意思，例如：quarter—四分之一即是同源字。square 原指測量直角的工具。

straight [stret] *adj.* 直的；坦誠的；整齊的 / *adv.* 清楚地；直接

Go straight along this street and turn right at the third traffic light.
沿著這條街直走，然後在第三個紅綠燈右轉。

cross [krɔs] *n.* 叉號；十字架 / *v.* 越過；橫渡

The tourists will cross from Burma into Thailand on the third day.
觀光客將在第三天越過緬甸進入泰國。

pair [pɛr] *n.* 一對；一雙；一副 / *v.* 配對

Trainees were asked to do the exercise in pairs.
實習生被要求二位一組做練習。

part [pɑrt] *n.* 部份；零件 / *v.* 分開

The best part of the year-end party must be the lucky prize drawing.
尾牙最棒的部份一定是抽獎。

衍生字 **par·ty** *n.* 派對

piece [pis] *n.* 張；片；塊

This jigsaw puzzle has five pieces missing.
這套拼圖有五片不見了。

roll [rol] *n.* 捲；捲狀物 ／ *v.* 滾動；打滾

The miniature pig rolled over onto its back.
那隻迷你豬翻身仰臥著。

聯想字 **row** *n.* 列；排 ／ *v.* 划船

---

share [ʃɛr] *n.* 部份；股份 ／ *v.* 分享；分擔

Let me share my pizza with you two.
讓我和你們二人一起分享我的披薩吧。

記憶技巧
字源上，share 是 cut一切的意思，切開才能分享。

---

toy [tɔɪ] *n.* 玩具

Put away all the toys on the floor, and then go to bed.
把地板上所有的玩具收好，然後去睡覺。

---

doll [dɑl] *n.* 洋娃娃

My dog likes to bury the girl's dolls in the back-yard garden.
我的狗喜歡將女孩的娃娃埋在後院的花園。

---

gift [gɪft] *n.* 禮物；天賦；才能

The principal gave the gifted student a dictionary as his birthday gift.
校長送給那位資優生一本字典作為生日禮物。

衍生字 **gift·ed** *adj.* 聰慧的；有天賦的
同源字 **give** *v.* 給與；舉行
同義字 **pres·ent** *n.* 禮物；現在 ／ *v.* 展現；授予 ／ *adj.* 出席的

小試身手 ★ 出自 99 年第二次基測

I had a dream — a strange dream that has helped me to understand Eric much better.

In the dream, Eric looked angry and said, "Melissa, I have something to tell you."

I've lived with Eric for more than five years. He is the cutest thing I've ever seen. I buy him fish and milk and lots of toy mice once a week. I even bought a small house for him, because he sometimes likes to be left only by himself. I love him with all my heart, and **give** him all I love.

But what has gone wrong? In the dream Eric said angrily, "I don't like fish. I don't like milk. And toy mice? Are you crazy? I'm not a cat. And I don't want to be a cat, either!" Then he ran back to his small house.

After the dream, I know better: dogs don't like fish or milk. And surely they do not like **toy** mice. Most important of all, they will let you know when they are really angry!

_____1. What can we learn about Eric in the reading?

    (A) He likes cats.

    (B) He is Melissa's pet.

    (C) He is four years old.

    (D) He enjoys talking with Melissa.

_____2. Why was Eric angry in the dream?

    (A) He did not have many friends.

    (B) Melissa loved him the wrong way.

    (C) Melissa did not take him out for a long time.

    (D) There were too many mice in Melissa's house.

_____3. Why did Melissa buy a house for Eric?

    (A) Eric did not sleep well in her room.

    (B) Eric needed more space for his toys.

    (C) Eric was too big to share a bed with her.

    (D) Eric did not always like to be with others.

答案：1. (B)；2. (B)；3.(D)

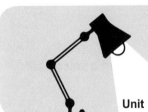

Unit 36　金錢買賣

🎧 Track 143

mon·ey　[`mʌnɪ]　　*n.* 錢；貨幣

The man took out some money from his wallet and handed it over to the homeless guy.
那名男子從皮夾掏出一些錢，然後遞給那位無家可歸的人。

聯想字　**wal·let**　*n.* 皮夾

- -

dol·lar　[`dɑlɚ]　　*n.* 元

There are one hundred cents in a dollar.
一美元有一百美分。

- -

to·tal　[`totl]　　*n.* 總數；合計 ／ *adj.* 總計的

A total of 45 dogs will be entered in the race.
總計有 45 隻狗會參加比賽。

- -

price　[praɪs]　　*n.* 價格；價錢；代價

The young guy chose to pay the price to buy the prize.
那名年輕人選擇支付那價錢來買獎品。

同源字　**prize**　*n.* 獎賞；獎品

- -

bor·row　[`bɑro]　　*v.* 借入；借貸

English has borrowed a number of words from French.
英文從法文借用了很多字。

反義字　**lend**　*v.* 借出

buy [baɪ] *n.* 合算 ╱ *v.* 買

Gina bought a set of kitchen knives on sales from a salesman.
Gina 從一位銷售員買了一整組廚房刀具。

| 衍生字 | **buy·er** | *n.* 買家 |

反義字	**sell**	*v.* 賣；銷售
	sale	*n.* 賣；出售
	sales·man	*n.* 男銷售員

---

or·der [`ɔrdɚ] *n.* 訂單；順序；指令 ╱ *v.* 點菜；訂購；指示

I would like to place an order for a model car 1936 Mercedes Benz Maharaja Holkar.
我想下一張購買一輛 1936 年賓士馬哈拉加霍克模型車的訂單。

---

pay [pe] *n.* 薪水；工資 ╱ *v.* 付費；薪資

You can pay for one in cash and get one for free.
你可以現金支付一件，然後一件免費。

| 聯想字 | **free** | *adj.* 免費的；空閒的；自由的 |

| 衍生字 | **pay·ment** | *n.* 支付 |
| | **re·pay** | *v.* 償還 |

---

spend [spɛnd] *n.* 開銷 ╱ *v.* 花費；度過

Their son spent a lot of money on video games before.
他們的兒子以前花費很多錢在電動玩具上。

| 衍生字 | **spend·ing** | *n.* 支出；開銷 |

記憶技巧

字源上，spend 是 to draw—拖拉的意思，也就是將錢支付出去—pay out。

cost [kɔst]　*n.* 費用；成本／*v.* 花費；值……錢

It costs a lot to buy an apartment in this part of Taipei.
在臺北這個地段買一間公寓要花很多錢。

記憶技巧
字源上，cost 是字首 com—together 及字根 st—stand 構成，某物值多少錢表示該物站立在哪一價位上。

charge [tʃɑrdʒ]　*n.* 收費；控告／*v.* 收費；記在帳上；控告

Charge the bill to my account, please.
請將帳單記在我帳上。

聯想字 **o·ver·charge** *v.* 多收錢；索費過高
　　　und·er·charge *v.* 少收錢

ex·pen·sive [ɪk`spɛnsɪv]　*adj.* 高價的；昂貴的

The blanket feels very expensive, and not cheap at all.
這毛毯感覺昂貴，一點也不便宜。

聯想字 **cheap** *adj.* 廉價的；便宜的

記憶技巧
expensive = expense + ive，expense 是花費的意思，ex = out，字根 pense 是支付一pay 的意思，支付出去的錢是花費，花費的就是昂貴的。

bank [bæŋk]　*n.* 銀行；堤；岸

In the bank, there are many people sitting on the bench and waiting for their number to be called.
銀行裡，許多人坐在長椅上等待叫號。

同源字 **bench** *n.* 長凳；長椅

記憶技巧
bank 原意是堤岸，水邊天然的土坡，而 bench 原是手工的土製座位。

few [fju] *adj.* 少數的／ *pron.* 一些 ／ *det.* 少數的

Last but not least, there are fewer people who are willing to take this job.

最後但同樣重要的是願意接這份工作的人較少了。

| 同源字 | lit·tle | *n.* 少許 ／ *adj.* 少的；年幼的 ／ *det.* 不多的 |

less *adv.* 較少地 ／ *pron.* 更少 ／ *det.* 較少

least *adv.* 最少地 ／ *pron.* 最少 ／ *det.* 最少

---

man·y [ˋmɛnɪ] *adj.* 許多的 ／ *pron.* 許多 ／ *det.* 許多的

There are at least twice as many blue cards as there are red ones.

藍色卡片的數量至少是紅色卡片的兩倍多。

| 相關字 | much | *adj.* 許多的 ／ *adv.* 非常 ／ *pron.* 許多 ／ *det.* 多的 |

most *adj.* 最多的 ／ *pron.* 大多數 ／ *det.* 最多的

al·most *adv.* 幾乎，字首 al = all。

小試身手 ★ 出自 105 年會考

It was 11 p.m. and Molly walked out of her bakery. She turned and looked at her store one last time. She wanted to remember what it ___(1)___ at the moment. A few hours later, people would come and clean out everything in the store. A young man had **bought** it. He ___(2)___ it into a flower shop.

Before it was a bakery, this place ___(3)___ a small coffee shop. Molly worked in the shop as a waitress. But taking **orders** was never Molly's dream; **baking** was. When she knew her boss planned to **sell** the shop, she **borrowed money** and **bought** it.

Her bakery had been open for thirty years. Thirty very wonderful years. However, it would all come to an end tonight. Molly ___(4)___ the bakery to be a family **business**. But her daughter was never interested in **baking**. Molly did not want her **business** in a stranger's hands, so after some serious thinking, she decided to close it.

"Goodbye, my dear old friend," Molly looked at the store, whispering.

_____1. (A) had looked like
       (B) looked like
       (C) would look like
       (D) has looked like

_____2. (A) had changed
       (B) changed
       (C) was going to change
       (D) has changed

_____3. (A) used to be
       (B) would be
       (C) has been
       (D) is

_____4. (A) had wanted
       (B) has wanted
       (C) would want
       (D) will want

答案：1. (B)；2. (C)；3.(A)；4.(A)

Unit **37** 魔法

🎧 Track 147

ma·gic [ˋmædʒɪk] *n.* 魔法；魔術 ／ *adj.* 有魔力的；神奇的

The witch put a magic spell on the princess and turned her into a spider.
女巫對公主施魔咒，然後把她變成一隻蜘蛛。

衍生字 **ma·gi·cian** *n.* 魔術師
　　　 ma·gic·al *adj.* 有魔力的

---

strange [strendʒ] *adj.* 奇怪的；陌生的

The man gave me a strange look, which made me really scared.
男子給我一個奇怪的眼神，令我非常害怕。

衍生字 **strang·er** 陌生人

---

witch [wɪtʃ] *n.* 女巫；巫婆

A witch on a broomstick was flying high in the sky, with a wizard following.
掃帚上的女巫飛翔在高空中，後面跟著男巫。

反義字 **wiz·ard** *n.* 男巫；術士

---

club [klʌb] *n.* 社團；俱樂部；夜總會

My cousin has just joined a board game club in town.
我表哥剛加入鎮上的一個桌遊社團。

com·ic   [ˋkɑmɪk]   *n.* 漫畫／*adj.* 連續的

Many students in Asia spend their free time reading comics.
許多亞洲學生把他們的空閒時間花在看漫畫書。

---

ghost   [gost]   *n.* 鬼；鬼魂

Many people believe in ghosts and show their respect to them.
很多人信仰鬼魅，對祂們表示敬畏。

---

fire   [faɪr]   *n.* 火；射擊／*v.* 開火；發射；解雇

The firefighter was badly burned when putting out the fire.
該名消防隊員在滅火時嚴重燒燙傷。

聯想字 **burn**   *n.* 燒傷；燙傷／*v.* 燃燒；燒、燙傷

---

smoke   [smok]   *n.* 煙／*v.* 抽煙；冒煙

Hundreds of buildings went up in smoke when a huge fire spread around the city.
數百棟建築物在一場蔓延全市的大火時化為飛煙。

---

gas   [gæs]   *n.* 瓦斯；汽油；氣體

We stopped and got some gas at the gas station.
我們在加油站停車加一些汽油。

衍生字 **gas·sy**   *adj.* 起氣泡的；脹氣的

---

can·dle   [ˋkændḷ]   *n.* 蠟燭

I will light a candle in memory of the brave firefighter.
我將點燃蠟燭以紀念那位勇敢的消防隊員。

mud [mʌd] *n.* 泥巴

Several cars got stuck in the mud after the heavy rains.
大雨過後,幾部車子陷在泥巴裡。

衍生字 **mud·dy** *adj.* 泥濘的;灰暗的

---

gar·bage [`gɑrbɪdʒ] *n.* 垃圾

A lot of garbage was removed from the coast during the beach cleanup.
淨灘期間很多垃圾從海岸清走。

同義字 **trash** *n.* 垃圾

---

break [brek] *n.* 中斷;休息 ╱ *v.* 斷裂;破壞;違反

The vase broke during the break time.
花瓶在下課時破掉了。

---

fill [fɪl] *v.* 充滿;填充

The truck was filled with bags full of rice and corn.
卡車塞滿了裝滿稻米和玉米的袋子。

衍生字 **ful·fil** *v.* 完成;實現
同源字 **full** *adj.* 飽的;滿的

---

mir·ror [`mɪrɚ] *n.* 鏡子;反映

The dog barked loudly when looking at himself in the mirror.
那隻狗在鏡中看著自己時大聲吠叫。

Last Sunday, at about 4 o'clock in the morning, my family and I were woken up by our dog. We were ___(1)___ to see **smoke** everywhere. Dad ran to the bathroom to get everyone a wet towel, and Mom told us to crawl on the floor. It was hard to see clearly in the dark, but we were very lucky to be able to ___(2)___ and get out quickly.

We lost everything in the house. I was very sad. But Mom and Dad said that they were thankful because ___(3)___. Maybe they were right; I did not lose my family-the most important thing in my life.

_____1. (A) bored

      (B) proud

      (C) ready

      (D) surprised

_____2. (A) get to the door

      (B) check the e-mail

      (C) turn off the light

      (D) answer the phone

_____3. (A) nothing was burned

      (B) no one got hurt in the **fire**

      (C) we kept all our money at home

      (D) our house was big and comfortable

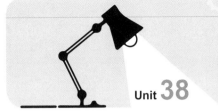

手部動作

🎧 Track 150

hold   [hold]   *n.* 握;抓 ／ *v.* 握著;抱著;舉行

The man kept holding a gun as he lay dying on the ground.

該名男子倒臥地上氣絕時,手裡仍握著一把槍。

聯想字 **keep**   *v.* 保持

---

pull   [pʊl]   *n.* 拉;拖 ／ *v.* 拉;拖;吸引

You push the table forward, and I'll pull it toward me.

你把桌子往前推,我會往我這邊拉。

反義字 **push**   *n.* ／ *v.* 推;促使;推銷

---

bring   [brɪŋ]   *v.* 帶來;導致

Tom brought me his notebook, but took away mine.

Tom 把他的筆記本帶來給我,但卻拿走我的。

反義字 **take**   *v.* 拿走;花費;搭乘

---

pick   [pɪk]   *n.* ／ *v.* 挑選;摘採

Fred picked up the doll and put it on the shelf.

Fred 撿起洋娃娃,然後放在架上。

聯想字 **put**   *v.* 放置

raise　[rez]　*n.* 加薪／*v.* 舉起；提高；養育；引起

The soldier rose from his seat and raised his right hand.
那位士兵從他的座位躍起，舉起他的右手。

同源字　**rise**　*v.* 上升；升起；上漲

---

throw　[θro]　*v.* 投擲；拋扔

I threw the frisbee, and my dog jumped up to catch it.
我擲出飛盤，我的狗跳起來把它接住。

聯想字　**catch**　*v.* 接住；抓住；逮住；捕獲
　　　　catch·er　*n.* 捕手，catch + er

---

o·pen　[`opən]　*v.* 打開／*adj.* 打開的；營業的

The teacher left the window wide open and closed the front door.
老師讓窗戶開得很大，然後關上前門。

衍生字　**o·pen·er**　*n.* 開罐器
反義字　**close**　*n.* 結尾；結局／*v.* 關上；結束／*adj.* 近的；密切的

---

pass　[pæs]　*n.* 及格；通行證／*v.* 經過；通過；傳遞

My secretary passed a piece of note paper to me during the meeting.
我的祕書會議期間遞一張便條紙給我。

衍生字　**pas·sage**　*n.* 通道；段落

---

knock　[nɑk]　*n.* 敲擊／*v.* 敲擊；碰撞

I heard someone knocking on the window just now.
我剛才聽到有人在敲打窗戶。

brush [brʌʃ] n. 刷子；畫筆／v. 刷；拂去

You had better brush your hair before you step onto stage.
妳步上舞臺之前，最好先梳一下頭髮。

---

dig [dɪg] v. 挖掘；理解

The students dug several small holes and planted these flowers.
學生挖了幾個小洞，然後種了這些花。

衍生字 **dig·ger** n. 挖掘機；掏金者

---

shake [ʃek] n. 搖動；奶昔／v. 搖動；握手

The waitress shook some powdered chocolate over coffee.
女服務生搖了一些巧克力粉在咖啡上。

---

col·lect [kə`lɛkt] v. 收集；聚集；領取／adj. 對方付通話費的

Rainwater collects in the pond to be used for various purposes.
雨水聚集在池子以供各種不同目的的使用。

衍生字 **col·lec·tion** n. 收集
col·lec·tor n. 收集者

記憶技巧

collect = col + lect，字首 col = com，together，字根 lect 是 gather—蒐集的意思，蒐集一起的動作就是 collect。

---

hang [hæŋ] v. 把……掛起；懸掛；吊著；絞死

A pearl necklace hung around the lady's neck.
一串珍珠項鍊掛在那位女子的脖子上。

衍生字 **hang·er** n. 衣架

fight [hɪt] *n.* 打架；戰鬥／*v.* 打鬥；作戰

Some animals can fight to the death for mating rights.
一些動物會為了交配權而打鬥至死。

聯想字 **hit** *n.* 非常成功的人或事／*v.* 打；打擊；碰撞
at·tack *n.* 攻擊；突然發作／*v.* 進攻；襲擊

小試身手 ★ 出自 106 年會考

　　Englishman Robert Scott is known for leading two trips to Antarctica. The first one made him a star; the second ___(1)___.

　　After his first successful trip, Scott decided to be the first person to stand on the South Pole. However, ___(2)___. He would be in a race with Roald Amundsen, from Norway. Both left their countries by ship in June of 1910 and arrived in Antarctica in January of 1911.

　　About ten months later, both teams started their trips down to the South Pole. ___(3)___. Amundsen's team used dogs, and Scott's team used horses. Because horses weren't good at traveling on snow, it took Scott's team 77 days to arrive at the South Pole. They got there on January 17,1912, and were surprised to find that Amundsen was ahead of them. The news **hit** Scott very hard, but what he didn't know was that ___(4)___. His team began their long trip home with **broken** hearts. After days of terrible weather and little food, Scott lost his men one after another, and he himself was the last one to meet the end of his life. No one on his team lived to go back home and tell their story. It was only learned through Scott's diary.

_____1. (A) hurt his health

　　　(B) **opened** his eyes

　　　(C) cost him his life

　　　(D) made his dream come true

_____2. (A) he didn't want to **take** this trip with others

　　　(B) he wasn't the only one who had this dream

　　　(C) he wouldn't let anyone else **take** his prize away

　　　(D) he couldn't miss the chance to make his country proud

_____3. (A) And Scott used a popular way for his men to travel fast

　　　(B) But there were problems to deal with before they traveled

　　　(C) But Amundsen didn't know better about animals than Scott

　　　(D) And their ways of traveling decided which team would win

_____4. (A) there was still hope

　　　(B) no one ever believed him

　　　(C) the worst had not come yet

　　　(D) Amundsen had not been honest

答案：1. (C)；2. (B)；3.(D)；4.(C)

Unit **39**　**移動**

🎧 Track 154

move　[muv]　*n.* 遷移；行動；措施／*v.* 移動；感動；提議

Could you help me move this bookshelf to the right side?

麻煩幫我把這個書架移到右邊嗎？

衍生字　**move·ment**　*n.* 動作
　　　　mov·er　*n.* 搬運工人；提議者

---

go　[go]　*v.* 去；離去；變成

Mr. Lin went to that country in his youth, and finally became a successful businessman.

林先生年輕時去到那個國家，後來成為一名成功的商人。

複合字　**churchgoer**　*n.* 定期上教堂的人
　　　　moviegoer　*n.* 常看電影的人

反義字　**come**　*v.* 來
　　　　be·come　*v.* 變成；成為
　　　　wel·come　*v.* 歡迎

記憶技巧

1. become = be + come，字首 be 是 by─around 的意思。

2. welcome = wel + come，字根 wel 是 will─意願的意思，welcome─歡迎是為迎合他人意願或願望而來。

leave [liv] *n.* 假；假期 ／ *v.* 離開；遺留；使保持

Tom left for Hong Kong yesterday, and he will stay there for three days.

Tom 昨天離開前往香港，他將在那裡停留三天。

| 聯想字 | **off** *adv.* 離開；走開；關掉 |
| 反義字 | **stay** *n.* 停留時間 ／ *v.* 停留；暫住；保持 |

記憶技巧

stay 與站立—stand 同源，原意是維持站立，後來衍伸為停留在一地方的意思。

---

en·ter [`ɛntɚ] *v.* 進入；輸入；報名參加

Two police officers entered the building through the back door.

兩名警官經由後門進入這棟建築物。

| 衍生字 | **en·trance** *n.* 入口；登場 |

記憶技巧

字源上，enter 與字首 inter--between、among 有關，表示連結二物體。

---

fly [flaɪ] *n.* 蒼蠅 ／ *v.* 飛；駕駛飛機；搭乘飛機

Flying in space is exciting, but it is also dangerous.

在太空飛行很刺激，但也很危險。

| 同源字 | **flight** *n.* 飛行；班機 |

---

hur·ry [`hɝɪ] *n.* 匆忙 ／ *v.* 趕快

Are the guests in a hurry to leave?

賓客要匆忙離開嗎？

send [sɛnd] *v.* 寄發；送

I'll send my friend, Jack, an invitation by airmail tomorrow.

我明天會以航空郵件寄送一份邀請函給我的朋友 Jack。

---

set [sɛt] *n.* 套；組；集合 ／ *v.* 設定；放置

The secretary set a pile of handouts on the counter.

秘書放置一疊資料在櫃臺上。

(記憶技巧)

字源上，set 與 sit 同源，安置猶如坐下而使身體固定於一處。

---

a·broad [əˋbrɔd] *adv.* 在國外；到國外

The sales manager is currently abroad on business.

業務經理目前在國外出差。

(記憶技巧)

abroad = a + broad，字首 a 是 at、on、in，字根 broad 是寬的，處於寬的狀態，原指彼此的距離，後來譬喻為出門、離家，現代英文中則表示離開祖國到海外的意思。

---

for·eign [ˋfɔrɪn] *adj.* 外國的；外來的

The foreign engineer has a good command of several foreign languages.

那位外國工程師精通數種外國語言。

衍生字 for·eign·er *n.* 外國人

---

turn [tɝn] *n.* 轉彎；輪流 ／ *v.* 使轉動；轉彎；變得

We will take turns driving on our way to the vacation spot.

我們在前往渡假勝地的途中會輪流開車。

walk [wɔk] *n.* 步行 ╱ *v.* 步行；遛

My sister is a fast walker. She walks fast all the time.
我姐姐是個快速步行者，她總是快速步行。

衍生字 **walk·er** *n.* 步行者；散步者

---

run [rʌn] *n.* 跑 ╱ *v.* 跑；運作；經營

The runner keeps fit by running and jogging every morning.
那位跑者藉由每天早上快跑和慢跑來保持身材。

聯想字 **jog** *v.* 慢跑
衍生字 **run·ner** *n.* 跑者

---

jump [dʒʌmp] *n.* 一躍而起 ╱ *v.* 跳躍

The jumper was hopping over the jump rope with either foot continuously.
那位跳躍者連續單腳交換跳繩。

聯想字 **hop** *v.* 單足跳；齊足跳
衍生字 **jump·er** *v.* 跳躍者

---

here [hɪr] *adv.* 這裡；在這裡

There are Christmas cards hanging on the tree here and there.
樹上到處都掛著聖誕卡片。

反義字 **there** *adv.* 在那裡；到那裡

Dear Wendy,

You asked me to **send** you a picture of my family. Here it is.

The picture was taken in our garden by me cousin. It took me some time to get everyone together. My younger sister, Gigi, was so excited about taking pictures. She made my mom stand between my two brothers, and made my dad walk to the back and then to the front. Finally, <u>she</u> had him sit down under the tree. She even made our dog, Rover, **move** three times, but Rover did not like the idea of taking pictures, so he ran into his doghouse. I am the one behind the doghouse. As for Gigi, can you see where she is?

Karen

_____1. Which is the picture that Karen sent Wendy?

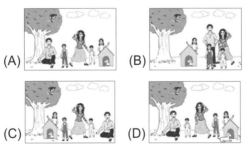

(A)   (B)

(C)   (D)

_____2. Who is <u>she</u> in the second paragraph?

(A) Karen's mother.

(B) Wendy.

(C) Karen.

(D) Gigi.

Unit 40 程度

all [ɔl] *det.* 所有的;全部的 / *pron.* 全體;一切;全部

Not all the students have good writing skills.
不是所有的學生都擅長寫作技巧。

---

an·y [ˋɛnɪ] *det.* 任何的 / *pron.* 任何一個

I'm afraid there isn't any lemon cake left.
恐怕沒有任何檸檬蛋糕還留著。

聯想字	**anything**	任何事物
	anyone	有人;任何人
	anybody	有人;任何人
	anywhere	任何地方
	anyhow	無論如何

記憶技巧
字源上,any 是不定冠詞 an 黏接字尾 y 而構成的限定詞,表示不確定的對象。

---

oth·er [ɛls] *det.* 其他的 / *pron.* 其他的人或物

I have three cellphones. One is a Samsung Galaxy, another is an iPhone, and the other is a Sony.
我有三支手機,一支是 Samsung Galaxy, 一支是 iPhone, 另一支是 Sony。

聯想字	**an·oth·er**	*det.* 另一個 / *pron.* 另一個
	else	*adv.* 其他;否則

記憶技巧
another = an + other,一個其他的就是另一個。

238

some [sʌm] *det.* 一些的 ／ *pron.* 一些

It will take us somewhere between two and three hours to reach the island by sea.

我們搭船到那座小島大約要花上二到三小時。

聯想字	**something**	某事；大約
	someone	某人
	somebody	某人
	somewhere	在某處
	somehow	以某種形式
	sometime	某個時候
	sometimes	有時候

next [ˋnɛkst] *adv.* 接下去；然後 ／ *det.* 下一個

Take the next street on the left.

在下一條街左轉。

sev·er·al [ˋsɛvərəl] *pron.* 幾個 ／ *det.* 幾個的

I have seen that movie several times.

那部電影我看了好幾次。

of·ten [ˋɔfən] *adv.* 常常

It's not often that you get more than you pay for.

那是不尋常的，就是得的比付出的還多。

ev·er [ˋɛvɚ] *adv.* 曾經

Have you ever been to Angkor Wat?

你去過吳哥窟嗎？

No, I have never been there before.

不，我以前從未去過那裡。

聯想字	nev·er *adv.* 從未；決不
	how·ev·er *adv.* 然而；可是；不過

記憶技巧

never = n + ever，字首是 ne，not 的意思，賦予 ever 否定的意涵，為避免二母音字母相鄰，ne 的 e 便省略。

---

just [dʒʌst] *adj.* 公平的；正義的 ／ *adv.* 正好；僅僅；只是；剛才

I met the principal just now in the hall.

我剛才在大廳遇到校長。

反義字 unjust *adj.* 不公平的；不正義的，un = not

---

still [stɪl] *adj.* 靜止的 ／ *adv.* 仍然

The student is still standing still in front of the blackboard.

那位學生仍然靜止地站在黑板前面。

---

to·geth·er [təˋgɛðɚ] *adv.* 一起；共同

I will pack these items in a zip lock bag together, and that'll be 2,500 dollars altogether, please.

我將這些物品一起打包在一個夾鏈袋，總共是二千五百元，麻煩你了。

衍生字 al·to·geth·er *adv.* 完全；全部

記憶技巧

1. together = to + gether，字根 gether 是 gather—聚集的意思，去聚集一起就是 together。
2. altogether = all + together，全部聚集一起就是總共。

ve·ry [ˋvɛrɪ] *adv.* 很;非常

There are quite a few teenagers using Twitter. It seems to be very popular with them.
相當多青少年在用推特,它似乎非常受他們的歡迎。

聯想字 **quite** *adv.* 相當;頗

----

yet [jɛt] *adv.* 尚未;還

The mechanic hasn't finished fixing the machine yet.
機械工還沒完成修理那部機器。

----

a·gain [əˋgɛn] *adv.* 再一次

Could you spell that word again, please?
麻煩再拼一次那個字,好嗎?

----

al·so [ˋɔlso] *adv.* 也;並且

Also, Davis was so tired that he could fall asleep while sitting in this chair!
還有,Davis 如此地疲累,坐在這把椅子上時就睡著了。

記憶技巧

also = al + so,字首 al = all,字根 so 表示這麼、如此、所以。

I was jogging with my dog this morning when I saw John Archer at a street corner. He was sitting on a bike with **one** of his feet on the ground. "He's waiting for someone," I thought. John and I were **both** in the **ninth** grade. He was a basketball player on our school team and was **very** popular with **many** girls. But I **never** talked to him before. He was not my type.

John saw me, too. He smiled. For a moment I thought he was smiling at someone else. But he was not. "Hi, Mary Jones," he said to me. "You have a cute little dog." I smiled but did not say **anything**, because I did not know what to say. "I'm here waiting for you. Would you... would you like to go to the movies with me?" he asked. I was **very** surprised. I **never** thought he would do <u>this</u>, and I **never** thought about going out with him.

I said "no," of course. But he seemed nice and friendly. Maybe I would go to watch him play basketball **some** day.

_____1. What was John doing on the street when Mary saw him?

    (A) Jogging.

    (B) Talking to a girl.

    (C) Riding a bicycle.

    (D) Waiting for someone.

_____2. What does <u>this</u> mean in the second paragraph?

    (A) Smiling at Mary's dog.

    (B) Being surprised to see Mary.

    (C) Playing basketball with Mary.

    (D) Asking Mary to go to movie.

_____3. What do we know about John and Mary from the reading?

    (A) They are in the same school.

    (B) They like each **other very much**.

    (C) They are **both** interested in movies.

    (D) They **both** enjoy jogging in the morning.

附錄

1. Test 1 ～ Test 5 單字測驗試題
2. 1200 單字詞素（字首／字根／字尾）整理
3. 單字學習的核心知識
4. 多功能字卡效益／製作說明
5. 詞素卡功用／遊戲解說

Test 1

_____ 1. The _____ is an animal in Africa that looks like a
horse.
(A) lion   (B) monkey   (C) zebra   (D) goose

_____ 2. A(n) _____ can grab leaves from a tree with its
long trunk.
(A) koala   (B) giraffe   (C) hippo   (D) elephant

_____ 3. The children must make their room _____ before
they can get a red envelope.
(A) clean   (B) strong   (C) young   (D) hairy

_____ 4. Will Smith is a(an) _____ actor from the USA.
(A) famous   (B) dirty   (C) favorite   (D) angry

_____ 5. I go to the beach every _____ vacation, even
though it is very hot.
(A) spring   (B) summer   (C) fall   (D) winter

_____ 6. My father took me to a _____ to watch teams of
dancers compete for money.
(A) show   (B) picture   (C) story   (D) photo

_____ 7. Strawberries are my favorite _____ and apples are
my least favorite.
(A) fruit   (B) forest   (C) fish   (D) food

_____ 8. I bought this _____ to remember my trip to Taipei.
(A) landmark (B) tour guide (C) postcard   (D) footprint

_____ 9. I studied hard, so my math test was _____ to get a good grade.

(A) beautiful   (B) different   (C) late   (D) easy

_____ 10. My wife and I are proud of our beautiful _____.

(A) wife   (B) husband   (C) son   (D) daughter

_____ 11. He's a(n) _____ that sells shoes at the department store.

(A) housewife   (B) actress

(C) clerk   (D) farmer

_____ 12. The mother, father and children are a _____ that enjoys traveling together.

(A) group   (B) member   (C) family   (D) people

_____ 13. People need to study, so please don't _____ in the library.

(A) wear   (B) talk   (C) tell   (D) wait

_____ 14. _____ our summer vacation, we traveled to Japan.

(A) Behind   (B) Over   (C) Into   (D) During

_____ 15. Don't play with the _____ or you might cut off your finger.

(A) knife   (B) bowl   (C) dish   (D) plate

_____ 16. Ireland is a beautiful _____ in Europe that is next to England.

(A) house   (B) world   (C) party   (D) country

_____ 17. It's difficult for Americans to use _____ to eat their
food.
(A) saucers　(B) spoons　　(C) chopsticks (D) forks

_____ 18. I love to play _____ games with my friends during
recess.
(A) delicious　(B) fun　　　(C) golden　(D) safe

_____ 19. Come in to the doctor's office and _____ a seat.
(A) bring　　(B) take　　　(C) hand　　(D) put

_____ 20. Will he _____ us to his birthday party?
(A) try　　　(B) use　　　(C) join　　(D) invite

_____ 21. After the rain ended, there was a _____ in the sky.
(A) problem　(B) rainbow　(C) meadow　(D) bamboo

_____ 22. Franks's favorite meat is _____, but he doesn't eat
it often.
(A) tea　　　(B) milk　　　(C) fish　　(D) beef

_____ 23. You will find Paul in his _____ taking a nap.
(A) bedroom　　　　　　(B) bathroom
(C) living room　　　　　(D) dining room

_____ 24. It was a big _____ when the puppy jumped out of
the box.
(A) show　　(B) joy　　　(C) love　　(D) surprise

_____ 25. My friends loved playing with my pet _____ after it
learned how to talk.
(A) mouse　(B) parrot　　(C) koala　　(D) panda

_____ 26. I couldn't wait to watch the new _____ on YouTube.

(A) statue   (B) video   (C) pin   (D) gift

_____ 27. The mother held the little girl's _____ when crossing the street.

(A) leg   (B) foot   (C) shoulder   (D) hand

_____ 28. Let's have _____ together tomorrow morning at 8 am.

(A) breakfast   (B) brunch   (C) lunch   (D) dinner

_____ 29. Please keep this secret _____ you and me.

(A) near   (B) between   (C) in front of   (D) inside

_____ 30. I have been a big _____ of his music for many years.

(A) speaker   (B) member   (C) winner   (D) fan

_____ 31. It's a little chilly outside, so you should put on a _____.

(A) jacket   (B) shirt   (C) skirt   (D) blouse

_____ 32. The movie was so exciting, that I wanted to watch it _____.

(A) again   (B) maybe   (C) so   (D) just

_____ 33. I'm in the _____ cooking dinner for my family.

(A) market   (B) kitchen   (C) garage   (D) garden

_____ 34. I like to go to the pool and _____ when it is hot outside.

(A) tour   (B) hunt   (C) work   (D) swim

_____ 35. Next time, let's go eat at the new _____ downtown.
　　　　(A) theater　　(B) museum　　(C) restaurant　(D) shop

_____ 36. After I wake up in the _____, I eat breakfast and
　　　　brush my teeth.
　　　　(A) morning　　(B) afternoon　　(C) evening　　(D) night

_____ 37. I bought a _____ to watch the Mayday concert.
　　　　(A) snack　　　(B) line　　　(C) ticket　　　(D) check

_____ 38. Our family likes to _____ whenever we visit a park
　　　　on a sunny day.
　　　　(A) enjoy　　　(B) picnic　　　(C) feed　　　(D) paint

_____ 39. My father planned to go hiking up a _____ next
　　　　weekend in Nantou.
　　　　(A) tomb　　　(B) mountain　(C) plaza　　　(D) bridge

_____ 40. The fireman went into the burning house to _____
　　　　the woman's life.
　　　　(A) save　　　(B) move　　　(C) attack　　　(D) enjoy

_____ 41. The man yelled at the taxi driver because his driving was
　　　　too _____.
　　　　(A) fast　　　(B) well　　　(C) many　　　(D) yummy

_____ 42. During Chinese New Year, there's a full _____ in the
　　　　sky at night.
　　　　(A) Earth　　　(B) moon　　　(C) star　　　(D) sun

_____ 43. Taiwan is a large _____ surrounded by water.
　　　　(A) island　　　(B) river　　　(C) lake　　　(D) sea

_____ 44. He did not like the idea of taking a boat, because he felt the sea was full of _____.

(A) trouble　　(B) danger　　(C) flash　　(D) rainbow

_____ 45. Please eat your ice cream quickly before it starts to

_____.

(A) lose　　(B) rise　　(C) freeze　　(D) melt

_____ 46. A monkey is a(n) _____ animal that can make tools to solve problems.

(A) dear　　(B) even　　(C) super　　(D) smart

Test 2

_____ 1. I went to church on _____ evening, and the next day I had to go to school.

(A) Sunday   (B) Monday   (C) Friday   (D) Wednesday

_____ 2. _____ was a better day than today, because I went to watch a new movie with my friend.

(A) Today   (B) Yesterday   (C) Tomorrow   (D) Weekday

_____ 3. My mother was pleased, because I got a _____ on my math test.

(A) hundred   (B) thousand   (C) million   (D) billion

_____ 4. Don't run down the stairs, or you might _____ and hurt yourself.

(A) find out   (B) fall down   (C) throw away   (D) put on

_____ 5. It looks like it will be a _____ day, so I will take an umbrella.

(A) snowy   (B) cloudy   (C) rainy   (D) windy

_____ 6. I _____ my grandmother yesterday and had a great time with her.

(A) visited   (B) carried   (C) booked   (D) planned

_____ 7. I _____ you when you said you would never lie to me.

(A) scanned   (B) knew   (C) believed   (D) meant

_____ 8. I _____ you so many times on your cell phone, but you didn't answer.

(A) chatted   (B) fought   (C) called   (D) marked

_____ 9. My birthday is on _____ 29th, so I celebrate it once every four years.
(A) January   (B) February   (C) March   (D) April

_____ 10. Father's Day in Taiwan is on _____ 8th.
(A) May   (B) June   (C) July   (D) August

_____ 11. I dressed as a zombie for Halloween last _____.
(A) September   (B) October
(C) November   (D) December

_____ 12. I caught a taxi on the _____ of 5th Avenue and Miller Boulevard.
(A) road   (B) block   (C) corner   (D) street

_____ 13. Summer is the best _____ of the year for swimming.
(A) week   (B) month   (C) season   (D) year

_____ 14. This was the _____ time I entered a speech contest, so I was very nervous.
(A) first   (B) second   (C) third   (D) last

_____ 15. I _____ practice basketball after school, so you can find me at the basketball court every evening.
(A) always   (B) often   (C) seldom   (D) sometimes

_____ 16. I don't know what to expect, because I have _____ been here before.
(A) usually   (B) never   (C) once   (D) twice

_____ 17. My eight-year-old cousin studies at a(n) _____ in Taipei.
(A) nursery school   (B) elementary school
(C) junior high school   (D) senior high school

_____ 18. Mr. Lin is the new _____ who will take over at the elementary school.

(A) reporter (B) athlete (C) volunteer (D) principal

_____ 19. Harry and Sally went to the _____ on Saturday to watch the new movie.

(A) hotel (B) charity

(C) movie theater (D) bank

_____ 20. My _____ hurts, and I think I might have a headache.

(A) face (B) foot (C) finger (D) head

_____ 21. It looked like it might _____, so I brought an umbrella with me.

(A) sky (B) rain (C) cloud (D) wind

_____ 22. Taking a _____ is a more convenient way to travel throughout Taipei or Kaohsiung.

(A) train (B) boat (C) metro (D) sleigh

_____ 23. I _____ on my bike to school yesterday because my father was too busy to take me.

(A) rode (B) took (C) walked (D) swam

_____ 24. It's _____ for anyone to stay out late at night by themselves.

(A) dangerous (B) wrong (C) awesome (D) useful

_____ 25. I always liked the smell of _____ baking in the oven in the bakery.

(A) rice (B) pork (C) bread (D) chicken

____ 26. I put all of the groceries in the _____ and walked
to the cashier to pay for them.
(A) bucket   (B) tank   (C) rope   (D) basket

____ 27. She _____ I was not feeling well and asked me if
I needed to see a doctor.
(A) asked   (B) trained   (C) cheered   (D) noticed

____ 28. The driver _____ at the red light and waited for
the color to change.
(A) started   (B) won   (C) cared   (D) stopped

____ 29. After winning the basketball competition, our team was
given a large _____.
(A) carpet   (B) screen   (C) trophy   (D) map

____ 30. The birthday boy made a _____ before he blew
out the candles on his cake.
(A) will   (B) wish   (C) peace   (D) luck

____ 31. We like our homeroom teacher, but there are some
_____ students who do not.
(A) another   (B) other   (C) the other   (D) else

____ 32. It is so _____ today that using a fan is not enough
to cool off.
(A) warm   (B) hot   (C) cool   (D) cold

____ 33. The fish soup was too _____, which made me
very thirsty for water.
(A) salty   (B) sweet   (C) meat-free   (D) sour

_____ 34. I told you to throw away the _____ yesterday, so
why is it still in the trash can?
(A) salt　　　(B) powder　　(C) gas　　　(D) garbage

_____ 35. I haven't seen my friend in ten years, and when I saw him,
he looked so _____.
(A) the same　(B) gone　　　(C) special　　(D) different

_____ 36. Sally lost her car _____, and without it she
couldn't go to work.
(A) robot　　　(B) key　　　(C) letter　　(D) paper

_____ 37. If you feel dehydrated, you should drink some
_____ right away.
(A) weather　　(B) water　　　(C) waterfall　(D) wind

_____ 38. I went to the doctor for a _____ when I was not
feeling well.
(A) check in　　　　　　　　(B) check out
(C) check mate　　　　　　　(D) check-up

_____ 39. I'd like to _____ to many countries around the
world one day.
(A) turn　　　(B) trip　　　(C) travel　　(D) tour

_____ 40. I started collecting stamps when I was young, and I have
_____ about a hundred already.
(A) boiled　　(B) collected　(C) tasted　　(D) made

_____ 41. I'm sorry but there's _____ we can do to help you
with your problem.
(A) everything (B) something　(C) anything　(D) nothing

_____ 42. Steve woke up _____, because he needed to finish his homework before his first class.

(A) then   (B) early   (C) almost   (D) finally

_____ 43. The child ate too _____ candy and cried because his stomach hurt.

(A) enough   (B) much   (C) half   (D) many

_____ 44. If you're _____, we can go out to try the new restaurant.

(A) bloody   (B) stinky   (C) hungry   (D) sick

_____ 45. There are only seven _____ in a week and 52 weeks in a year.

(A) seconds   (B) hours   (C) minutes   (D) days

_____ 46. I'd love to go with you, _____ I have to finish my homework first.

(A) and   (B) but   (C) or   (D) so

_____ 47. I went on a(n) _____ in the mountains with my uncle almost every week during my summer vacation.

(A) event   (B) sport   (C) magic   (D) hike

_____ 48. The ladies enjoyed taking a jog _____ the river side.

(A) along   (B) over   (C) across   (D) under

_____ 49. If you scratch the _____ of a dog near it's tail, it will be very happy.

(A) right   (B) left   (C) front   (D) back

_____ 50. The _____ said her hobby was going shopping with her friends.

(A) human   (B) woman   (C) animal   (D) mate

_____ 51. KFC is famous for its _____ chicken, but it also sells sandwiches.

(A) fried   (B) heated   (C) cooked   (D) boiled

_____ 52. I want _____ in my tea, because I am really hot after exercising.

(A) yogurt   (B) ice   (C) cake   (D) chocolate

_____ 53. The crowd cheered for the runner after he ran 100 _____ in 12 seconds.

(A) inches   (B) centimeters
(C) kilometers   (D) meters

_____ 54. The students and the teacher argued about the correct answer to the math _____.

(A) question   (B) health   (C) thing   (D) team

_____ 55. It's important to have good _____, so your team can win the race.

(A) paperwork   (B) teamwork
(C) housework   (D) homework

_____ 56. Please be _____ next time, or we will leave without you.

(A) at a time   (B) at times   (C) in time   (D) on time

_____ 57. Chinese New Year is my favorite _____, because I receive many red envelopes with money inside.

(A) holiday   B) festival   (C) celebration (D) life

答案詳見 P.283

Test 3

_____ 1. Our family went to Kenting to go _____ in the sea, and we took many photos of beautiful fish.
(A) skating   (B) surfing   (C) snorkeling (D) shopping

_____ 2. Many people like to take a break from work by taking a _____ in another country.
(A) beach   (B) tide   (C) vacation   (D) mountain

_____ 3. The best way to experience a place while traveling is to try out their _____ food.
(A) local   (B) low   (C) real   (D) later

_____ 4. Mary wrote in a _____ every night, so she could remember her thoughts when she got older.
(A) prize   (B) award   (C) diary   (D) album

_____ 5. Growing up, I've always _____ junk food, because it's not healthy.
(A) picked up   (B) stayed away from
(C) woke up   (D) took up

_____ 6. The neighbors lined up with bags of _____, waiting for the garbage truck that plays a beautiful song.
(A) message (B) trash   (C) death   (D) fire

_____ 7. The farmer carried a load of corn in the back of his _____ and unloaded it at his barn.
(A) car   (B) van   (C) scooter   (D) truck

_____ 8. Sally was a _____ student at school, because she
was good looking and friendly.
(A) whole　　(B) popular　　(C) best　　(D) interesting

_____ 9. After the player got _____ on the basketball court,
an ambulance took him to the hospital.
(A) coughed　(B) broke　　(C) heated　　(D) hurt

_____ 10. After we _____ at our destination, I needed to make
sure I took all of my belongings off the bus.
(A) shouted　(B) laughed　　(C) happened　(D) arrived

_____ 11. The _____ began when the official shot a gun into
the air, and all of the runners took off.
(A) path　　(B) tattoo　　(C) comic　　(D) race

_____ 12. The festival always ends with a large display of
_____ over the lake.
(A) firefighters　　　　　(B) fireflies
(C) firecrackers　　　　　(D) fireworks

_____ 13. To prepare our delicious dinner, we stopped by the
_____ to gather all the ingredients.
(A) supermarket　　　　(B) superstar
(C) supercomputer　　　(D) supermodel

_____ 14. We invited our friends over for an outdoor party and
_____ steaks, hot dogs and hamburgers over the
grill.
(A) fry　　(B) boil　　(C) bake　　(D) barbecue

_____ 15. People in northern California were _____ out of their beds by a strong earthquake.

(A) failed   (B) built   (C) pasted   (D) shaken

_____ 16. I _____ the perfect birthday party for my friend, but forgot to buy the birthday cake.

(A) guessed   (B) hoped   (C) thought   (D) planned

_____17. It's crazy how quickly the _____ tickets were sold out, so I missed my chance to watch the singer's performance.

(A) concert   (B) present   (C) reason   (D) e-mail

_____ 18. Terry _____ to have vanilla ice cream this time, because last time he had strawberry.

(A) sent   (B) chose   (C) gave   (D) brought

_____ 19. You _____ be crazy to think that Cindy will go out on a date with you!

(A) can   (B) must   (C) may   (D) should

_____ 20. It's a _____ to be at your service, sir, and let me know if you need anything.

(A) message   (B) news   (C) pleasure   (D) advice

_____ 21. Afraid of catching the latest flu, she _____ going to any crowded places.

(A) became   (B) avoided   (C) agreed   (D) texted

_____ 22. The driver was terrified when her car _____ a dog crossing the road.

(A) filled   (B) hit   (C) held   (D) drew

_____ 23. My friend played a _____ on me and gave me an empty iPhone box for my birthday

      (A) rule   (B) ghost   (C) magic   (D) trick

_____ 24. Our school has finally opened up a new _____ for students to study.

      (A) part   (B) area   (C) office   (D) ground

_____ 25. People often say I have a loud _____, because I can't stop talking.

      (A) shoulder (B) mouth   (C) knee   (D) eye

_____ 26. Do you _____ that amazing smell coming from the kitchen?

      (A) smell   (B) feel   (C) taste   (D) sound

_____ 27. Most _____ restaurants have fat customers, because they serve unhealthy food.

      (A) frozen food   (B) canned food

      (C) junk food   (D) fast food

_____ 28. To make a cake, you must add 2 eggs, 2 cups of _____ and 3 cups of flour.

      (A) hamburger   (B) French fries

      (C) brown sugar   (D) green salad

_____ 29. My grandpa got really sick, and we took him to the _____.

      (A) epicenter   (B) grass

      (C) playground   (D) hospital

_____ 30. When you catch a cold, don't forget to drink water and take

_____.

(A) picture   (B) nap   (C) rest   (D) medicine

_____ 31. He _____ the correct password to log in to the

Facebook account.

(A) left   (B) lay   (C) pressed   (D) entered

_____ 32. Many tourists come to Taiwan to experience Chinese

_____ through temples, festivals and food.

(A) tradition   (B) experience   (C) effect   (D) culture

_____ 33. In recent years, it has become _____ to have a

cellphone at an early age.

(A) common   (B) difficult   (C) careful   (D) convenient

_____ 34. After Alex had his first date with Mary, she never

_____ him back on the phone.

(A) texted   (B) used   (C) hopped   (D) tried

_____ 35. Last night, my wife had a _____, so I got a cold, wet

towel and put it on her forehead.

(A) cold   (B) sneeze   (C) headache   (D) fever

_____ 36. The food tasted so bad, my body wouldn't let it go down my

_____.

(A) throat   (B) ankle   (C) neck   (D) tooth

_____ 37. He is really good at putting puzzles together, because he

can memorize the _____ of all the pieces.

(A) board   (B) shape   (C) dream   (D) stair

_____ 38. At night, my little brother would sleep with my parents
because he's scared to be in a _____ room.
(A) middle (B) shining (C) dark (D) crazy

_____ 39. After reminding him so many times, he finally _____
to turn off the lights.
(A) remembered   (B) noticed
(C) minded   (D) learned

_____ 40. She would always sing _____ taking a shower and
dream of becoming a famous singer.
(A) while (B) because (C) where (D) though

_____ 41. You only finished a _____ of your work, which
means you still didn't finish 75 percent of the work.
(A) half (B) quarter (C) whole (D) zero

_____ 42. Remember to always bring an _____ with you in
case it rains.
(A) cutter (B) hat (C) umbrella (D) comb

_____ 43. There was enough cake to give everyone _____ for
Robert, so he did not have dessert.
(A) below (B) except (C) as (D) through

_____ 44. Steve was a _____ of a dating app, and met his wife
online.
(A) seller (B) miner (C) user (D) lover

_____ 45. Tim _____ on the "LIKE" button, after watching
one of his favorite YouTubers.
(A) set (B) clicked (C) typed (D) worked

_____ 46. On his way back home, Tom crashed his bike and
_____ his ankle.
(A) twisted　　(B) ordered　　(C) kept　　(D) built

_____ 47. Not knowing what to do, I _____ his advice and
took the job offer.
(A) finished　(B) followed　(C) began　(D) stopped

_____ 48. It's really easy to buy things _____ now, since many
stores have free shipping.
(A) Facebook (B) online　(C) bookstore (D) keyboard

_____ 49. The _____ in the desert was unbearable, even
though I was under an umbrella.
(A) safety　　(B) note　　(C) heat　　(D) meal

_____ 50. When I finally met my date, she was more beautiful
_____ than in her photo.
(A) not at all　　　　　(B) right away
(C) in person　　　　　(D) face to face

_____ 51. Before ordering a _____, I usually ask what type of
beef they use.
(A) steak　　(B) salad　　(C) soup　　(D) spaghetti

_____ 52. I have to stay on _____, if I want to make it to the
movies on time.
(A) schedule　(B) choice　　(C) example　(D) country

_____ 53. When leaving the area, please stay _____ and don't
push other people!
(A) safe　　(B) calm　　(C) traditional　(D) main

_____ 54. Ice cream is only for _____, so don't eat it before the main meal.

(A) butter   (B) milk   (C) dessert   (D) dressing

_____ 55. Don't forget to bring the housewarming present with you when you visit his _____ on the 14th floor.

(A) town   (B) department

(C) apartment   (D) house

答案詳見 P.283

Test 4

_____ 1. A healthy dinner can include _____, bread, vegetables, and fruit.
(A) meat   (B) sky   (C) clothing   (D) tale

_____ 2. Bungee jumping is a _____ hobby, and I would never want to try it.
(A) expensive   (B) comfortable
(C) excellent   (D) dangerous

_____ 3. You may be surprised to know that electric vehicles can actually reach a high _____.
(A) speed   (B) size   (C) display   (D) idea

_____ 4. In order to provide a refreshing dessert for five people, I brought a large _____ to the picnic.
(A) banana   (B) peach
(C) watermelon   (D) mango

_____ 5. Some people enjoy eating a yellow _____, but I find it to sour for my taste.
(A) peach   (B) lemon   (C) guava   (D) papaya

_____ 6. My parents went out to a party on New Year's _____ in order to take part in the countdown to the new year.
(A) nighttime   (B) eve   (C) evening   (D) midnight

_____ 7. He chose to get a job at the well-known company that offered the latest _____ in computers.
(A) credit   (B) creativity   (C) stuff   (D) technology

_____ 8. Peter's father went to the animal shelter to _____
         for a puppy to give his son.
         (A) sell   (B) fit   (C) cheer   (D) search

_____ 9. Taiwan has many _____ workers from different
         countries, working in the factories.
         (A) silly   (B) free   (C) foreign   (D) heavy

_____ 10. Many people chose to order gifts on _____ to
         avoid the huge crowds.
         (A) websites   (B) gyms   (C) spots   (D) squares

_____ 11. In the beach resort, _____ twelve people were
         missing after the tsunami hit.
         (A) in fact   (B) ever after
         (C) at least   (D) in that case

_____ 12. At the ski resort, almost everyone wears a _____
         underneath their coats for extra warmth.
         (A) T-shirt   (B) vest   (C) shirt   (D) sweater

_____ 13. The _____ design of new school building makes it
         look a school of the future.
         (A) true   (B) bright   (C) modern   (D) pretty

_____ 14. Collecting stamps was my uncle's longtime _____,
         and now his collection is worth a lot of money.
         (A) prince   (B) drawer   (C) price   (D) hobby

_____ 15. He was _____ tall for a sixth grade student, making
         many people think he would play in the NBA one day.
         (A) besides   (B) especially   (C) quickly   (D) early

_____ 16. If you buy a t-shirt for me, please choose the _____ size, because I am neither big nor small.

    (A) medium   (B) large   (C) fresh   (D) amazing

_____ 17. If you ask me, the French fries at this restaurant taste _____ than the hamburgers.

    (A) good   (B) better   (C) best   (D) well

_____ 18. There were _____ students at this school who had a perfect score on the college entrance exam, which surprised the teacher.

    (A) quite a few   (B) a few

    (C) few   (D) very few

_____ 19. In Taipei City, there is a _____ on almost every corner, and they are always open every day, 24 hours a day.

    (A) tourist spot   (B) building

    (C) convenience store   (D) bakery

_____ 20. A man in a suit knocked on the door to _____ a debt, and my father was afraid to respond.

    (A) act   (B) live   (C) rise   (D) collect

_____ 21. Less than a _____ from the school was a fire department, so we felt safe.

    (A) kilometer (B) inch   (C) centimeter (D) meter

_____ 22. The weight of a package of meat in the USA is measured in _____ instead of using the metric system.

    (A) tons   (B) pounds   (C) kilograms (D) grams

_____ 23. The woman's daily exercise _____ was to take a jog in the park before breakfast.

(A) aisle   (B) routine   (C) route   (D) elevator

_____ 24. My parents often fought with the next-door neighbors and told me to stay away from their son, who was my

_____.

(A) engineer   (B) princess   (C) enemy   (D) teenager

_____ 25. The _____ expert in AI technology was hired to give a speech at the university.

(A) leading   (B) young   (C) lovely   (D) tired

_____ 26. During the massive fires in Australia, millions of _____ were killed.

(A) kangaroos   (B) hippos

(C) oxen   (D) foxes

_____ 27. Not many foreigners know that Taiwan has sixteen _____ tribes, each with their own culture and lan guage.

(A) natural   (B) aboriginal   (C) dragon   (D) giant

_____ 28. There are only 24 hours per day, so there is a _____ to how many masks the factory can produce.

(A) limit   (B) job   (C) sight   (D) role

_____ 29. The overcrowding at the basketball game was _____ after the principal brought in more benches for seating.

(A) led   (B) lost   (C) decided   (D) solved

_____ 30. In an _____ on the television show, the movie star talked about his new movie.

(A) interview　(B) difficulty　(C) chance　(D) direction

_____ 31. For a birthday gift, I want an iPhone more _____ anything else.

(A) rather　(B) than　(C) quite　(D) straight

_____ 32. Thousands of people visit Penghu every year to enjoy water sports and diving in the _____.

(A) candle　(B) nature　(C) ocean　(D) star

_____ 33. The couple went to the _____ to buy tickets for the movie they wanted to watch.

(A) factory　(B) theater　(C) post office　(D) station

_____ 34. The price of fresh fish _____ twice as much as it did last year, because the supply has been reduced.

(A) cost　(B) spent　(C) took　(D) paid

_____ 35. There have been many stories of _____ saving swimmers from drowning.

(A) flying fish　(B) sharks　(C) dolphins　(D) whales

_____ 36. During their road trip, Harvey pulled into gas stations to let his family use the _____.

(A) toilet　(B) oven　(C) light　(D) air

_____ 37. My cell phone battery was dead, so I asked to _____ a stranger's phone to call my parents.

(A) shine　(B) lend　(C) rent　(D) borrow

_____ 38. Before traveling to Australia, my mother went to the bank to exchange her money for Australian bank _____.

(A) notes　　(B) dimes　　(C) dollars　　(D) cents

_____ 39. Both of us have the same grandfather _____, so I think we are actually related to each other.

(A) in total　　　　　　(B) in the beginning

(C) in common　　　　　(D) in reality

_____ 40. _____ math can be very difficult, it remains my favorite subject, because I like to solve problems.

(A) If　　(B) Though　　(C) Because　　(D) Since

_____ 41. I read a book about a(n) _____ female scientist who won the Nobel Prize.

(A) public　　(B) successful　(C) inspiring　　(D) serious

_____ 42. The man broke his arms and legs in a horrible skiing accident, and the doctors worked all night to repair his

_____.

(A) fingers　　(B) nails　　(C) toes　　(D) limbs

_____ 43. There was a time I _____ worry about my math tests, but now that I have good understanding of the subject, I no longer worry.

(A) gave up　　(B) used to　　(C) fell asleep　(D) felt sleepy

_____ 44. In order to fit more clothes in my suitcase, I _____ my shirts and pants neatly before I put them inside.

(A) folded　　(B) ironed　　(C) hung　　(D) burned

_____ 45. Mr. Lin opened a _____ in the USA selling pearl milk tea and Taiwanese snacks.

(A) energy　　(B) fear　　(C) hope　　(D) business

_____ 46. Vicky ordered a box of special candies for her aunt online, and later she went to pick up the _____ which was delivered to the nearby 7-11.

(A) letter　　(B) package　　(C) mail　　(D) lamp

_____ 47. Steve hates going to the _____, but he had no choice but to visit when he had a toothache.

(A) mail carrier　　　　(B) dentist

(C) businessman　　　　(D) soldier

_____ 48. After the _____ paid for her meal, the cashier chased the woman outside and returned her purse.

(A) secretary　　　　(B) boss

(C) customer　　　　(D) shopkeeper

_____ 49. The wealthy _____ took trips to Africa to shoot buffalo and elephants.

(A) refrigerator　　　　(B) speaker

(C) hiker　　　　(D) hunter

_____ 50. Superman is a superhero who can fly and wears a long, red _____ over his back.

(A) coat　　(B) jacket　　(C) skirt　　(D) cape

_____ 51. Ted took a long walk on the warm, tropical beach, wearing a pair of white _____ that did not quite reach his knees.

(A) pants　　(B) shorts　　(C) socks　　(D) jeans

_____ 52. Ken took out his _____ from his pocket and pulled out a dollar to give to the homeless man.
(A) scarf   (B) cap   (C) towel   (D) wallet

_____ 53. Taiwan grows a type of _____ grape, known as Muscat, which makes a sweet wine.
(A) purple   (B) brown   (C) pink   (D) gray

_____ 54. In a period of six months, Jay _____ his physical disability and learned to walk without assistance.
(A) overcame (B) fixed   (C) hired   (D) swept

_____ 55. Visitors to the museum were asked to take a _____ in the auditorium to watch a short film.
(A) bench   (B) seat   (C) sofa   (D) chair

_____ 56. The trainer always gave the dog he trained a _____ whenever it listened to his commands.
(A) pot   (B) courage   (C) treat   (D) hate

_____ 57. Needless to say, when my son accepted the award for outstanding achievement, I was a _____ father.
(A) proud   (B) impossible (C) honest   (D) able

_____ 58. As the earthquake shook the house, I jumped out of bed, hugged my wife, and _____ that we would be safe.
(A) saw   (B) prayed   (C) heard   (D) forgot

_____ 59. I cried when my pet goldfish died, but I became angry when my mother _____ it down the toilet.
(A) erased   (B) painted   (C) flushed   (D) brushed

Test 5

_____ 1. During Lunar New Year vacation, I _____ with my best friend online for hours every day.

(A) nodded　　(B) chatted　　(C) cried　　(D) smiled

_____ 2. My father chose not to go to college and _____ did my mother.

(A) abroad　　(B) either　　(C) neither　　(D) too

_____ 3. Before buying my VR game, I didn't know how _____ it was to set up.

(A) international　　　　(B) simple

(C) magnificent　　　　(D) virtual

_____ 4. I saw a child chase a ball onto the street, so I _____ and saved him from being hit by a bus.

(A) turned away　　　　(B) took action

(C) put off　　　　　　(D) signed up

_____ 5. There were so many toys at the store that I wanted to buy, _____ I had no money to purchase any.

(A) already　　(B) yet　　(C) perhaps　　(D) super

_____ 6. Sam wouldn't stop playing with his phone, _____ his mom took it away.

(A) so　　(B) until　　(C) whether　　(D) since

_____ 7. When I asked Joy what foreign _____ she wanted to learn, she said French.

(A) celebration　　　　(B) climate

(C) language　　　　　(D) fable

275

_____ 8. Hanging from the roof of my house is a _____ that shows my family's loyalty to our country.

(A) flag   (B) post   (C) mask   (D) headset

_____ 9. My family visits a _____ at midnight on Lunar New Year to pray for good fortune.

(A) bathhouse   (B) court

(C) temple   (D) track

_____ 10. The night before the trip to the amusement park, I was so _____, and I couldn't sleep.

(A) surprised   (B) interested   (C) excited   (D) worried

_____ 11. Before I left the house, I put a piece of _____ on the table to notify my mom where I was going.

(A) bin   (B) paint   (C) paper   (D) glue

_____ 12. She makes a lot of writing mistakes, so she always prepares a(n) _____ in her pencil case.

(A) ruler   (B) marker   (C) eraser   (D) caller

_____ 13. Our classmates planned a(n) _____ to show appreciation for our homeroom teacher.

(A) exercise   (B) relationship (C) event   (D) wedding

_____ 14. During our last vacation, our family took a _____ country trip in our car.

(A) full   (B) thick   (C) golden   (D) cross

_____ 15. Breaking news! A local celebrity _____ due to a disastrous car crash.

(A) smoked   (B) bowed   (C) died   (D) married

_____ 16. The dog got hurt from falling down the stairs, so it can't wag her _____ now.

(A) lap   (B) tail   (C) lip   (D) heart

_____ 17. I've been doing this job for so many years, that every day I think my work is so _____.

(A) interesting (B) surprising   (C) exciting   (D) boring

_____ 18. The school rules require that all students arrive at school in their _____.

(A) machines (B) uniforms   (C) napkins   (D) medals

_____ 19. I took a walk in the park all alone, feeling _____ and desperate for a companion.

(A) quick   (B) colorful   (C) lonely   (D) greedy

_____ 20. The recipe for the salad requires us to use _____ eggs that we chop into small pieces.

(A) boiled   (B) bottled   (C) animated   (D) satisfied

_____ 21. My favorite animal is the _____, because it has the ability to fly in total darkness.

(A) ant   (B) grasshopper

(C) bug   (D) bat

_____ 22. Betty has a dream to become a _____, because she enjoys dancing in unison to improve a team's morale.

(A) winner   (B) cheerleader

(C) coach   (D) runner

_____ 23. We have to stop logging the trees in this _____, because soon will no longer sustain animal life.

(A) smoke   (B) forest   (C) goodness (D) planet

_____ 24. The 100 meter _____ is known for its display of
intense speed and competition.
(A) tug-of-war (B) dash　　(C) marathon　(D) relay race

_____ 25. According to the story, a scary _____ comes out at
night and kills people.
(A) beast　　(B) sheep　　(C) goat　　(D) goose

_____ 26. Once the battle ended, the soldiers raised a white flag to
ask for _____.
(A) art　　(B) truth　　(C) peace　　(D) gold

_____ 27. I _____ that I had a big exam tomorrow, so I refused
his offer to go out to watch a movie.
(A) hung up　　　　　(B) kept in mind
(C) sat on the fence　　(D) took aside

_____ 28. I truly _____ it when I said that you were my best
friend.
(A) cancelled　(B) received　(C) meant　(D) comforted

_____ 29. There is now a new _____ built for local residents of
the apartment building to swim in.
(A) planet　　(B) airplane　(C) lake　　(D) pool

_____ 30. Books help expand people's _____ of the world, but
fewer people read books these days.
(A) age　　(B) health　　(C) fantasy　(D) knowledge

_____ 31. Civics is probably my favorite _____ of all, because
my teacher makes it interesting.
(A) theme　　(B) topic　　(C) subject　(D) recipe

_____ 32. The terrorists forced the _____ to fly the airplane to a different country.

(A) host   (B) chef   (C) judge   (D) pilot

_____ 33. What do you have recommended on the _____? It's so hard to choose.

(A) menu   (B) bowl   (C) fork   (D) ingredient

_____ 34. The young man was asked to prepare for dinner by setting the _____ and plates in the dining room.

(A) toast   (B) sauce   (C) tableware   (D) pot

_____ 35. To make good tea, you first need a decent _____ to pour the liquid.

(A) pan   (B) mat   (C) lid   (D) teapot

_____ 36. Eggs usually come in a _____, with a container that holds twelve safely.

(A) pair   (B) dozen   (C) roll   (D) copy

_____ 37. Didn't your mom teach you to have good _____ when you are at someone's house?

(A) wishes   (B) manners   (C) gloves   (D) dumplings

_____ 38. The student gave the _____ spelling of the word to win the contest.

(A) correct   (B) possible   (C) national   (D) loud

_____ 39. If you want people to have a good impression of you, it helps to be _____ when you first meet them.

(A) polite   (B) mad   (C) glad   (D) stupid

_____ 40. My chicken finally _____ eggs, so now I feel it is more useful.

(A) laid   (B) born   (C) killed   (D) quit

_____ 41. Even though she had to have two jobs, the single mother _____ two children by herself.

(A) allowed   (B) matched   (C) raised   (D) pushed

_____ 42. If you want to access your _____ online, you will need to know your user name and password.

(A) radio   (B) account   (C) tap   (D) button

_____ 43. My mom has always told me never to open the door to a _____ who knocks on the door.

(A) lawyer   (B) stranger   (C) recorder   (D) reporter

_____ 44. The sound of my mother's _____ made me calm when she sang to me.

(A) noise   (B) volume
(C) voice   (D) information

_____ 45. She _____ her emotional story with the whole class, and everyone cried.

(A) cheated   (B) stole   (C) belonged   (D) shared

_____ 46. These shirts were so _____ that if I gotten there later, they would have been sold out.

(A) wet   (B) cheap   (C) sharp   (D) clear

_____ 47. The huge _____ is about to hit Japan, so citizens must be prepared for unexpected floods.

(A) guest   (B) hurry   (C) climate   (D) typhoon

_____ 48. It's important for us to _____ our plastic waste, otherwise too much of it will end up floating on the ocean.

(A) destroy   (B) recycle   (C) produce   (D) deliver

_____ 49. Take your _____ in line and someone will call for you when it is your turn.

(A) outside   (B) center   (C) circle   (D) position

_____ 50. If you attend a funeral in Taiwan, you can offer money placed into a white _____.

(A) envelope   (B) stamp   (C) letter   (D) company

_____ 51. Please look at the round table and count the chairs, so you know _____ how many people can sit there.

(A) carefully   (B) usually   (C) luckily   (D) exactly

_____ 52. In every good restaurant, there will be a _____ to serve your meal.

(A) waiter   (B) firefighter   (C) salesman   (D) fisherman

_____ 53. I sometimes put _____ on my cooked meat, but sometimes it makes me sneeze.

(A) salt   (B) oil   (C) pepper   (D) sugar

_____ 54. Something knocked over my garbage can, but these footprints didn't come from a(n) _____.

(A) human   (B) keeper   (C) artist   (D) adult

_____ 55. More stores are no longer offering free _____ bags for their customers.

(A) elementary   (B) digital

(C) unclean   (D) plastic

_____ 56. After a heavy rain shower, you can spot a beautiful
_____, if you are lucky.
(A) rainbow   (B) wind   (C) sun   (D) mud

_____ 57. The older couple took a luxury cruise _____ from
Los Angeles to Hawaii.
(A) ship   (B) boat   (C) ferry   (D) train

_____ 58. Gas powered vehicles can _____ the air with up to
10 liters of carbon dioxide a day, which can increase
climate change.
(A) fuel   (B) pollute   (C) create   (D) protect

_____ 59. Sir, if you don't mind, someone will be here to _____
you soon.
(A) serve   (B) pass   (C) clean   (D) appear

_____ 60. There is _____ in the world that can separate the
two lovers, not even their parents.
(A) everything (B) anything   (C) something (D) nothing

答案詳見 P.284

Test 1 解答

1. (C)	2. (D)	3. (A)	4. (A)	5. (B)	6. (A)	7. (A)	8. (C)
9. (D)	10. (D)	11. (C)	12. (C)	13. (B)	14. (D)	15. (A)	16. (D)
17. (C)	18. (B)	19. (B)	20. (D)	21. (B)	22. (D)	23. (A)	24. (D)
25. (B)	26. (B)	27. (D)	28. (A)	29. (B)	30. (D)	31. (A)	32. (A)
33. (B)	34. (D)	35. (C)	36. (A)	37. (C)	38. (B)	39. (B)	40. (A)
41. (A)	42. (B)	43. (A)	44. (B)	45. (D)	46. (D)		

Test 2 解答

1. (A)	2. (B)	3. (A)	4. (B)	5. (C)	6. (A)	7. (C)	8. (C)
9. (B)	10. (D)	11. (B)	12. (C)	13. (C)	14. (A)	15. (A)	16. (B)
17. (B)	18. (D)	19. (C)	20. (D)	21. (B)	22. (A)	23. (A)	24. (A)
25. (C)	26. (D)	27. (D)	28. (D)	29. (C)	30. (B)	31. (B)	32. (B)
33. (A)	34. (D)	35. (D)	36. (B)	37. (B)	38. (D)	39. (C)	40. (B)
41. (D)	42. (B)	43. (B)	44. (C)	45. (D)	46. (B)	47. (D)	48. (A)
49. (D)	50. (B)	51. (A)	52. (B)	53. (D)	54. (A)	55. (B)	56. (D)
57. (B)							

Test 3 解答

1. (C)	2. (C)	3. (A)	4. (C)	5. (B)	6. (B)	7. (D)	8. (B)
9. (D)	10. (D)	11. (D)	12. (D)	13. (A)	14. (D)	15. (D)	16. (D)
17. (A)	18. (B)	19. (B)	20. (C)	21. (B)	22. (B)	23. (D)	24. (B)
25. (B)	26. (A)	27. (D)	28. (C)	29. (D)	30. (D)	31. (D)	32. (D)
33. (A)	34. (A)	35. (D)	36. (A)	37. (B)	38. (C)	39. (A)	40. (A)
41. (B)	42. (C)	43. (B)	44. (C)	45. (B)	46. (A)	47. (B)	48. (B)
49. (C)	50. (C)	51. (A)	52. (A)	53. (B)	54. (C)	55. (C)	

Test 4 解答

1. (A)	2. (D)	3. (A)	4. (C)	5. (B)	6. (B)	7. (D)	8. (D)
9. (C)	10. (A)	11. (C)	12. (D)	13. (C)	14. (D)	15. (B)	16. (A)
17. (B)	18. (A)	19. (C)	20. (D)	21. (A)	22. (B)	23. (B)	24. (C)
25. (A)	26. (A)	27. (B)	28. (A)	29. (D)	30. (A)	31. (B)	32. (C)
33. (B)	34. (A)	35. (C)	36. (A)	37. (D)	38. (A)	39. (C)	40. (B)

41. (C)   42. (D)   43. (B)   44. (A)   45. (D)   46. (B)   47. (B)   48. (C)

49. (D)   50. (D)   51. (B)   52. (D)   53. (A)   54. (A)   55. (B)   56. (C)

57. (A)   58. (B)   59. (C)

Test 5 解答

1. (B)   2. (C)   3. (B)   4. (B)   5. (B)   6. (B)   7. (C)   8. (A)

9. (C)   10. (C)   11. (C)   12. (C)   13. (C)   14. (D)   15. (C)   16. (B)

17. (D)   18. (B)   19. (C)   20. (A)   21. (D)   22. (B)   23. (B)   24. (B)

25. (A)   26. (C)   27. (B)   28. (C)   29. (D)   30. (D)   31. (C)   32. (D)

33. (A)   34. (C)   35. (D)   36. (B)   37. (B)   38. (A)   39. (A)   40. (A)

41. (C)   42. (B)   43. (B)   44. (C)   45. (D)   46. (B)   47. (D)   48. (B)

49. (D)   50. (A)   51. (D)   52. (A)   53. (C)   54. (A)   55. (D)   56. (A)

57. (A)   58. (B)   59. (A)   60. (D)

1200 單字詞素
（字首／字根／字尾）整理

字首 篇

▶ uni = one

❶ unite 聯合

❷ united 聯合的 = unite + ed

❸ uniform 制服 = uni + form 形式

▶ bi = two

❶ between 之間 = by + two

❷ bicycle 自行車 = two + wheel

❸ dozen 一打 = two + ten

❹ two 二

❺ twelve 十二

❻ twelfth 第十二

❼ twenty 二十

❽ twentieth 第二十

▶ al = all

❶ almost 幾乎 = all + most 大部份的

❷ already 已經 = all + ready 預備好的

❸ also 並且 = all + so

❹ always 總是 = all + way + s

▶ a = in、on

❶ abroad 在外國 = a + broad 寬廣的

❷ above 在上面 = a + over 在……上面

❸ across 跨越 = a + cross 跨越

❹ ahead 前面 = a + head 頭部

❺ aloud 大聲地 = a + loud 大聲的

❻ around 周圍 = a + round 圓的

❼ away 離開 = a + way 道路

▶ ad = to

❶ apartment 公寓 = to separate 分開 + part 部份 + ment

❷ appear 出現 = to + come forth 前來

❸ arrive 抵達 = to + river 河流

▶ de = down、apart

❶ decide 決定 = apart + cut 切

❷ department 部門 = apart + part 部份 + ment

❸ different 不同的 = away + carry 攜帶 + ent

▶ pre = before、forward

❶ present 出席 = before + to be 存在

❷ prepare 預備 = before + make ready 預備好的

❸ problem 問題 = forward + cast 丟擲

❹ prince 王子 = first + go 去

❺ princess 公主 = prince + ess

▶ re = back、again

❶ remember 記得 = again + mindful 留心的

❷ repeat 重複 = again + to rush 倉促

▶ in = in

❶ inside 裡面 = in + side 邊

❷ enjoy 喜愛 = en + joy 喜樂

❸ enjoyment 樂趣 = enjoy + ment

▶ ex = out

❶ outside 外面 = out + side 邊

❷ example 例子 = out + take 拿

❸ eraser 擦子 = ex + scrape 擦；刮 + er

❹ excellent 優秀的 = excel 擅長 + ent

❺ excuse 藉口、原諒 = ex + cause 訴訟

❻ exercise 練習 = out + enclose 圍住；附上

❼ expensive 昂貴的 = ex + weighed 衡量 + ive

▶ super = over 在……上方；超越

❶ super 極好的

❷ supermarket 超級市場 = super + market 市場

❸ surprise 驚訝 = over + to seize 抓

▶ sub = under

❶ subject 學科 = under + ject 投擲

❷ understand 了解 = under + stand 站立

▶ inter = between、among

❶ Internet 網際網路 = between + net 網

▶ be = by、upon

❶ become 成為 = upon + come 來

❷ before 前面 = by + fore 前面

❸ behind 後面 = by + hind 後面

❹ belong 屬於 = by + go 去

❺ below 下面 = by + low 底下

❻ beside 旁邊 = by + side 邊

▶ tele = far off

❶ telephone 電話 = tele + sound 聲音

❷ television 電視 = tele + vision 視線

▶ com = together

❶ comfortable 舒適的 = together + force 力量 + able

❷ computer 電腦 = together + think 思考 + er

❸ correct 正確的 = together + straight 直的

❹ convenient 便利的 = together + go 去 + ient

▶ un = not，ne 否定

❶ unhappy 不快樂 = not + happy 快樂

❷ never 從不 = not + ever 曾經

❸ neither 二者皆非 = not + whether 是否

❹ none 無一 = no + one 一

▶ mis = wrongly 錯誤地

❶ mistake 錯誤 = wrongly + get 拿取

字根篇

 字根篇

▶ **port = carry 攜帶**

❶ **port** 港口

❷ **airport** 機場 = air + **port**

❸ **important** 重要的 = in + **port** + ant

❹ **sport** 運動 = out + **port**

▶ **cept = take 拿**

❶ **case** 盒子、案例

❷ **catch** 抓

❸ **except** 除外 = out + **take**

▶ **fact = make、do 製造、做**

❶ **fact** 事實

❷ **factory** 工廠 = **make** + place 地方

❸ **difficult** 困難的 = not + easy to **do** 容易做到

❹ **office** 辦公室 = work + **do**

▶ **mov = move 移動**

❶ **move** 移動

❷ **movie** 電影

❸ **moment** 時刻 = **move** + ment

▸ cess = go 去

❶ successful 成功的 = from under + go + ful

❷ necessary 必需的 = not + go + ary

▸ grad = go 去

❶ grade 年級、成績

❷ degree 程度 = down from + go

▸ sta = stand 站立

❶ cost 成本 = together + stand

❷ post 郵政

❸ postcard 明信片 = post + card

❹ rest 休息、其餘 = back + stand

❺ restroom 洗手間 = rest + room

❻ stand 站立

❼ understand 了解 = under + stand

❽ understanding 理解 = understand + ing

❾ station 車站 = stand + tion

❿ fire station 消防隊

⓫ police station 警察局

⓬ stay 停留

⓭ store 商店、儲存

▶ cycle = cycle 循環、wheel 輪子

❶ cycle 循環、自行車

❷ bicycle 自行車 = two + wheel 輪子

❸ motorcycle 機車 = motor 馬達 + wheel

▶ med = middle 中間的

❶ middle 中間的 = mid + le

❷ midnight 午夜 = mid + night

❸ mean 意義

❹ medium 中等的、媒介 = med + ium

▶ fin = end 結束

❶ fine 好的

❷ finish 完成 = fin + ish

❸ finally 最後、終於 = fin + al + ly

▶ part = part 部分

❶ apartment 公寓 = apart 分離 + ment

❷ department 部門 = depart 離開 + ment

❸ part 部分

❹ party 派對 = part + y

▶ vid = see 看

❶ television 電視 = far off 遠離 + see

❷ video 錄影

❸ visit 拜訪、參觀

▶ cite = call 喊叫

❶ excite 使興奮 = out + call

❷ exciting 刺激的 = excite + ing

❸ excited 感到興奮的 = excite + ed

▶ cuse = reason 原因、lawsuit 訴訟

❶ cause 原因、引起

❷ because 因為 = be + cause 原因

❸ excuse 原諒 = out + cause 訴訟

▶ not = know 知道

❶ know 知道

❷ note 筆記

❸ notebook 筆記簿 = note + book

❹ notice 注意、告示

▶ us = use 使用

❶ use 使用、用途

❷ useful 有用的 = use + ful

❸ usually 經常 = usual 經常的 + ly

▶ popul = people 人

❶ popular 受歡迎的 = **people** + ar

❷ public 公開的 = **people** + ic

▶ nat = birth 出生

❶ national 國家的 = **nat** + ion + al

❷ nature 大自然 = **nat** + ure

▶ cent = hundred 百

❶ cent 分

❷ hundred 百

字尾 篇

▶ ence

ence 與 ance 同源，大多黏接動詞而形成名詞，表示該動詞的狀態或事實。黏接 ence 的動詞也常黏接 ent 而衍生成形容詞，並且形成名詞與形容詞對應。

❶ convenience 便利，convenient 便利的

❷ excellence 優秀，excellent 優秀的

❸ appearance 外觀，apparent 明顯的

❹ importance 重要性，important 重要的

❺ experience 經驗，體驗

❻ sentence 句子

▶ ing

ing 有存在、持續、主動等意涵，存在即是動名詞，持續、主動則是現在分詞，因此，ing 可形成名詞或形容詞。

形成名詞

❶ building 建築物 = build 建造 + ing

❷ clothing 衣物 = clothe 穿衣 + ing

❸ dining 用餐 = dine 進食 + ing

❹ evening 晚上 = even 均分的 + ing

❺ living 生活 = live 生活 + ing

❻ meeting 會議 = meet 會面 + ing

形成形容詞

① boring 令人厭煩的 = bore 使厭煩 + **ing**

② exciting 刺激的 = excite 使興奮 + **ing**

③ surprising 令人驚訝的 = surprise 使驚訝 + **ing**

④ hard-working 努力的 = hard 努力地 + work 工作 + **ing**

⑤ interesting 有趣的 = interest 使感興趣 + **ing**

▶ ed

ed 有被動、完成等意涵，表示被動時可視為 ing 的反義字尾。

① bored 感到厭煩的 = bore + **ed**

② excited 感到興奮的 = excite + **ed**

③ interested 感到興趣的 = interest + **ed**

④ married 已婚的 = marry 結婚 + **ed**

⑤ surprised 感到驚訝的 = surprise 驚訝 + **ed**

⑥ tired 疲累的 = tire 使疲累 + **ed**

▶ ion

ion 常表示狀態或動作，tion、ation 與 ion 同源，其中 ation = ate + ion。

① dictionary 字典 = say 說 + **ion** + ary

② education 教育 = out + tow 拖吊 + **ation**

③ question 問題 = quest 尋求 + **ion**

④ television 電視 = far off 遠離 + see + **ion**

⑤ vacation 假期 = empty 空出 + **ation**

▶ ment

ment 表示動作的結果、手段,多黏接動詞。

❶ apartment 公寓 = apart 分開 + **ment**

❷ department 部門 = depart 分離 + **ment**

▶ ure

ure 多黏接動詞,表示動作的抽象名詞。字母串 ture 唸 /tʃɚ/。

❶ future 未來、未來的

❷ nature 自然 = birth 出生 + **ure**

❸ picture 圖畫 = paint 繪畫 + **ure**

▶ y

字尾 y 可形成名詞,也可黏接名詞而形成形容詞,表示具有該名詞性質的。

❶ city 城市

❷ country 國家

❸ party 派對 = part 部分 + **y**

形容詞字尾

❶ angry 憤怒的 = anger 憤怒 + **y**

❷ catchy 動聽易記的 = catch 抓住 + **y**

❸ cloudy 有雲的 = cloud 雲 + **y**

❹ dirty 髒的 = dirt 灰塵 + **y**

❺ easy 容易的 = ease 容易、安逸 + **y**

❻ funny 樂趣的 = fun 樂趣 + **y**

❼ healthy 健康的 = health 健康 + **y**   health = heal 治療 + th

❽ hungry 飢餓的 = hunger 飢餓 + **y**

⑨ lucky 幸運的 = luck 運氣 + **y**

⑩ rainy 有雨的 = rain 雨 + **y**

⑪ sunny 晴朗的 = sun 太陽 + **y**

⑫ thirsty 渴的 = thirst 渴 + **y**

⑬ windy 有風的 = wind 風 + **y**

▶ **er**

er 表示產生動作的人、器具或工具，除了動詞，還可黏接形容詞。

❶ carrier 攜帶者、運輸工具 = carry 攜帶 + **er**

❷ driver 駕駛人 = drive 駕駛 + **er**

❸ farmer 農夫 = farm 耕種 + **er**

❹ foreigner 外國人 = foreign 外國的 + **er**

❺ leader 領導人 = lead 領導 + **er**

❻ player 選手、播放器 = play 比賽、播放 + **er**

❼ reader 讀者 = read 閱讀 + **er**

❽ scooter 輕型機車 = scoot 飛奔 + **er**

❾ shopkeeper 店主 = shop 商店 + keep 經營 + **er**

❿ singer 歌手 = sing 唱歌 + **er**

⑪ stranger 陌生人 = strange 陌生的 + **er**

⑫ teacher 教師 = teach 教學 + **er**

⑬ waiter 侍者 = wait 等待 + **er**

⑭ waitress 女侍者 = waiter 侍者 + **ess**

⑮ worker 工人 = work 工作 + **er**

⑯ writer 作者 = write 寫作 + **er**

⑰ ruler 統治者、尺 = rule 統治 + **er**

▶ man

❶ businessman 商人 = business 商業 + **man**

❷ fireman 消防員 = fire 火 + **man**

❸ mailman 郵差 = mail 郵件 + **man**

❹ policeman 警察 = police 警方 + **man**

▶ ery = place for

名詞性質的 ery 表示場所，ary、ory 是同源字尾，同樣表示場所。

❶ bakery 麵包店 = bake 烘焙 + **ery**

❷ factory 工廠 = fact 製造 + **ory**

❸ library 圖書館 = libr 書 + **ary**

▶ able

除了 full of，able 還可表示能夠、允許、值得等意涵。

❶ comfortable 舒適的 = comfort 舒適 + **able**

❷ possible 可能的 = power 力量 + **ible**

▶ ful

ful 與形容詞 full—充滿的同源，意思是 full of—充滿……的，黏接名詞，形成形容詞，表示充滿該名詞的性質的。

❶ **full** 滿的

❷ beautiful 美麗的 = full of beauty 美

❸ careful 小心的 = full of care 小心

▶ ous

黏接名詞，同樣表示 "full of" 名詞性質的狀態。

❶ dangerous 危險的 = danger 危險 + **ous**

❷ delicious 美味的

❸ famous 有名的 = fame 名聲 + **ous**

▶ ly

ly 表示狀態，黏接名詞，形成形容詞；黏接形容詞，形成情態副詞。

形成形容詞

❶ friendly 友善的 = friend 朋友 + **ly**

❷ lonely 獨自的 = lone 獨自的 + **ly**

❸ lovely 可愛的 = love 愛 + **ly**

形成情態副詞

❶ finally 最後、終於 = final 最後的 + **ly**

❷ really 真實地 = real 真實的 + **ly**

❸ usually 經常地 = usual 經常的 + **ly**

單字學習的核心知識

詞素

1. 構詞上，英文單字是由詞素，即字首、字根、字尾所構成，其語意與詞素息息相關，例如：unusable—不能用的，字首 un，表示否定，字根 use 是使用的意思，字尾 able 表示可以被……的。

un	us	able
字首	字根	字尾

2. 詞素分為可獨立詞素與不可獨立詞素二類，可獨立詞素就是未黏接字首或字尾的單字（可獨立字根），例如 book、desk、nice、fast 等。

3. 不可獨立詞素包括字首、字尾、不可獨立字根，例如 com 是字首，有一起的意思；cept 是不可獨立字根，有拿的意思，ful 是字尾，充滿的意思。

4. 單字除了詞素之外，還可能包含填補字母—詞素黏接時（大多是黏接字尾），為了唸音順暢而插入音（大多是母音）並增加的字母，例如 centimeter 的 i 是填補字母，唸音 /ə/；actual 的 u 是填補字母，唸音 /u/。

cent	i	meter
字根	填補字母	字根

act	u	al
字根	填補字母	字尾

5. 詞素與單字的語意關係密切，因此應以語意作為詞素的辨識依歸，例如辦公室—office 是由 of（work）與 fice（do、make）二詞素所構成，若分析為 off（分離）與 ice（冰）則因語意不符而貽誤。

6. 詞素衍生構詞是英文造字的一種方式，而詞素大多源自拉丁文或希臘文，其拼寫形式歷經長時流傳而多所變異，同源詞素之間常見字母更換或增減，例如詞素 ven、vent，clos、close 同源，單字 unit、unite 與字首 uni 同源，三者拼寫相似，語意明顯相關，易於辨識，因此不宜執著 uni 而將 unit、unite 細究分析為 uni-t、uni-te。

7. 一些詞素常與單字同源，彼此唸音相近、語意相關，因此，以同源單字辨識詞素誠為詞素學習的最佳方式，例如以 unit 學習字首 uni，unit 可視為 uni 的神隊友。

8. 學習上，建議依照字尾、字首、字根（不可獨立字根）順序逐步精進。先從字尾著手是因為字尾大多黏接單字，而單字易於辨識，因此較易學習。字首黏接字根時，常因相鄰字母唸音順暢考量而改變拼字，辨識不易，例如 computer、convenient、collect、correct、co-worker 等單字的字首都是 com，但尾字母不同。另外，字首常黏接不可獨立字根，單字構詞不易辨識、理解，例如，以上單字的字根 pute、vent、lect、rect 都是不可獨立。熟悉字尾、字首與構詞衍生之後，再行嘗試陌生而又變化多端的不可獨立字根，成功學習的可能性應該較高。

9. 字尾的學習要點除了語意、字源詞性之外，還有字尾對字重音的影響，例如，字尾 ic 的字重音都置於其前一音節，例如 historic；explain 黏接字尾 ation 衍生名詞 explanation，explain 的重音節母音弱化，對應的拼字縮減。另外，字尾黏接所形成的特定字母串唸音也是學習焦點 -- 正確，甚至預測唸音應與拼字同樣重要。

10. 不同於字尾，一個字首常有多個語意，而且不同的衍生字常見不同的語意，例如，re 主要有 back、again 二語意，repay 的 re 是 back，repeat 的 re 則是 again。因此，學習時字首時，除了要知道有那些語意，還是了解因字而異的語意對應。唸音方面，知曉黏接字根時的同化現象是學習字首的另一要點，例如，上述 com、con、col、cor、co 等變化。

音節

英語是拼音文字，單字的唸音都是拼音而成，而拼音的單位就是音節，由母音搭配子音組合而成。一個單字至少包含一個音節，而每個音節包含一個母音，例如 day 有一個音節，today 有二個音節，yesterday 則有三個音節。

為了使單字的唸音清楚，音節具有基本的音量，因此，音節有結構的考量，這就是音節結構的由來。當然，單字若包含多個音節，音量充足，每一音節不需符合單音節基本音量的要求。

英語的音節包括音節首子音與韻腳兩大部分，而韻腳又包括核心音（母音）與音節尾子音二部分：

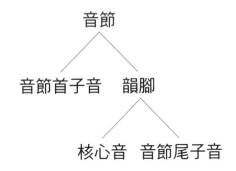

1. 音節尾子音缺項的音節是開放音節，例如：me、toe、now；包含音節尾子音的音節是封閉音節，例如：long、length、lengths。

2. 音節首子音可缺項，至多三個，例如：and、hand、please、spring。

3. 音節尾子音也可缺項，至多也是三個，第三個是文法相關的字尾，例如：too、tool、hand、hands。

4. 我們設定短母音的音量是一，子音的音量也是一，長母音的音量是二。為使一個單字擁有起碼，單音節的韻腳音量不能只有一，也就是說，一個單字若是單音節，且是開放音節，母音必須是長母音。

單字節單字	音節類型	韻腳結構	韻腳音量
bee	開放音節	長母音	2
beer	封閉音節	短母音 + 1 子音	2
beat	封閉音節	長母音 + 1 子音	3
beats	封閉音節	長母音 + 2 子音	4

5. 音節的劃分方式：

(1) 劃分音節的目的在於標示重音節母音是長母音或是短母音：

- 若是長母音，重音節是開放音節，無音節尾子音。
- 若是短母音，重音節是封閉音節，有音節尾子音。
- 音節與拼音無關，拼音不受音節的限制。

(2) 劃分音節的步驟：

- 確認音節數—找出母音發音的字母組合

  單母音字母：b**a**t

  二合母音字母：b**oa**t

  w, y 與母音字母的字母串：n**ow**、b**oy**

  非音節首的字母 y：c**y**cle

  r, m, n 等音節性子音：list**en**、penc**il**

- 分配字母：

  子音部分

  → 重音節母音若是長母音，子音切給右側音節以形成開放音節：

  pa‧per、va‧ca‧tion

→ 重音節母音若是短母音，子音切給重音節以形成封閉音節：
rec·ord、el·e·phant

→ 重複或連續的子音字母，分配左右音節，左側為封閉音節：
pep·per、ap·ple

母音部分：

→ 重複而各自唸音的母音字母應劃為二音節：
vac·u·um

(3) 劃分音節的考量因素：

- 固定唸音的字母串：va·ca·**tion**、mu·si·**cian**、spe·**cial**
- 詞素要完整：**stand**·ing、bus·y、lat·er（比較 lat·ter）

同源字

　　同一詞源的字彙互為同源字，彼此唸音相近，尤其是音節首子音；另外，同源字與詞源的語義相關，彼此語義相通—「音相近、義相連」是同源字的歷史痕跡、主要特徵，更是字彙學習的一大助力。

1200 字表中的同源字組（表一）：

beef	cow	
black	blue	
cake	cookie	
car	horse	run
cent	hundred	
cook	kitchen	
green	grow	grass
move	movie	
salad	salt	
shirt	skirt	
sing	song	
three	third	
vest	wear	
visit	video	wise
water	wet	winter

不規則動詞三態變化彼此同源，且常包含名詞同源字（表二），例如：

原形	過去式	過去分詞	名詞
bleed	bled	bled	blood
feed	fed	fed	food
give	gave	given	gift
sell	sold	sold	sale
sit	sat	sat	seat
sing	sang	sung	song

多功能字卡
─單字教學／學習的恩物

　　多功能字卡是吾等寓教於樂，友善學習等理念的實踐，致力語言知識與表現接軌的產物，更是教學者與學習者共創雙贏的恩物。視覺導向的多功能字卡以不同顏色分別標示詞素、連結字母及字根語意或同源字等語素，圓點劃分音節，粗體大字標示重音節，教學者一卡在手，完整教授語素、構詞音韻、超音段（suprasegmental features）等字彙元素，有效引導學習者輕鬆唸音、辨識拼字、培塑字彙學習力度。

多功能字卡的效益

1. 語音方面

　　(1) 學生依音節拼音，減少單字唸音壓力。

　　(2) 清楚標示重音節，正確唸出單字發音。

2. 構詞方面

　　(1) 顏色標示字根首尾，減緩單字拼字壓力。

　　(2) 有效推測單字語意，準確掌握單字詞性。

　　(3) 了解語音詞素關聯，統整構詞音韻訊息。

　　(4) 輕鬆建立構詞概念，強化單字學習力度。

3. 運用方面

(1) 學期前共備製作，檔案永續使用。

(2) 團體或個別教學，情境布置素材。

(3) 搭配桌遊及 app，消弭個別差異。

4. 功能字卡的製作流程

(1) 開一 WORD 新檔

(2) 版面設定橫向，邊界上下左右 2

(3) 插入方格 3 x 3

(4) Calibra 字型 36 號字鍵入單字

(5) 插入音節圓點

符號(S)	特殊字元(P)																	

字型(F)：(一般文字)　　　　　　　　　　　子集合(U)：拉丁文-1補充

L	M	N	O	P	Q	R	S	T	U	V	W	X	Y	Z	[	\	]	^	_	`	a
b	c	d	e	f	g	h	i	j	k	l	m	n	o	p	q	r	s	t	u	w
x	y	z	{			}	~		¡	¢	£	¤	¥	¦	§	¨	©	ª	«	¬		®
¯	°	±	²	³	´	µ	¶	·	¸	,	¹	º	»	¼	½	¾	¿	À	Á	Â	Ã	Ä

(6) 確認查詢：Longman Dictionary

(7) 重音節字母調 48 粗體

(8) 顏色標示字根、字首、字尾、連結字母

- 字根紅色、字首黑色、字尾綠色、連結字母紫色
- 字根左右的圓點紅色、字首之間的圓點黑色、字尾之間的圓點綠色
- 圓點 36 大小不粗體
- 確認查詢：Etymology Online Dictionary

（多功能字卡範例下載）

★ 因各家手機系統不同，若無法直接掃描，仍可以電腦連結 https://tinyurl.com/w5k75ct 雲端下載

詞素卡的功用

　　多功能字卡呈現一個單字的詞素與語音結構，以視覺觀察、辨識、記憶其組成要素，較為適合培塑構詞概念的啟蒙階段。詞素卡則是多功能字卡的應用與延伸，二卡接軌，彌足珍貴。

1. 詞素卡援用多功能字卡的詞素顏色標示—字首黑色、字根紅色、字尾綠色。

2. **每張詞素卡僅含一詞素**，然為增加卡牌組合的字數，同源詞素將以較小字型列於字源拼寫的下方，構詞效力一致。

3. 詞素卡明確呈現單字的構詞過程，有效增進詞素與單字學習力度。

4. **詞素卡以卡牌取代手寫或紙本文字，藉由視覺、觸覺、活動（同儕互動）**等多元操作與體驗，期能降低負向學習因素、刺激學習意願與動機，進而建構正向的詞素學習歷程，成為單字的成功者。

5. 詞素卡活動首重單字構詞分析的衍生組合，足以建構單字的構詞概念。

 （完整詞素卡片下載）

★ 因各家手機系統不同，若無法直接掃描，仍可以電腦連結 https://tinyurl.com/romu7qm 雲端下載

詞素卡卡牌遊戲解說

遊戲一 **單字接龍** 不限

道具：字首卡－18 張（黑色）
　　　字根卡－20 張（紅色）
　　　字尾卡－16 張（綠色）
　　　紙，筆

玩法

❶ 玩家進行分組（可以單人或多人同時進行）家長（老師）各抽一張字首、字根或字尾卡發給玩家，或是由玩家三種卡牌自行各抽一張，每人或每組共 3 張（有字的一面必須先朝下且不可預覽）。

❷ 待「開始」的口令下達之後才可以翻卡牌進行比賽；利用該 3 張具有任何該字首、字根或字尾卡牌的單字，在紙上造出文法正確及內容有意義的句子。

❸ 計分方式採積分制，含有卡牌字首、字根及字尾的單字各得 2 分；文法正確得 2 分；句子內容有意義再得 2 分，總分 10 分。如果有錯誤出現（例如拼字、文法、句子未在規定時間內完成或句子內容不合邏輯等），則酌情扣分。

❹ 每回合大約進行 3 到 5 分鐘，時間到必須停止作答，進行幾回合之後再統計總得分，最高分的則獲勝。

（遊戲一──單字接龍教學影片）

★ 因各家手機系統不同，若無法直接掃描，仍可以電腦連結 https://tinyurl.com/u49lpgl 雲端下載

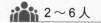 2～6 人

道具：字首卡－ 18 張（黑色）

字根卡－ 20 張（紅色）

字尾卡－ 16 張（綠色）

鬼牌－ 9 張（當成「功能牌」使用；其中設定 4 張為「變色牌」，

3 張為「禁止牌」，2 張為「迴轉牌」）。

玩法

❶ 首先將所有卡牌（共 63 張）充分洗牌及決定發牌順序，由裁判或其中一名玩家依順時鐘方向發牌，每人領取 5 張卡牌，剩下的卡牌則是牌堆（牌堆的卡牌如果抽完了，則把玩家打出來的所有卡牌重新洗牌，做為新牌堆繼續進行遊戲），每位出牌者可依照情況將字首卡、字根卡、字尾卡或功能卡打出，每次只可以出 1 張牌，若無牌可出時，則必須從牌堆中取走 1 張牌，最先將手中的所有卡牌出完者，則是該次比賽贏家。

❷ 出牌順序一開始是依順時鐘方向，第一位出牌者如果出的是字首、字根或字尾卡時，出牌時必須喊出一個具有該字首、字根或字尾的單字，下一位玩家則根據前一位玩家出的卡牌也打出相同類型的字首、字根或字尾卡，並喊出合適的單字，如果喊不出來或是該單字不合規定（該單字裡面沒有包含該字卡的字首、字根或字尾）的話，則該名玩家不能出牌，同時必須從牌堆取走 1 張牌，後序的玩家一樣照前面玩家的出牌模式進行比賽。

❸ 如果玩家手中有功能牌的話，可以將該卡牌拿來使用，三種功能牌的使用方式為：

變色牌－指定下一位玩家必須出黑色（字首卡）、紅色（字根卡）或綠色（字尾卡）；

禁止牌－出牌者的下一位玩家將不能出牌，必須等到下一輪才能出牌；

迴轉牌－原本輪到出牌者的下一位玩家出牌，改成出牌者的上一位玩家出牌，將順時鐘方向的出牌順序改成逆時鐘，或是將逆時鐘方向的出牌順序改成順時鐘。

另外，如果前一位玩家出的是功能牌，下一位玩家也可以打出功能牌，例如：連續兩位或以上玩家皆打出變色牌，最後一位出牌者才可決定接下來的卡牌要變成什麼顏色；連續兩位或三位玩家皆打出禁止牌（被禁止牌限制無法出牌的玩家如果手中剛好也有禁止牌，則仍可出禁止牌限制再下一位玩家不能出牌），最後一位出禁止牌的下一位玩家才會被限制不能出牌一輪；連續兩位玩家皆打出迴轉牌的話，則出牌順序不用改變。

❹ 只要有其中一位玩家先把手上的卡牌都出完的話，就算結束一個回合的比賽；或是玩到只剩一位玩家仍未將手上的卡牌全部出完，也算遊戲結束。建議可以請該名玩家負責下一回合洗牌及發牌。

（遊戲二—單字 99 教學影片）

★ 因各家手機系統不同，若無法直接掃描，仍可以
電腦連結 https://tinyurl.com/v7py8pt 雲端下載

單字對對碰　　　　 不限

道具：字尾卡－ 16 張（綠色；因字尾是英文學習者辨別單字詞性的主
　　　要方式，故此遊戲以字尾卡來進行）

玩法

❶ 玩家們（可預先分組）進行搶答活動，指派一個人擔任出題者。

❷ 將字尾卡洗牌洗好，然後任意抽選其中一張卡牌，先回答正確詞性
　並舉例說出有該字尾單字的那位學生可獲得該張字尾卡

❸ 得到最多卡牌的人即為比賽贏家。

　（遊戲三─單字對對碰教學影片）

★ 因各家手機系統不同，若無法直接掃描，仍可以
　電腦連結 https://tinyurl.com/wwp43uw 雲端下載

遊戲四 **單字抽抽樂**　　　　 不限

道具：字首卡－ 18 張（黑色）
　　　字根卡－ 20 張（紅色）
　　　字尾卡－ 16 張（綠色）
　　　紙或黑、白板，筆

玩法

❶ 先將玩家分成數組。

❷ 家長（老師）再任意抽出字卡當作題目，玩家可以在黑、白板或紙
　上寫出具有該字首、字根或字尾的單字，一個正確的單字以一分
　計算，寫出正確的字數越多，則分數越高。

❸ 每題的回答時間可限制在 1 到 2 分鐘左右，最後則是以累積總分最
　高的獲勝。

　（遊戲四─單字抽抽樂教學影片）

★ 因各家手機系統不同，若無法直接掃描，仍可以
　電腦連結 https://tinyurl.com/sm93auo 雲端下載

遊戲五 **單字心臟病**　　　　　　　　　　不限

道具：字首卡－ 18 張（黑色）

　　　字根卡－ 20 張（紅色）

　　　字尾卡－ 16 張（綠色）

玩法

❶ 將玩家分組以及所有字首、字根和字尾卡牌混合，進行搶答。

❷ 由牌堆最上面一張開始翻牌，回答時必須說出一個具有該卡牌字首、字根或字尾的單字，回答正確者可獲得該張卡牌。

❸ 遊戲時間可設定為 5 到 10 分鐘為一回合，不需將全部卡牌都用來比賽，以避免遊戲時間冗長，降低遊戲的刺激性。

❹ 遊戲結束時，擁有最多張卡牌的獲勝。

（遊戲五—單字心臟病教學影片）

★ 因各家手機系統不同，若無法直接掃描，仍可以電腦連結 https://tinyurl.com/w5j3sfo 雲端下載

語研力 *E035*

全方位英語大師 1200 單字學習寶典：
詞素卡×多功能字卡，唯一一本雙卡牌單字書，完整解構基礎單字，增強記憶學習效果

字彙學習的房角石，流暢閱讀的起手式

作　　者	蘇秦、周儀弘
審　　定	楊智民
顧　　問	曾文旭
出版總監	陳逸祺、耿文國
主　　編	陳蕙芳
文字校對	翁芯琍
內文排版	吳若瑄
封面設計	陳逸祺
法律顧問	北辰著作權事務所

印　　製	世和印製企業有限公司
初　　版	2020 年 04 月
初版二刷	2021 年 05 月
出　　版	凱信企業集團 - 凱信企業管理顧問有限公司
電　　話	（02）2773-6566
傳　　真	（02）2778-1033
地　　址	106 台北市大安區忠孝東路四段 218 之 4 號 12 樓
信　　箱	kaihsinbooks@gmail.com

定　　價	新台幣 349 元 / 港幣 116 元
產品內容	1 書

總 經 銷	采舍國際有限公司
地　　址	235 新北市中和區中山路二段 366 巷 10 號 3 樓
電　　話	（02）8245-8786
傳　　真	（02）8245-8718

本書如有缺頁、破損或倒裝，
請寄回凱信企管更換。
106 台北市大安區忠孝東路四段218之4號12樓
編輯部收

【版權所有　翻印必究】

國家圖書館出版品預行編目資料

全方位英語大師 1200 單字學習寶典：詞素卡 X 多功能字卡，唯一一本雙卡牌單字書，完整解構基礎單字，增強記憶學習效果 / 蘇秦著 . -- 初版 . -- 臺北市 : 凱信企管顧問 , 2020.04
　　面；　公分
ISBN 978-986-98690-0-3(平裝)

1. 英語 2. 詞彙

805.12　　　　　　　　　　　108023177

凱信企管

用對的方法充實自己，
讓人生變得更美好！

凱信企管

用對的方法充實自己，
讓人生變得更美好！